HOLD ON TO
MY HEART

~ Maine Sullivans ~

Ashley & Nash

Bella Andre

HOLD ON TO MY HEART

~ Maine Sullivans ~

Ashley & Nash

© 2021 Bella Andre

Sign up for the New Release Newsletter

bellaandre.com/newsletter

www.BellaAndre.com

Facebook ~ Instagram ~ Twitter

facebook.com/bellaandrefans

instagram.com/bellaandrebooks

twitter.com/bellaandre

Ashley Sullivan's whole world changed when she got pregnant at seventeen. After the father of her child ditched her and their son, she bypassed college, shelved her plans to see the world, and went straight to managing the family café in Bar Harbor, Maine. For the next eleven years, she poured her entire heart into raising her amazing son, Kevin. But when her brother invites her to the grand opening of his new hotel in Vienna, she decides it's finally time to experience a little of the adventure she still secretly longs for. She isn't planning on doing anything crazy, of course. Especially not something as wild and reckless as ending up in bed with one of the sexiest music superstars in the world...

Nash Hardwin has been on the road full time since leaving his rough childhood behind when he was sixteen. Beloved by millions of fans around the world, he's never had a real home and never trusted anyone enough to fall in love. Not until he meets Ashley Sullivan. After she unexpectedly steps in to help him out of a very tricky situation, he ends up having the best day of his life with her in Vienna. Ashley is sweet, beautiful, and intelligent...with the biggest heart of anyone he's ever met.

When their perfect day inevitably turns into an even more perfect night, there's no denying that they make incredibly beautiful music together. But is there even the slightest chance that the small-town single mom and the road-warrior rock star can make things work? Or will the realities of lives that are polar opposites make it impossible to hold on to each other's hearts?

A note from Bella

Ashley Sullivan is my favorite kind of heroine. Though her life as a single mom hasn't always been easy, she's never let it keep her down, and she's forever grateful for her amazing son. Of course, I had to make sure that after so many years of going it alone, she would fall head over heels for the sexiest, most wonderful hero imaginable! Rock star Nash Hardwin meets all those criteria, and then some...

I absolutely loved writing *Hold On To My Heart* and I hope you enjoy reading their love story just as much!

If this is your first time reading about the Sullivans, you can easily read each book as a stand-alone—and there is a Sullivan family tree available on my website (BellaAndre.com/sullivan-family-tree) so you can see how the books are connected!

Happy reading,
Bella

P.S. More stories about the Maine Sullivans are coming soon! Please be sure to sign up for my newsletter (BellaAndre.com/newsletter) so that you don't miss out on any new book announcements.

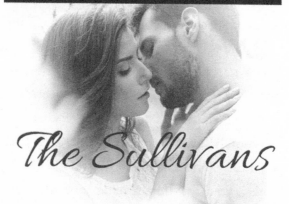

CHAPTER ONE

Ashley Sullivan stretched under the wonderfully soft duvet in her rental apartment, then threw off the covers. Vienna, Austria waited just outside her door. Her six siblings had traveled overseas multiple times. But this was her first time leaving the United States. She loved Bar Harbor, Maine, and couldn't imagine living anywhere else. But for the next forty-eight hours, she was thrilled to have the chance to explore one of the most beautiful cities in Europe.

When her brother Brandon had suggested she travel abroad for one of his hotel launches, she'd thought he was joking. After all, Ashley was not only a single mom to her eleven-year-old son, Kevin, she also managed the Sullivan cafés and Irish-themed boutiques throughout Maine. What's more, she was constantly playing defense against Kevin's father, Josh, pivoting again and again to try to stop disaster before it struck. Thankfully, they'd never married, despite the shocking discovery at seventeen that she was pregnant. What a disaster marrying Josh would have been...

Every day, however, Ashley thanked her lucky stars for Kevin. Her son was the light of her life. Being his mom was worth any and all sacrifices—missing out on her senior prom, not moving away from home or going to college at eighteen, never flying to Europe for fantasy vacations.

As a child, Ashley had loved reading about faraway lands and watching *National Geographic* TV specials. She'd dreamed of being a travel writer, at least until she'd realized that it wasn't writing that she loved, but the chance to have adventures in exotic places.

At long last, she was living out her dream! Ashley had long been fascinated by what she'd read in travel guides about the wonders of Vienna—Empress Sisi, the Spanish Riding School's Lipizzaner horses, and Schönbrunn Palace and its gardens. She could hardly believe that she was here, ready to embark on the forty-eight-hour whirlwind city tour that she'd meticulously planned back in Bar Harbor.

After flying in late the night before, she'd taken a taxi straight to her rental apartment. Brandon had offered to set her up at his swanky new hotel, but though she was grateful for his offer, she wanted this trip to be entirely on her terms. Her timetable. Her dime.

She'd saved a good sum of money over the years from her job running her family's business. Normally, she spent her savings on new clothes and shoes for Kevin, as he outgrew them every few months. This weekend, she was looking forward to splurging on a few small treats for herself. Things to remember Vienna by.

She walked to the French doors, pulled them open, and stepped out onto a small balcony. Even as she lifted her face to the bright morning sun, she felt a pang in her heart. Of course she knew her parents were going to take good care of Kevin during her absence. Her siblings were more than willing to help out too. And she wasn't under the misapprehension that she was indispensable at work either.

What worried her was having *zero* faith in Kevin's father.

The endless nonsense Josh pulled when it came to their son boggled her mind. Josh's latest crazy idea had been to suggest that Kevin stay at his place while she was gone. While that might be perfectly okay for most co-parents, Josh ate nothing but junk food, played video games all night long, was barely holding down his latest job, and couldn't even keep a goldfish alive. Her ex was completely out of his mind asking her to trust him with their son for the weekend.

Fortunately, Josh had been offered the "chance of a lifetime" at the last second to go ATVing with some of his friends. It was only then that she'd booked her flight to Austria. Kevin had been disappointed that he couldn't stay with his dad, and though Ashley hated it when her son was upset, she was hugely relieved that he'd be safe and sound with her parents instead.

Even so, she found it nearly impossible to stop worrying about Kevin. How could she, when her entire world had revolved around him since she was seventeen? It was the reason none of the guys she'd dated had turned into anything serious. Not a single one of them had been good enough to be Kevin's stepfather.

Granted, most of her dates ran as fast as they could once they found out that she was a single mom. As for the ones who claimed Kevin "wasn't a problem" for them? Ashley would much rather be alone for the rest of her life than settle for a man who looked at Kevin as a potential *problem* in the first place.

Her sisters, Cassie and Lola, were constantly trying to persuade her to date more. But as far as Ashley was concerned, everything in her and Kevin's life (apart from Kevin's father) was going just fine, so why risk both of their hearts on some guy who surely wouldn't end up being worth it?

She took a deep breath. *Kevin is going to be just fine*, she reminded herself. *You're here to have a fantastic weekend abroad.*

Working hard to push away her concerns, determined to make the most of her mini-break, she focused her attention on the streets of downtown Vienna.

Ashley had lucked out in finding an apartment that overlooked Michaelerplatz, a circular street with a fountain at the center of it, in the heart of the city. The door to her building was accessed through a narrow cobblestone walkway, and though it hadn't been easy to carry her heavy suitcase up three flights of stairs, it had been worth it. Looking out over the city center, she felt at once safe and secure from the crowds, while still being a part of it all.

There were plenty of people up and about in early-morning Vienna. The café tables were full of tourists and local business people having coffee or tea and eating what looked like delicious Viennese breakfast specialties.

She had been nervous about looking like a tourist, so she'd packed carefully, erring on the side of elegant versus casual, when she normally lived in jeans and T-shirts in Bar Harbor. Though she'd never manage to pull off the slightly edgy looks of the beautifully dressed local women heading off to work, she was glad she'd carefully curated her wardrobe for the next couple of days.

Ashley grinned, thinking about how her family would react if she came home with a Vienna-inspired platinum-blond pixie cut, instead of her usual shoulder-length, wavy brown hair. For a few moments, it was fun to imagine being someone else. A hotshot CEO. A television star. Or even a take-no-prisoners man-eater who dazzled with sex appeal.

She laughed at the preposterousness of being anyone other than a small-town single mom. Hearing her laughter, a handsome man looked up at her from the street below. His suit was smooth, his hair slick, and his flirtatious smile told her he had a well-earned reputation as a lady-killer. But for all his good looks, he didn't make her heart race.

Ashley had always been attracted to rugged-looking men who didn't necessarily shave every day or feel at home in a suit and tie. Though she hadn't had any serious relationships since high school, she had just as many needs as anyone else. The big difference between her and other women was that at seventeen, she had made her son the center of her world. And since there weren't any men she trusted not only with her heart, but also with her son's, she accepted that the closest she would get to being with a man for the foreseeable future would be her secret late-night fantasies about musician Nash Hardwin.

She'd never been one to pay much attention to celebrities or pop culture, but there was something about his music that always tugged at her. After seeing him in concert on a rare night out several years ago, she'd found herself falling asleep dreaming about sharing his bed. Some women dreamed about movie stars, others about professional athletes. Her late-night fantasies about Nash were her little secret.

Maybe once Kevin was eighteen, and Ashley had successfully launched him into the world, she might consider putting her own needs as a sensual woman a little higher on the list. But definitely not before then.

There was no point in denying that getting pregnant her very first time in bed with a guy had left her scarred. Scarred enough that since then, she'd preferred to keep her life on the straight and narrow in order to keep both herself and Kevin safe and sound. For now, her late-night fantasies about a sexy rock star she would never meet would have to be good enough.

Stepping back inside, she headed for the shower. Thirty minutes later, she was dressed in a beautifully printed wrap dress that her sister Lola had given her as a birthday present last year. Putting on her ballet flats, she did a twirl in front of the mirror, feeling pretty and happy. She was ready to soak up as many wonders of Vienna as she possibly could during the next two days.

She was just walking out the door when a text came in from Brandon.

Hey, Ash, hope your flight was good and that you slept well last night. Since you wouldn't agree to

stay in my hotel, I insist on taking you to breakfast.
Text me once you're awake, and I'll meet you at the
café across from your apartment.

Brandon, like everyone else in her family, was determined to take care of her. It was why she hadn't
wanted to stay in his newest hotel, even though she
knew it would be incredibly luxurious. For once, she
wanted to do exactly what *she* wanted to do. She hoped
having a little separation would keep her brother from
trying to babysit her on her first trip abroad. Plus, she
knew how busy he was during one of his hotel launches. She didn't want him to feel like he had to take his
eye off his own ball because of her.

Nonetheless, she was happy to have breakfast with
him this morning. Before she headed off into the
unknown, it would be nice to share a cup of coffee
with the brother she adored and saw far too rarely.

She texted back that she'd love to see him, and he
let her know he'd be there shortly. She headed down
the stairs as if there were wings on her feet. Amazingly,
her brother was already there by the time she made it
to the nearest café.

Brandon gave her a hug. "Welcome to Vienna,
Ash."

"Thanks." She spun in a slow circle to take in the
beautiful fountain and cobblestones and old stone

buildings. "I love it here already."

Her brother grinned at her excitement, then guided them to an open table. As he motioned for a waiter to bring over menus, he said, "I knew you would love Vienna. Honestly, I can't believe it's taken this many years to get you out of the US."

"You try raising a kid by yourself, and then let me know how much free time you have left over to gallivant all over the world."

"I can't argue with that. Although you know I'm probably going to try, just because I like being contrary."

She laughed. "You wouldn't be Brandon Sullivan if you didn't." When the waiter tried to hand her the menu, she pointed two tables over. The apple strudel the man was eating looked gorgeous. "I'll have what he's having. And an espresso, please."

"Ah," the waiter said with a smile, "our *Apfelstrudel* is considered the best in Vienna."

"I can't wait to taste it."

Though he'd already taken her order, the waiter stared into her eyes for a few seconds. She got the sense he was flirting with her, perhaps considering asking for her number when they'd finished their breakfast?

She glanced at Brandon to see if he had noticed this too, but after telling the waiter he'd have the same thing, he proceeded to scroll through messages on his phone.

Of course her brother wouldn't notice someone flirting with her. How could he when in his mind, she would forever be the naïve little sister who had gotten knocked up in high school?

Despite the fact that she had an eleven-year-old son, she doubted Brandon—or any of her older brothers, for that matter—realized she was now a fully grown woman. They didn't mean to be dismissive, so she didn't take it personally. But she sometimes wondered if they would ever look at her as a peer, rather than as the baby sister they needed to constantly watch over.

"What are you planning to see first?" Brandon asked. "I'm assuming you've put together a spreadsheet for your weekend in Vienna?"

Brandon knew her well enough to have guessed right. She did have a spreadsheet in her bag, with opening times for the museums and gardens she planned to visit. But suddenly, she didn't want to be the same predictable Ashley she'd always been.

Instead of pulling out her itinerary, she waved a hand in the air. "I'm not sure where I'll go first. I'll just see which way the wind blows me."

Brandon looked at her like she had lost a screw. "*You* are just going to go wherever the wind takes you?

The woman who practically sleeps with a spreadsheet under her pillow at night?"

"That's right, Brandon. I'm going to be totally spontaneous today." His disbelief that she could have a nice day without pre-planning every second of it rankled. "I'm here having breakfast with you, aren't I? That certainly wasn't in any plan."

He held up his hands. "No need to get bent out of shape, Ash. I guess I'm just a little worried about you because you've never wandered around a foreign city by yourself. I wish I could hang out with you today, but inevitably, no matter how much work goes into one of these launches, something always ends up—"

The ringing of his phone cut him off in mid-sentence.

"Speak of the devil, that's an SOS call from my assistant. Which means something must have already hit the fan."

Giving Ashley an apologetic look, he took the call. "What's up?" The color fell from his cheeks as he listened. "I'll be there ASAP." He jammed the phone into his pocket and stood up, putting twenty euros on the table.

"What happened?" Ashley asked as she also stood, a little sad that she wasn't going to get to taste *Apfelstrudel* just yet, but knowing it was far more important to support her brother.

"Someone who works for me must have leaked the news of my VIP guest for tomorrow night's launch party." Brandon looked furious as they quickly headed down the street in the direction of his newest SLVN hotel.

"Who is it?"

"Nash Hardwin. Evidently, there's a growing crowd on the street outside the hotel, blocking traffic and making a lot of noise. The police are demanding we take care of the problem immediately."

A little thrill went through Ashley at the sound of Nash's name. She'd had no idea he would be here in Vienna, on the very same weekend she was in town. And she definitely hadn't realized that Brandon was doing business with him.

Even though he was her secret fantasy man, she didn't know much about Nash's life beyond the fact that his music blurred the lines between rock, pop, and country—and appealed equally to each audience.

Though her brother was none the wiser about her fantasies, she found herself fighting to keep from blushing at the thought that Nash was at Brandon's hotel. If she wanted to meet him, she suspected her brother could arrange it. But since coming face-to-face with him would likely ruin the fantasy for her—she'd surely end up being tongue-tied and awkward and wishing a hole in the ground would swallow her up—

she wouldn't be asking Brandon for any favors on that count.

"Sorry we had to leave before we got a chance to eat, Ash, but since we're headed to the hotel, if you can wait for me to iron things out with Nash and the police, I'll have the kitchen rustle you up something to eat and show you around the new hotel."

"Sounds great," she said as they picked up their pace. "Did you know Nash before he came to Vienna?"

"I've met him a few times over the years. We've shared a bottle of beer or two. I know he's got a bit of a reputation, but he always struck me as a good guy, despite his less-than-upstanding past."

Again, while Ashley wasn't up on the comings and goings of celebrities, she was aware that Nash had had a few brushes with the law. She wasn't okay with people breaking the law, but there was a tiny part of her that found his bad-boy past a little sexy.

"What exactly did he do to gain his reputation?"

"From what I can recall reading in the papers years ago, he did the trifecta—theft, fights, and drugs."

"Wow." She'd had no idea. "Sounds like he was into a lot of bad things."

"Maybe he was. Or maybe he wasn't, and the stories from when he was younger were blown out of proportion." Brandon shrugged. "Honestly, who knows what the truth is? Smith, Ford, Nicola, and

Tatiana have all been lied about in the press many, many times over the years. I wouldn't be surprised if the same thing were true about Nash."

Her brother was right. For her famous cousins, and the celebrities some of her cousins had married, there was a big difference between the truth of who they really were and the fiction of who the press made them out to be.

Ashley wondered what was *actually* true about Nash.

"Like I said," Brandon added, "the couple of times I've met Nash, I liked the guy. Plus, I got really lucky that tonight's launch fit into his crazy schedule. After tomorrow night, he'll be touring for six weeks, and then he goes straight into the studio to record a new album. I'd hate for him to regret agreeing to play at my launch."

They were still two long blocks from Brandon's hotel when they started to understand why the Viennese police had received so many calls from upset locals. The noise coming from the street outside the hotel was loud.

Really loud.

Ashley could make out a woman screaming, "Nash, I love you!" A beat later, another yelled, "Nash, marry me!" And then a third chimed in with, "Nash, I want to have your baby!"

Ashley knew she shouldn't laugh. Not when this was no laughing matter for her brother on the eve of his hotel launch. But despite her own secret fantasies about Nash, she couldn't imagine ever crying out that she wanted to have his baby.

Nope. She'd been there, done that with another guy who hadn't stuck around. As far as she was concerned, it would be *awful* to become pregnant with a roving rock star's baby.

Okay, so her cousin Mia had married a loving, steadfast rock star, Ford Vincent. And her cousin Marcus was married to Nicola, a brilliant musician who had made Ashley's cousin the happiest man in the world. But Ford and Nicola were the exceptions.

There couldn't possibly be another famous musician who would give up everything for love.

"This is worse than I anticipated," Brandon muttered.

But Ashley was fully confident he'd find a way out of this mess. Brandon was a brilliant problem-solver, he always had been. As children, whenever they were on the verge of getting caught being naughty, he'd come up with a way to get away from the scene of the crime without penalty.

Her brother looked at the size of the crowd with a frown. "Nash is going to need to leave out the back exit. *If* he can even get away with doing that, consider-

ing his fans are bound to scent him from a mile away."
Brandon looked grimmer by the second, which was no
wonder, given that the decibel level kept rising as more
and more fans joined the crush on the street. "Right
now, he's got to want my head on a platter. Especially
after I promised him total privacy."

From the street, Brandon led Ash to a back alley
with a service elevator. He flashed his all-access badge
at the touch screen, and that was when she realized
that Brandon intended that she should accompany him
upstairs to meet with Nash.

"I should wait in the lobby," she said. Surely her
presence would only complicate things. Especially if
she got all drooly when she saw Nash live and in the
flesh.

Brandon pulled her into the elevator. "I'm afraid I
need you to be my human shield, Ash."

"What?" She had no idea what on earth he was
talking about.

"Until I can figure out a plan B," he explained, "I'm
hoping Nash won't want to pound me to smithereens
in front of my sister."

Before she could protest, they were on the top
floor, and the elevator door was opening.

Brandon knocked on the lone door on the entire
floor. "Nash," he called out, "it's Brandon Sullivan."

Nash yanked the door open. "What the hell is going on outside? It sounds like the Beatles came to town."

It instantly struck Ashley that Nash Hardwin was by far the best-looking man she'd ever set eyes on. She'd always thought he was ruggedly attractive, of course. But seeing him in person? All she could do for the moment was stare.

"As soon as I figure out who leaked the news that you're here," Brandon was saying, "I promise you that he or she will be barred from all future hotel jobs, in every city in the world, for the rest of time. And my team is already working with the local authorities to safely send your fans home. But because that could take some time, it's imperative that we get you out of here as soon as possible and to a secret location." He ran a hand through his hair. "If only I could figure out how to get you past the fans who are literally stationed at every exit."

Ashley didn't know what prompted her to speak up, only that the words were out before she could pull them back. "What if Nash wore a disguise?"

Nash turned to her, and she realized that in his initial fury, he hadn't seen her standing behind her brother. His eyes smoldered as he looked at her.

She almost started laughing at the word *smolder* popping into her head. But there was no other way to describe it. Without trying, Nash was shockingly sexy.

And she knew he most definitely *wasn't* trying, because unlike the waiter at breakfast, there was nothing whatsoever about Nash's current expression that could be read as flirtatious.

"Who are you?"

"Ashley Sullivan, Brandon's sister." She could feel her brother bristling at the tone that Nash had used while speaking to her, so she put a hand on Brandon's arm to stop him from saying something he might later regret. "I was just thinking that if you looked more like a tourist than a superstar musician..." She gestured to his black jeans and black T-shirt and black boots. "Maybe you could escape unnoticed."

"I've tried to disguise myself before, and it has never worked," he said, instantly discounting her idea. "The fans always know it's me."

Well, that was her told. Which didn't make him any less sexy, she had to admit to herself. Just as she also had to admit that actually coming face-to-face with him might very well fuel some hot new late-night fantasies. Ones where his scowls turned into kisses... Feeling a flush rise to her cheeks, she worked to push down her inappropriate thoughts.

"Actually, Nash," Brandon said as he moved his gaze from Nash to her and then back again, "I think Ashley's on to something." For some reason, her brother suddenly looked a great deal more positive. "If you'll let us in, I can explain why I think a disguise might work this time."

Ashley wondered what her brother had in mind. And why he kept looking at her this way. She knew when Brandon was up to something.

Still, she couldn't imagine how his plans for Nash could possibly involve her.

CHAPTER TWO

Though he didn't look happy about it, Nash stepped aside to let them into his luxurious penthouse suite. The deeper they went into the room, the louder the crowd outside sounded.

"These are the best soundproof windows money can buy," Brandon grumbled, "and it is still ridiculously loud in here. No wonder the police are calling with complaints from every neighbor within a half-mile radius." He looked at Nash. "Why the hell are so many women nuts for you?"

Nash shrugged with the nonchalance of a man who had clearly never had a woman turn him down. "It's the music. Doesn't matter who's at the mic or holding the guitar. It's not me they're crazy for."

While it was a surprisingly modest thing to say, Ashley didn't think Nash was right about his appeal being solely about the music. Yes, his songs were great. But there was something special about Nash. Something that made it hard to look away from him. Something that made even a straight-and-narrow-walking woman like Ashley fantasize about him.

"What's your big plan?" he asked Brandon.

Brandon shot another look at Ashley, one she didn't at all care for. Not when her brother's scheming brain seemed to be working overtime.

Finally, he explained, "The key is that you won't leave the building alone. Instead, you and Ashley will walk out of the hotel as a couple, looking like a husband and wife who have come to Vienna for the European vacation of their dreams."

"*No.*" Ashley was the first to respond, the single word clipped and overly loud as it left her lips. "There's no way you're roping me into this." She glared at her brother, wondering how he could be so deluded as to think his idea would actually work. "No one would *ever* believe Nash and I are married, no matter how good our disguises are."

"I don't see why not," Nash said.

She turned to stare at him in shock. Was he actually considering Brandon's crazy idea? "Everything about you screams *star*," she said to Nash. "Whereas everything about me screams *normal*. Disguise or not, neither of those things is going to change." She had no idea why she had to explain something so obvious to Nash and Brandon. "Which is why I am going to leave now to let the two of you find another way to work this out."

She was halfway to the door when Nash said, "You playing the part of my wife would really help me out, Ashley."

Trying to ignore the way her name on his lips sent warmth running through her, she slowly turned around to try, one more time, to make both men see reason. "Of course I wish you all the best in getting out of here in one piece, Nash. And I'm also truly sorry that you have to deal with stuff like this, because it can't possibly be fun. But the fact remains that I am *not* the woman for you."

Before Nash could speak again, Brandon moved to put his arm around her shoulders, looking at her in an imploring way. "Don't you see, Ash? That's exactly why you're *perfect* for this. Since no one would ever think the two of you are an item, if you're with a disguised Nash, that means he can't possibly be who he is."

Ashley wasn't insulted by her brother's logic. Brandon didn't mean any harm. He was simply agreeing that she checked the *normal* box, as opposed to the *superstar girlfriend* box.

"You're wrong, Brandon," Nash said. "Dead wrong." He gazed into her eyes, holding her momentarily spellbound with an extra helping of *smolder*. "You're gorgeous, Ashley. Any guy you agreed to be with would be lucky as hell."

Brandon's growl came from deep in his chest as he rounded on his VIP guest. "Don't even think about looking at my sister as another one of your conquests."

Truthfully, Ashley didn't know how to react. Not to any of this. She had come here to check tourist destinations off her life list, not to spar with her brother and a larger-than-life musician.

How had her first day in Vienna gone so quickly off the rails?

Granted, when this was all over, she would never forget that giddy feeling in her stomach at being called *gorgeous* by Nash Hardwin.

She was surprised to find Nash still staring at her, rather than turning to deal with Brandon's threatening comment. The smolder was still there, but again, she got the sense that he wasn't putting it on to try to sway her decision. His breathtaking sex appeal was simply a natural part of him, like how she had hazel eyes and brown hair.

"I'd really appreciate your help," he said again, having to speak quite loudly to be heard over the women screaming his name outside. "If there's anything I can do for you in the future, I promise to pay it forward."

While being a single mom had done an awful lot to toughen Ashley up over the years, she still found it impossible to turn her back on someone who genuinely needed help. And given that the noise out on the streets below kept increasing, Nash clearly needed help.

"Okay." She let out an audible sigh. "I'll help. But if it all goes sideways—"

"It won't." Nash held her gaze a moment longer before finally turning to speak to Brandon. "Will you be able to source clothes, hats, glasses, and shoes for both of us?"

Though he nodded, Brandon still didn't look happy as he took another threatening step closer to Nash. "I meant it when I said you'd better keep your hands off my sister. She's helping us out today. So don't get any ideas. Or else."

Fed up with her brother's behavior—especially on the heels of Brandon having previously told her how much he liked Nash despite his past—Ashley got between the men and moved Brandon away from Nash, using the flat of her hands on his chest. She could only imagine what a disaster it would be if they started brawling in the hotel. It was one thing for Brandon to grapple with her other brothers. It would be another for him to start something with his VIP guest all because he seemed to think she hadn't moved beyond being his vulnerable little sister.

"I can take care of myself," she told her brother, even though she suspected he might never be able to see that that was true. "And I'm sure Nash has absolutely no intention of impinging on my honor in any way," she added, suddenly feeling like a heroine in a historical drama. "Please go and find us some disguises so that we can get Nash out of here before the crowd gets any bigger. I'd hate for anyone to get hurt out there."

"I would too," Nash said, frowning as he looked out the window at the ever-growing crowd of his fans. "There's nothing worse than hearing that one of my fans got hurt at a show. If someone got injured today—"

"I won't let that happen," Brandon said. "You have my word. And I'll also make certain that a crowd won't form outside the hotel again." With one more warning look at Nash, he turned and left the room.

"The good news is that my brother has always been as good as his word," Ashley said to Nash once they were alone. "So I'm positive your fans outside will all be okay." Then she added, in a slightly apologetic tone, "The bad news, however, is that he's always been overprotective with me and my two sisters. Our dad is pretty overbearing too. So are my other brothers—and a few of my cousins, come to think of it. Please don't take it personally." Even though they both knew it *had* been personal.

But Nash simply smiled and said, "It's good to have family looking out for you."

It was the last thing she'd expected him to say, and

she appreciated that he didn't seem to have taken any offense at Brandon's behavior. For a moment, she thought Nash might say something more—perhaps to tell her about his own family?

Instead, he gestured to the buffet breakfast laid out on a side table. "Are you hungry? Thirsty?"

Her grumbling stomach answered for her. She hadn't had a chance to eat breakfast, and the meal on the plane had been a lifetime ago. "As you just heard for yourself, I'm starved."

She thought she saw laughter in his eyes as he said, "Help yourself to whatever you want."

She picked up a plate and put some fruit salad and a delicious-looking pastry on it. Nash did the same, and then they both sat at the dining table in his suite.

She supposed they could sit and eat in silence until Brandon came back, but she couldn't stop wondering about something. "Is it hard? To have so many people want to see you? Talk with you? Breathe the same air as you?" She left off how many of them wanted to have his baby, saying instead, "Is it hard for you to always have to put on disguises to leave your hotel room?"

He didn't answer for a few moments, giving her ample time to pop a piece of the pastry into her mouth. Gosh, it was good. Light and flaky and full of flavor. She'd have to ask Brandon to ask his chef what it was. Maybe she could give the recipe to her mother for the café back home.

Finally, Nash spoke. "There's nothing worse than a celebrity complaining about his or her fans."

Fans who were, at that very moment, still screaming his name at the top of their lungs.

She smiled across the table. "How about if I ask the question differently so your reply can't be construed as complaining? Is it weird to be in your position, even though you truly appreciate the people who helped make you a success?"

She was surprised by how comfortable she was talking with Nash. She wasn't nearly as socially adept as the other women in her family. Her mom could happily chat with anyone in her lovely lilting Irish accent. Her sister Cassie was a ray of sunshine, and everyone loved her. And her sister Lola was so confident and beautiful that she never had trouble connecting with strangers. Whereas Ashley spent her days in the back office of the Sullivan café, alone with her spreadsheets.

What's more, she couldn't shake the feeling that the stories about Nash's dark and dangerous past had to be wrong. He didn't strike her as a troublemaker. Although, she supposed he could have been different in his youth. After all, she'd been different, hadn't she? Back then, she'd felt free to dream and seek adventure in a way she never would now.

"Yes," he said with a nod, "it can be weird." He smiled at her before adding, "*Very* weird."

She was speechless for a moment, her heart pounding a million miles a minute from nothing but his super-sexy grin.

"Thanks again for doing this, Ashley."

Thankfully, she found her voice in time to say, "I get what it's like to be in a jam." More than he'd ever know, given that she doubted her teenage pregnancy was going to come up in conversation anytime soon. After all, once they put on their disguises and left the hotel, she'd never see him again. "I have to admit, though, that I'm still worried we're not going to be able to pull this off. Even if we can temporarily change the way you look, if you end up needing to speak with anyone on our way out, they'll know it's you in an instant."

"Don't be so sure about that." He'd replaced the distinctive low rumble of his voice—the sexiest faintly southern drawl she'd ever heard—with a spot-on East Coast accent.

"How did you do that?" She still could barely believe what she'd just heard. "You sound exactly like one of my suppliers in Connecticut."

"Accents and impressions are a hobby of mine," he explained, in a British accent this time, looking pleased at having surprised her.

But then something occurred to her. "Does anyone know you can do different accents?"

"I've got to have some secrets." He gave her another extremely charming—and yes, smoldering—smile. "The only one who knows this secret is *you*."

Trying to act like her heart wasn't madly racing again, she told him, "Having secrets in my family—with six siblings, dozens of cousins, and parents I have dinner with nearly every Friday night—is pretty much impossible." In fact, her only true secrets were her late-night fantasies about Nash, she thought with a blush she couldn't quite hold back.

"Six siblings? That must be interesting."

"'Interesting' is a good word for it," she agreed.

"Do you like being part of such a big family?"

Though she wasn't sure why he wanted to find out more about her, she said, "I do like it. At times like this, however, when one of my brothers decides to act like a Neanderthal, it can be a little grating. Although," she felt she should add out of fairness, "Brandon is the one who convinced me to come to Vienna. I've never been to Europe before, so this trip is a big deal for me."

"I'm sorry about throwing your day off course." To his credit, he truly did look remorseful about it, rather than acting like someone around whom the whole world revolved. Which she was certain it always did.

Not wanting him to feel bad—she wouldn't want

to be fed to the adoring mob outside, so she couldn't blame him for trying to avoid that fate for himself—she told him, "I've decided it's part of my European adventure. After all, what could be more exciting than putting on a disguise and pretending to be someone else for a little while?"

"What were your plans before I begged you to get me out of this mess?"

There was a part of her that felt embarrassed about being the ultimate, itinerary-toting geek tourist. But something told her Nash wouldn't laugh at her for it. He might be the most famous person she'd ever set eyes on—apart from Smith, Ford, Nicola, and Tatiana—but nothing about Nash indicated he'd be cruel.

How, she found herself wondering, had he ever ended up in jail? Because he didn't seem threatening either.

Just downright sexy as sin…

"This is my plan for the next forty-eight hours," she said, reaching into her bag and handing over the list she'd told her brother she didn't have. "I've read so much about Vienna over the years, I can't wait to finally see it with my own eyes. I have two days to see as much as I can before I go back to Bar Harbor."

"Any chance you're looking for a new job?" he said after he'd scanned her spreadsheet. "You're so organized, I'd sign you up to be my tour manager in a heartbeat."

"Thanks for the offer, but I'm happy with my job." And not just because she worked for her family. She truly loved making the Sullivan Cafés and stores bigger and better year after year.

"I've been to Vienna countless times for shows," he said as he looked at the list again, "but I've never seen any of these places."

"Seriously? Not one single museum or garden or palace?"

"As soon as I land in a new city, I either head straight to the venue, or sit down with press for an interview, or the local label we've licensed the record to wants to meet with me, or I'm trying to catch up on sleep. Sightseeing never makes the list." But then he shook his head. "Forget I just said that, will you? The only thing worse than a celebrity complaining about his fans is a celebrity complaining about his five-star travel."

"You don't need to apologize for anything," she insisted. "I'm close with a few celebrities, so I get that fame and massive career success aren't always easy to deal with. Do you happen to know Ford Vincent and Nico?"

"I've run into both of them on the road at music festivals a few times over the years. How do you know them?"

"They're married to my cousins Mia and Marcus." Something else occurred to her. "I have a feeling you might also know one of my other cousins—Smith Sullivan?"

"Smith asked me to do a walk-on role in one of his movies recently," Nash told her, obviously surprised to hear about her famous family members, "but I couldn't fit it into my tour schedule."

A knock on the door startled Ashley. She'd been so drawn into their conversation. She couldn't remember the last time she'd found it so easy, or enjoyable, to spend time with a man. Who would have thought that when she finally let her guard down around someone, he would be a global superstar? Not to mention her secret fantasy...

Nash got up to let Brandon back into the suite. Her brother was holding two bags of clothes, shoes, and accessories.

"I got plenty of options for both of you, so hopefully something here will work."

Nash's suite had separate bedrooms and bathrooms on each side of the living room. It wasn't until she went into one of the sumptuous bedrooms that she fully took in how fancy the hotel was.

Her brother's SLVN hotel brand always provided the height of luxury. She'd been to other launches, on the East Coast of the United States, so she wasn't surprised, but she had never actually stayed in one of his hotels. Though Brandon owned a Bar Harbor waterfront home, he lived full-time in various hotel suites around the world. She held out hope that one day he'd be able to spend some time at home with the rest of the family. Kevin absolutely adored his uncle and loved it whenever Brandon was able to visit.

She nearly laughed out loud as she imagined what it would be like to switch places with her brother for twenty-four hours. Frankly, it was impossible to imagine Brandon living in her little cottage, cleaning up dirty socks and making grilled cheese sandwiches and pizza. Just as it was impossible for her to imagine being surrounded by five-star luxury. In any case, she loved living in her cozy cottage with Kevin, dirty socks and all, so she wouldn't want to swap lives with Brandon even if she could.

She laid out the wardrobe options on the bed and grimaced. She'd never seen quite so much beige, gray, and brown in her life. So much for her carefully curated wardrobe and the cute wrap dress she'd chosen to wear today. She and Nash were supposed to blend in when they left the hotel, not stick out due to their terrible fashion sense. But maybe these clothes were so awful that no one would ever consider, in a million years, that Nash could be with someone wearing them?

She was drawing the line at the shoes, however.

Thankfully, her ballet flats wouldn't throw off her new look.

Deciding it would be better to get it over with quickly, she took off her pretty dress, then slipped into the least offensive outfit of the bunch—a midcalf beige skirt that bunched at the waist and a floral blouse that stopped at her elbows and poofed slightly at the shoulders.

When she turned to look at herself in the mirror, she broke out laughing. Wanting to show her sisters her disguise, she took a quick selfie and planned to send the photo later, when they would be awake in Maine. Honestly, she couldn't wait to see what Nash looked like. Carefully folding her wrap dress into her bag so that she could change into it as soon as they'd finished making their escape, she headed back to the living room.

Her brother couldn't hold in his laughter when he saw her. "Looking good, sis. Beige is definitely your color," he teased.

"I think you're right about these clothes. I wouldn't look twice at me in these. Not when I'm going to blend in perfectly with the stone buildings."

"That's the idea," Brandon said, still laughing.

Just then, the other bedroom door opened, and Nash walked out.

She tried not to laugh. She really did. But within

seconds, Brandon was laughing so hard that a gurgle of laughter escaped her throat too.

"I take it you both think this disguise will work," Nash said in a dry voice.

She tried to get her own mirth under control, but it was a lost cause. "I wouldn't have thought there was any disguise that would hide who you are. But seeing you now?" She giggled again as she took in his outfit. "It just might be possible."

Instead of being all beige like her, he was wearing varying shades of green. Ashley used to think green was a good color. But lime green, Army green, grass green, and pastel green definitely did *not* go together.

Though his pants were a too big around his hips, they seemed to fit at the waist. They were also a little short. But not in a fashionable way. She was pretty sure his clothes were made of the same polyester she was wearing.

Still grinning, Brandon explained, "I sent my assistant to the nearest charity shop, and I think she did a great job, especially on such short notice." Then he said, "Wait, there's more," and handed Nash a horrendous pair of leather slip-on shoes and a floppy sun hat.

Nash gamely put them both on. "How do these fit with the look?"

"Perfectly," Ashley replied, "although we still need to do something to disguise your face."

Brandon reached into yet another bag. The glasses her brother handed Nash were frameless and looked like something Benjamin Franklin might have worn. "Try putting these on. There's no correction to the lenses, they're just glass."

Nash put them on, and Ashley nodded. "Yes, that's perfect. If I wasn't trying so hard to recognize you, there's no way I would guess that Nash Hardwin is in that getup."

Meanwhile, the fans screaming Nash's name outside had only gotten louder.

Brandon's phone rang again, the same SOS ringtone. Without even picking it up, he said to Nash and Ashley, "It's time for you guys to go. Ash, I hope you don't mind, but until I figure out where to move Nash so that he won't be hounded, I was hoping I could temporarily move his stuff into your apartment. This way I can honestly tell the press to spread the word with the fans that he isn't here anymore. Plus that way he has his things to change back into once the two of you have gotten out of here."

"Ashley," Nash said before she could reply, "you don't have to put either me or my things up at your place. It's more than enough that you're helping me get out of the building."

But she was already in it with him this far. Why not keep helping out if she could? "I have no problem with moving your bags into my apartment. This way, you'll not only have a place to change out of that outfit, but your things will already be there."

"Thanks, again. I owe you big time after today."

"Okay, guys, enough chitchat." Brandon herded them out the door. "Call me if you run into any trouble. Just remember to act naturally, and you should be fine. And be sure to go out the front door of the hotel so no one questions why tourists are using the service entrance." Then he pinned Nash with a hard look. "And remember, my sister is off-limits."

Ashley couldn't resist slugging her brother in the gut—not hard enough to hurt him, but enough to wind him for a second—before getting into the elevator with Nash Hardwin by her side.

She'd told Brandon over breakfast that she was going to go wherever the wind took her today. Who would have thought it would blow her straight into the path of her secret celebrity crush?

CHAPTER THREE

Nash had done a lot of crazy things in his life. Some legal, some less so. But he'd never had a partner in disguise.

And he'd never felt so comfortable around someone so quickly either.

The more famous he became, the harder it was to trust people. Not that he'd been great at trusting people before fame. But during the past ten years, it had been easier to become more and more of a lone wolf.

Somehow, Ashley Sullivan had gotten over his walls. Maybe it was because she didn't treat him like a star? Instead, she treated him like any regular guy who was in a jam and needed her help.

This wasn't the way Nash had seen today going down. He had been looking forward to a rare day off from his packed tour schedule. For the next six weeks, he was booked to play a different European city each night. And then when the tour came to an end, he was planning to head straight into the studio to make a new record. An album for which he had yet to be inspired to write a single song.

This weekend in Vienna was supposed to give Nash some space from the grind of it all. No meetings. No interviews. And Brandon had assured him that the hotel would be the perfect place to get away. Before Ashley arrived, Nash had been irritated that his day wasn't going to plan.

Surprisingly, he wasn't irritated anymore.

He supposed he should be even *more* irritated, considering he was wearing ridiculous polyester clothes and had just been forced out of his luxurious hotel suite for the duration of his stay in Vienna. But as he glanced toward Ashley, he felt a budding sense of excitement. If they got away with their escape, maybe Nash could live for a few hours as a normal man in Austria—and maybe even see some of those tourist sights on Ashley's spreadsheet.

In the elevator, he spoke in his Connecticut accent. "Once we're out of the hotel, let's stay in these disguises and do your list."

"You want to join me sightseeing?" She looked shocked by his suggestion.

"I'll bet your itinerary is as good, if not better, than one a tour guide would have put together. So yes, that would be great...if you're up for letting me tag along with you today."

She blushed at his compliment before admitting, "I cross-referenced several guidebooks with online top-ten lists. I figured if I only have two days here, I should make the most of them." Then she smiled at him. "I'd be happy to have some company enjoying the wonders of Vienna."

On the ground floor, the elevator door slid open, and they stepped into the lobby. Gratifyingly, no one in the room gave them a second look, obviously assuming that they must be nothing more than a couple of very badly dressed tourists. But that didn't mean they were in the clear yet.

Nash took Ashley's hand, explaining, "This will make us look more like a real couple."

Though she gave a little intake of breath as he slid his fingers through hers, she didn't pull her hand away. And he was grateful that she didn't.

Not only because it would make their ruse seem more believable, but also because he liked holding her hand. He liked it a lot.

And yet, as they got closer to the hotel exit, he could feel the tension building inside of him. It was no longer that he simply wanted to get away from the crowd to keep mass pandemonium from ensuing.

He wanted to spend this day with Ashley more than he'd wanted anything in a long time.

Remarkably, Ashley seemed perfectly at ease with

her role as she smiled up at him in an adoring way. "I'm just so excited to finally be in Vienna. Thank you for bringing me here, honey bunny."

He couldn't stop his grin at her acting as he replied in his Connecticut accent, "Anything for my snuggle wuggle."

Her grin matched his. And as they headed past the fans, he was almost positive they were going to make it out without being spotted.

Until, suddenly, one of the women pointed at him. "Hey, do you think that man could be one of Nash's relatives coming to see him play tonight? Because I could swear his jawline and height are similar to Nash's."

Nash didn't stop to think, didn't pause to ask permission, before cupping his free hand around the back of Ashley's head and lowering his mouth to hers.

He'd meant to use the kiss as a way to hide his face from the fan who had almost figured out who he was. But as soon as his lips met Ashley's, desire took over.

Her lips were so soft.

Her taste was so sweet.

And her little hum of pleasure as his tongue found hers, drove him absolutely wild.

With great reluctance, he lifted his mouth from hers. When she looked into his eyes, her gaze was full of the same surprise he knew must be mirrored in his own.

Belatedly remembering they weren't yet in the clear, he tugged her hand and quickly propelled them both farther down the street. But long after they had made their escape, and the fans were far behind them, he continued to hold her hand.

He checked to make sure the coast was completely clear of fans before saying in his normal voice, "Sorry about kissing you back there. When I thought we were going to be caught out, I reacted without stopping to think about whether it would be okay with you." Especially given that a guy like him had no business messing around with a nice girl like her.

"I heard what the woman said," Ashley replied. "You made the right decision."

As she spoke, he couldn't tear his eyes away from her lips. Lips he was dying to kiss again. "Kissing you really did feel right, Ashley. More right than anything has for a very long time."

She looked a little stunned for a moment. But then she said, "So were you serious about wanting to be a tourist for the day?"

That was it? That was her response to his saying that kissing her felt right?

Any other woman would have taken him up on his not-so-subtle offer to kiss again right then and there. Whereas Ashley was acting like their kiss hadn't happened.

Was she not into him?

Had she been faking that desire he'd seen in her eyes?

But no, he had heard her moan of pleasure and had felt her kiss him back.

It suddenly hit Nash that thirty minutes ago, he'd been lamenting how he was tired of being nothing more than a piece of meat to every woman he met. Hadn't he wanted a break from it all, wanted to have one day where he wasn't a sex symbol? But then when he finally met a woman who didn't care about who he was or what he did for a living, his ruff immediately went up.

"Yes," he replied, "I was serious. After all, you can't deny that the two of us are dressed for a day of serious sightseeing."

They both laughed as they looked down at their clothes.

"What's our first stop?" he asked.

She pointed to a large building up ahead. "The Sisi Museum in the Hofburg. Empress Elizabeth was renowned in her day for being a great beauty, but also for being extremely difficult. She was murdered in her forties, unfortunately, dying from a stab wound. I've always been fascinated by her life, and the museum devoted to her is supposed to be phenomenal."

"Lead the way." Though a museum about a Viennese royal's life wouldn't normally have been at the top of his list, if it meant he got to spend more time with Ashley, he was all for it.

It didn't matter how ridiculous or drab her outfit, she was beautiful. Fresh and lovely without any makeup on, she had her hair down around her shoulders in a simple style, and he found everything about her to be incredibly appealing. She was completely different from the women he'd spent time with during the past decade. Hell, his whole life.

He'd never been with good girls. He'd always thought he wanted someone as wild as he was. By his thirties, however, he'd come to realize that wild got old real quick. Unless it was in bed, of course.

Nash couldn't think of the last time he'd done anything "normal." Five-star luxury was great. But Ashley seemed happier to him than any of the billionaires he knew.

She was imbued with a sense of peace, in her eyes, in the way she smiled so frequently, and in the ease with which she moved. The kind of peace that Nash had searched for fruitlessly his whole life.

Horse-drawn carriages full of tourists—some happy and looking blissfully in love, others looking angry as they sniped at each other—passed them on the street. He also noticed that the locals seemed to be in a rush, looking at their phones as they hurried down the streets, not seeming to notice the historic buildings all around them.

He'd made the same mistake all these years, hadn't he? As he'd toured the globe many times over, every city, every street had started to look the same.

This disguise was perfect. But his delight came from far more than just the clothes or the hat and glasses—it was the fact that Ashley was here with him.

Before they walked up to the ticket booth at the Hofburg, she said, "Why don't I do the talking today when we're doing things like buying tickets? Your accents are amazing, but I wouldn't want anyone to accidentally discover who you are and ruin your day. In fact, if you pull out your phone like everyone else right now, you'll blend in perfectly."

Knowing she was right, he did as she suggested, looking down at his phone as she got them two tickets. He'd missed a dozen calls in the past half hour, but he didn't care. He could be *Nash Hardwin* again tomorrow. For the next handful of hours, he just wanted the chance to be a normal guy with a normal girl, enjoying a vacation day.

When she returned, she was holding headphones. "I got us the audio tour," she explained. "That way, we won't miss out on anything important."

Nash hadn't been a great student in school. Okay,

that was the world's hugest understatement, given that he'd dropped out at sixteen. And he'd definitely never done an audio tour at a museum. As they looped the audio guides around their necks, Nash felt a little awkward. He wasn't a museum kind of guy, and surely everyone could tell, right? And yet, as he and Ashley made their way through the rooms filled with historical artifacts, old photos, historic dresses, and even the private train car that Empress Elizabeth had traveled in, he realized just how interesting the royal's life had been.

Sisi, as she was known, hadn't had a happy life. She'd had problems with love, with rarely letting herself eat enough, and with her family.

He understood family issues perfectly. No matter who you were or how much money you had—whether you were a superstar musician, or a woman who had been one of the most celebrated royals in Europe during her time—it didn't mean your happiness was guaranteed.

When Nash wrote a great song, or had a fan tell him how his music had helped them through a difficult time, or when he saw the smiles on people's faces at his shows, he felt happy.

But it was fleeting.

God, he hated sounding like he was whining or ungrateful. He *was* grateful. Music had pulled him out of a dead-end life. But the older he got, the less he could escape the thought that there had to be *more*.

Not more money or more adoration from fans, but more meaning. More peace. More happiness.

Only, he'd never been able to figure out how to achieve those things.

They came to the end of the museum tour and were routed to exit through the gift shop. Ashley pulled off her earphones, beaming from ear to ear.

"Oh my gosh," she exclaimed, "that was fantastic! Even better than I hoped it would be. Sisi's life was so interesting, but sad too." She cocked her head. "Did you like the museum?"

"I did. A lot, actually. And thanks for getting us the audio guides. You were right. That way, we didn't miss a thing."

Scanning the gift shop, she said, "I'm going to buy a deck of cards with her picture on it to remember today by."

"Good idea." He picked up a key chain that featured Sisi's face. Which was crazy, because he didn't need keys for anything. He was always driven around.

Once upon a time, his van keys had been his refuge. His escape. He'd been sixteen years old when he bought a run-down VW van. He'd spent every spare minute and every spare dollar fixing up the engine and building out the inside. The van was how he'd escaped his miserable life with his mother. It was where he'd written all of his early songs. It was where he'd slept after gigs.

That van had changed his life. And though he now traveled the world in the most expensive tour buses on the market, he'd never enjoyed any vehicle as much as he loved driving and living in that van.

A kernel of an idea suddenly sparked inside of him. What if he bought another old VW van and built it out the same way?

Shaking away the crazy thought—his touring and recording schedule was way too tight to deviate from for more than this one day with Ashley—he was about to offer to pay for their mementos when he realized he didn't have any cash on him and using a credit card would out his identity.

He was the worst caricature of a celebrity, wasn't he? He didn't drive anything, didn't pay for anything, didn't do his own laundry, didn't clean his own rooms.

"Ashley, I wish I could pay for these, but I don't have any cash on me and using a card with my name on it would be a bad idea. I'm sorry." He felt like a complete idiot.

She waved away his apology. "I'm sure you're good for a few museum tickets and a key chain," she teased him. "Besides, we already agreed that I'd do all the talking with people today, so I'm happy to do all of the buying too. In fact, it's my treat! I usually only spend money on endless bags of groceries. Buying these stellar tourist mementos is a lovely change of pace."

Instead of making him feel like a jerk, she had remained relaxed, cheerful, and easy to be with. What's more, she found the wonder of everything, even a deck of cards and a key chain with a long-dead Viennese empress's face on them.

She bought his key chain and handed it to him. "I'm sure you'll treasure this," she said, clearly teasing him.

But he would, more than she knew.

Grinning as he slipped the key chain into his green polyester pocket, he asked, "Where to next?"

"The Lipizzaner horses at the Spanish Riding School are world famous. The online tickets sold out ages ago, but I read that if you show up right before a performance, they sometimes have a few standing-only seats available. You wouldn't be interested in that, would you?"

"Sure I would." Didn't she realize he was totally and completely hers for the day, regardless of where they went or what they did? All he wanted was to spend time with her. He grinned. "Let's go see if they've got any nosebleed seats left for two well-dressed tourists."

In his regular life, Nash could have had tickets to a sold-out show in a millisecond. But today, he would try his luck like anyone else.

The riding arena was near the museum, and a few minutes later, Ashley was triumphant at the ticket booth. "They have two spots left! And the next show starts in just a few minutes. It was meant to be."

He loved seeing how happy she was. But when he saw the price of the tickets, he blanched. "I'll pay you back every cent," he said in a low voice as they walked inside.

Again, she waved away his concerns. "That's okay. It's fun having someone to see everything with. And like I said, this is the first time I've gotten to spend my savings on something fun and frivolous for myself and a friend. It's usually endless gallons of milk and cartons of eggs, or the mortgage, or repairs on my car."

He wanted to ask her who she was buying "endless" groceries for. Of course there was a guy waiting at home for her. Because there was no way on earth that a woman as beautiful, intelligent, and sweet as Ashley could be single. No wonder she'd ignored him when he'd said how good kissing her had been.

Before he could ask her any intrusive questions, he realized that she'd called him a friend. He felt it too—that they had become more than two strangers who had been thrown together. It was yet another excellent surprise for today.

The lights went down, and a quartet from the Vienna Philharmonic began playing "The Blue Danube" by Johann Strauss. Though Nash had no formal music training, over the years he'd taught himself to play everything from classical to jazz and country to rock. And as they stood in the stands above a horse arena, he'd never heard the waltz by Strauss played better. He made a mental note to have his manager contact the quartet to see if they could work together the next time he was in Austria.

And then, as the horses made their way into the arena, he was swept away by their artistry. Nash had never known animals could move with such precision, coordination, and beauty. They truly were dancing, with their riders helping to guide their movements.

Ashley grabbed his hand in excitement, then whispered in his ear, "Can you believe what the horses are able to do? This is so incredible!"

He agreed. The horses, the riders, and the musicians were all amazing.

But none of them was more incredible than Ashley.

She took delight in everything. She wasn't at all jaded. She was beautiful. Her kiss had been smoking hot. She was a breath of fresh air on every level.

And he was going to hate having to say good-bye to her when their day together came to an end.

CHAPTER FOUR

"That was one of the best performances I've ever seen," Ashley said when the show had come to an end. "Did you like it?"

"It was terrific. Thanks for bringing me here, and for buying my ticket. All these years, I tried to tell myself I wasn't missing out on much when I traveled to cities like Vienna, but now I know that isn't true. I'm going to start making it a priority to get out of my hotel and tour bus to see the places I'm traveling to."

"I'm so glad to hear that," she replied with a sunny smile.

Her smile made his heart beat faster. She was the complete opposite of any woman he'd ever been with. Was that the reason for her allure? The fact that a "nice girl" like her was unconquered territory? Or did her attractions go much deeper?

"Where to next?"

Ashley pulled out her list. "There's a tram that will take us to the summer palace and gardens, and I believe we can hop off midtrip to eat at the famous

Naschmarkt if you're hungry."

"You've read my mind. I'm starved."

"We should be able to pick up the red line touring bus around the corner from the State Opera House."

They walked together down the road to the bus stop, and though a handful of people did double takes, he knew it was simply because their outfits were so strange. No one suspected who Nash was.

"If I'd known green polyester would make me this unrecognizable," he said, "I would have switched out the contents of my closet a long time ago."

She laughed, but shook her head. "That's funny, because I was thinking just the opposite. You couldn't *pay* me to wear this outfit again after today."

"Why? You look great in it."

She shot him a look. "I'm not sure if that's a compliment or an insult."

"I meant it as a compliment."

"Thanks, I guess. Although I sure hope I looked better than this in my wrap dress earlier today."

"You looked beautiful in that dress," he confirmed.

When her eyebrows went up at his emphatic statement, he realized this was his chance to ask about her relationship status. "Your husband or boyfriend probably wouldn't like knowing how attractive I find you, would he?"

She looked more than a little surprised by his admission—even though he'd already said as much back at the hotel, and he'd also told her how much he'd enjoyed kissing her.

"What makes you think I'm in a relationship?"

"You mentioned buying gallons of milk."

"Those are for my son, Kevin. He's eleven." Her whole face lit up when she talked about her son, making her look even more beautiful. Which made his heart pound even faster. Too soon, her smile fell away. "I know he's in good hands with my parents and siblings for the weekend, but I still can't help but be a little worried. This is the first time I've gone somewhere without him."

Nash supposed he should have been surprised to hear that she had a kid. But somehow, that fit. He'd bet his entire fortune that she was a great mom. "Was Kevin upset that you were leaving for the weekend?"

"No, he was totally fine with it. In fact, I think he's pretty excited about getting to spread his wings without me around for once. It's just..." She sighed as she paused to buy their tickets for the tourist bus that had just pulled up. They got on board, heading up the stairs to the upper deck that was open to the sky before she continued. "His dad, Josh, is terribly unpredictable and irresponsible. I almost didn't come on this trip because he insisted that Kevin stay with him while I was out of town. I know that sounds like no big deal for a kid to stay over at his dad's house, but if you saw Josh's place and knew how he lived his life, you wouldn't want an eleven-year-old boy to stay with him either."

"How long were you two together?"

"We were never really *together*. We went out for a little while in high school. The first time we had sex, that was it—I got knocked up. And just like the classic story, the father of my child fled and was completely out of the picture until two years ago, when he decided he wanted to play at being a dad after the diapers and all-night colic sessions were done." Her cheeks colored. "I don't know why I just told you all of that."

"Believe me, I did far worse in high school," he said, in the hopes that she wouldn't regret sharing so much with him about her life. He'd loved hearing it and hoped she'd share more. "Heck, most of my late teens and early twenties were a mess. At least you never went to jail for anything you did." He'd been to jail for so many things. Trespassing. Fights. Theft. Even, at one of his lowest points, drugs. He wondered if Ashley knew about his past. He felt like he would never be able to fully live it down and was certain that people were constantly judging him by his arrest record.

"You're right that I never went to jail," she replied, "although sometimes it felt like I was in a prison of sorts when my whole life changed so drastically. I freaked out when I realized I was pregnant. Then Josh doubly freaked out when I told him. I knew there was no way I wanted to be with him long-term, so we broke up. Amazingly, my parents were really great about it all. They didn't shame me or make me feel bad." She paused before confessing, "I know this is going to sound strange, but they were so nice about it that I almost felt like I needed to beat *myself* up for the mistake I made."

When he was younger and getting into trouble over and over again, there hadn't been anyone who had cared about him enough to sit him down and try to help him figure his shit out. Sure, his manager and his record label had continually stepped in to bail him out of jail and get his record expunged, but ultimately they had done it to protect their investment. Not because they loved him like family. It wasn't until Nash woke up one day and realized he was sick of feeling sorry for himself—and thought about the many people out there who had it far worse than he ever had—that he'd finally stopped making such stupid decisions. That was also when he started giving money to charities, and schools, and families. Anonymously, of course.

"I know exactly what you mean," Nash said. "Sometimes you just want someone to say, 'You really screwed up, you shouldn't have done that, and I hope you'll make a better decision next time,' so that you can say you're sorry, promise you won't make another mistake that bad, and move on with your life."

Ashley looked stunned by his comments. "I don't think anyone has ever understood how I feel until you."

Nash had been given a million compliments over the years. He'd had people tell him he was a brilliant songwriter and that he was the best performer they'd ever seen. But no compliment had ever meant as much to him as hearing Ashley say she felt he understood her.

"What happened next?" he asked. "Did you stay in school and graduate? Or did you drop out?"

"I stayed, although I'm not going to lie to you and say it wasn't hard. Because it was. So very hard." She gave him a crooked half smile. "I had always been a good girl. I did my homework, studied for my tests, and made impressive plans for the future. After five minutes of god-awful sex, all of that was gone. My teachers were still nice to me, but I could tell they were looking at me differently. It felt like they had lost respect for me. All because I slept with someone I liked, but didn't love, and ended up having a baby at a really young age." She pushed her shoulders back. "But I survived."

"Don't take this the wrong way," Nash said, "but you are *a lot* tougher than you look."

"You're right," she agreed, "I am pretty tough. Even if my brothers and father often seem to forget that fact. But you know what? I'm also one of the luckiest people in the world, because I have Kevin." She smiled as she said, "I'm not saying it's all sunshine and butterflies in our house, because sometimes I lose it and yell about the dirty clothes all over his room, or how he was supposed to do his homework *before* playing video games. But if I had it to do all over again, I'd do it exactly the same way. There's no way I would want to live my life without my son in it."

Nash had never been the kind of guy who believed in love at first sight. Sure, he'd written songs about other people being in love, but he'd never met anyone who made *him* feel like he was falling. He'd never met a woman who, simply by telling him about her life, pierced him through the heart.

Not until Ashley.

His mother had also gotten pregnant at seventeen. But unlike Ashley, his mom had been anything but devoted to him. On the contrary, she had been downright dismissive, continuing to drink and party as if he didn't exist, while blaming his existence for everything bad in her life.

How different would his life have been if he had been raised by someone as loving as Ashley? Would he have made better decisions earlier in his life? Would he have stayed out of those fights? Would he have walked away from drugs and booze sooner? Would he never have known the inside of a prison cell so intimately?

As Nash watched her pull out her phone to take pictures from the tour bus, he found himself wishing another fan would nearly recognize him. Because then he could get away with stealing another kiss from the one woman he wanted to kiss more than he'd ever wanted anything in his whole life.

"We're here!" She hopped up, pulling on the cord to indicate that she wanted the bus to stop. "I am absolutely starving, so our timing is perfect."

They got off the bus and headed into the huge outdoor food market. Walking down the central pathway, they passed restaurants, produce stores, meat counters, and fish sellers.

Ashley stopped at a vibrantly colored candy stall. "The dentist is always saying Kevin shouldn't eat sour candy because it's bad for his teeth, but I've never seen sour candies that look like these." The tiny replica soccer balls and basketballs in big wicker baskets were actually sour candy confections. "Kevin would absolutely *love* these. So I'm going to break the rules for once and get them for him! I might even sneak some to eat myself."

As the proprietor of the stand bagged and weighed the candies, Nash marveled at how buying and eating sour candy was her version of *breaking the rules*. She'd be shocked if she knew how many actual rules he'd broken in his life…

After tucking the candy in her purse, she said, "All of the restaurants we've passed look great, but instead of eating at one of the Italian or Japanese places, what do you think about eating something traditionally Viennese?"

"Works for me." The day they were sharing was already unlike any other he'd experienced, so it made sense that the food they ate would be new to him too.

As luck would have it, there was a Viennese restaurant a hundred yards ahead. They were quickly seated outside under an awning and given two menus.

"I'm so hungry I could eat everything on the menu," Ashley said.

"I wonder what *Tafelspitz*, *Gulaschsuppe*, and *Erdäpfelsalat* taste like?" he asked.

"Only one way to find out," Ashley said. A few seconds later, she launched into a spirited conversation with the waiter about his favorite Viennese meals.

As she smiled her sparkling smile for the waiter, Nash grew increasingly jealous. Though he knew he was being ridiculous, he wanted her smiles and the light flush in her cheeks to be only for him.

"If the two of you don't mind sharing," the waiter finally said, "why don't you get all three dishes? I promise you won't be disappointed."

Nash couldn't remember the last time he'd shared food with anyone. Sure, he went out to eat with his band and people from his record label, but no one ever dared to eat off his plate. That was something you did with family or a girlfriend.

Which, he mused, must be why it felt so right with Ashley. In a matter of hours, she felt almost like his girlfriend. Even though they'd done nothing more than hold hands and share one perfect stolen kiss.

"Good idea," he said. "Let's get it all."

"I'm also going to have a *Gespritzter*," Ashley said, pointing to a wine spritzer–style drink on the menu. "Do you want one, Nash?"

"No, thanks. I don't drink." He hadn't touched alcohol or drugs in more than a decade. Not since he'd realized they turned him into someone he didn't like to be around. Someone like his mother.

Ashley excused herself to go the bathroom, and when she returned, her drink, his water, and their appetizer had been delivered. He lifted his glass to her in a toast. "To a great day together in Vienna with my snuggle wuggle."

She laughed as she clinked her glass against his. "Here's to my honey bunny." But then she frowned. "Although if you're dating anyone or are married, please let her know I'm not trying to horn in on her territory."

"I'm not dating anyone, and I've never come close to getting married."

"Me either," she told him. "In fact—and I can't believe I'm even admitting this to you, but since I'm already on a roll today, and this *Gespritzter* is so delicious my tongue will probably loosen even further once I've drained my glass—the truth is that I haven't dated much at all. Once I had Kevin, I threw my whole focus into raising him and helping to run my family's business. Before I knew it, I had a son going to kindergarten and was in a totally different place than everyone else my age."

"You had way more life experience than any of them. That should have been a bonus."

"It wasn't. Twenty-three-year-old men are terrified of dating someone with a five-year-old kid. And I didn't want any of them around Kevin when it seemed like they were barely more than kids themselves. All they cared about was partying and having fun. And there I was, helping with homework and having parent-teacher conferences." She shrugged. "Honestly, I'm okay with being alone. My family, however, is not nearly as okay with my solo status as I am. My sisters are always trying to set me up with someone. All of the dates have been epic fails, though, so I decided last year to stop going out with anyone."

"I've always preferred being alone over being with a boring date," he agreed.

This time, she was the one raising her glass in a toast. "To being alone."

He clinked his glass against hers as he echoed her words. "To being alone."

But it didn't feel quite right, not when he was having a *much* better time in Vienna with Ashley than he would have by himself.

"Actually, I'd like to amend that," he said. "To being alone together."

She laughed. "I like that. To being alone together."

They clinked glasses again and drank. When the food arrived, Nash decided neither the food nor the company could have been better than they were right here, right now, with Ashley Sullivan.

CHAPTER FIVE

As they left the restaurant and hopped back on the tour bus, Ashley couldn't stop smiling.

Though Nash was one of the most famous men in the world, and she should have felt nervous or awkward around him, somehow it was exactly the opposite. She had told him things she'd never said to anyone else. Not even her sisters. He was that easy to be with.

And yet, that didn't mean she wasn't also desperately attracted to him. He was her secret late-night fantasy hero, after all. Even in his ridiculous green polyester outfit, he was shockingly sexy.

It had momentarily thrown her to learn from Brandon that Nash had spent time in jail for a whole host of offenses. But the more time she spent with Nash, the less she understood how he could have done any of those things. Although she supposed the reason he didn't drink could be because he'd needed to stop. Whatever his past, or the reasons he stayed away from alcohol, she liked him a great deal.

In fact, whenever she thought about their kiss outside the hotel—even though it had been a fake kiss meant to throw his fans off the scent—her heart started galloping inside her chest.

The same thing happened every time his hand briefly moved to the small of her back when they were navigating a crowded area, or if their hands accidentally brushed as they were walking. She refused to beat herself up for her silly crush, though. After all, it was hugely unlikely that they would ever see each other again after she left Vienna. This was simply a very special day where she got to spend time with a very special man.

Why shouldn't she enjoy herself for one perfect day in Europe that no one but she and Nash would ever know had happened?

What surprised her the most, however, was that Nash also seemed to be having a great time. She could still hardly believe what he'd said. *Kissing you really did feel right, Ashley. More right than anything has for a very long time.*

Plus, given his success and wealth, she would have assumed he had seen the Seven Wonders, or at least spent time exploring the most wondrous places on the planet. Instead, she'd been surprised to learn that his tour, recording, and interview schedule was so intense, he'd never had a chance to have more personal adventures.

As they approached their stop for the summer palace and gardens, Ashley and Nash went to stand by the
bus doors, waiting for them to open. When she noticed
a group of teenagers gesturing to them and laughing,
she said to Nash in a low voice that only he could hear,
"If they only knew who they were laughing at."

Nash grinned. "When I was their age, I would have
been laughing my head off at us too. As you might
have guessed, I was a hell-raiser. I hope your son
doesn't put you through as many trials and tribulations
as I put my mom through."

As they got off the bus and made their way toward
the palace gates, Ashley said, "Regardless of what you
did when you were younger, your mom must be so
proud of you now."

Nash looked grim as he replied, "She passed away
not long after I signed my first record deal at eighteen.
But my music was never her thing. She was never
proud of me a day in her life."

"I'm sorry you lost her so young."

"It was a long time ago," he said with a shrug.

Though he was obviously trying to brush it off, she
could see from his grim expression that it didn't matter
how long ago it had been—his mother's lack of pride in
his achievements, along with losing her, hurt him.

"I'm still really sorry for what you went through,

Nash."

"You don't need to waste your pity on me," he insisted. "She was a single mom, like you. She got pregnant at seventeen, also like you. But that was where any similarities to you end. You're a great mom to Kevin. She wasn't a great mom to me. I get that her parents weren't good people and that she had some hard knocks early in her life, but..." He let out a harsh breath. "My childhood sucked. I couldn't wait to get away."

Though Nash wasn't asking for Ashley's thoughts about his mother's motivations, the two of them had already shared so much today that she felt compelled to give them to him anyway. "I wonder if part of why she acted that way was because she thought that if you left her, you'd be able to find something better. A better family. A better life."

He thought about it for a few moments. Then he shook his head. "Or maybe she was a drunk and junkie who never should have had a kid. When I was sixteen, I bought an old junker of a van, then built out the inside so I could live in it. I dropped out of school, packed my guitar, and hit the road. I've been moving from place to place ever since."

His difficult childhood surely must have been behind the troubles he'd had in his past, and it broke her heart. "I had a baby my senior year of high school, but at least I was lucky enough to be surrounded by my family. I can't imagine what leaving behind everyone and everything I knew at sixteen would have been like."

"I had it easy compared to you, Ash. You had a kid to take care of. Whereas I only had myself to worry about. If I didn't want to eat right, I didn't eat right. If I didn't want to sleep much, I didn't sleep much. I did whatever I wanted, whenever I wanted to do it."

She wondered if he realized that he'd just used her nickname. It felt right, though. "Is that when you started writing songs and playing shows?" she asked.

At last, his grim expression disappeared. "Do you have any idea how nice it is to be with someone who doesn't already know everything about my life?"

"I do know your music," she admitted. "I've just never been someone who reads celebrity magazines or watches much TV. And I didn't mean for my questions to feel like an interview. You don't have to answer, if you don't want to."

"Our conversation doesn't feel anything like an interview, Ash. First of all, I'm never friends with journalists. And I've sure as hell never kissed any of them."

She couldn't stop the smile from taking over her face, even if his reference to their kiss made her blush too. For a moment, his eyes did that smoldering thing, and she almost wondered if he was going to kiss her again. On purpose this time.

Instead, he answered her question. "Yeah, that's when I started playing shows. I needed money for gas and food, and I had all these songs I'd written that I'd never played for anyone, so I went to some open mics and ended up being offered the chance to play while people ate and drank and talked over my songs."

"I've always thought that must be hard for performers in restaurants. Did it hurt your feelings when they didn't listen?"

"Sure, it did. But it also helped me remember why I was doing it. I wrote music and played songs because I needed to write and play them. Other people liking them was a bonus, rather than the reason. Anyone making art to try to get validation from others is in for a rude awakening, because there will always be people who want to bring you down."

"You have such a healthy outlook on things," she said. "Although now that everybody loves your music, I can't imagine anyone would dare to be so rude if you were playing for them now."

"I don't know if that's necessarily true," he countered. "People aren't rude to *Nash Hardwin*. But if they didn't know who I was—" He broke off as he looked down at his outfit. "You know what? Let's try an experiment."

Before she had any idea what he intended to do, he approached a man busking in the garden and spoke with him. The next thing she knew, the man had handed Nash his guitar.

What on earth was Nash doing? If he played one of his songs live in the garden, he would surely blow his cover, regardless of his disguise.

But when he stepped up to the busker's microphone, which was attached to a small speaker, and began to play the guitar, though Ashley recognized the song, it wasn't because Nash had written it. It was a song her father had loved to sing to her when she was growing up: Simon & Garfunkel's "Scarborough Fair."

Nash's guitar playing was beautiful. And when he began to sing, his voice was so mesmerizing that a thrill ran through her from head to toe. Soon, people drifted closer, drawn in by his incredible voice and talent. Nash managed to infuse every word and every note of the song with emotion. Enough emotion to bring tears to her eyes.

Though she remained worried he might blow his cover if someone recognized his voice—causing pandemonium to erupt in the palace gardens, just as it had outside Brandon's hotel—she decided it would be worth it for this chance to hear him play "Scarborough Fair" in such a beautiful setting. She would never forget this one perfect moment in time.

By the time he finished, there must have been fifty people gathered around him. They applauded loudly, digging into their pockets for both coins and bills to throw into the open guitar case in front of him. They begged him to play another song, but he simply shook his head and handed the guitar back to the busker. He remained in conversation with the other man until everyone in the crowd had drifted away, and she could tell from Nash's body language that he was insisting the busker keep the small fortune in tips.

When Nash at last returned to Ashley's side, she told him, "That was beautiful."

"Thanks." He had a new spring in his step. "It felt good to be a random guy with a guitar standing in front of a microphone again."

"And you *definitely* proved that people want to listen to you because you're amazingly talented, not just because you're famous."

He shrugged as though he still wasn't quite convinced, then said, "Are you ready to head into Schönbrunn now?"

Though she appreciated his modesty, she hoped he understood just how special he, and his gift, really were.

"Actually," she replied, "I wouldn't mind getting a drink and hanging out in the garden for a while longer."

Though they hadn't yet entered the palace, she was enjoying being outside in the rose garden with Nash too much to continue rushing through her tourist list.

They collected two cups of steaming Viennese coffee and had just found seats in the waning sunlight when her phone rang with her son's ringtone. "It's Kevin," she told Nash before picking up.

"Hi, honey! I'm so glad you called." She was grinning from ear to ear. "What have you been up to with Grandma and Grandpa?"

"It's been off the hook," Kevin replied. "Grandpa took me to the skate park, and then we got pizza, and then I showed him how to play Minecraft. We're a wicked good team."

"Sounds super fun. I miss you."

"Miss you, too, Mom. Have you bought me any presents yet?"

She laughed. "I sure have."

"What is it?"

"Something small, but I have a feeling you're going to love it."

"I can't wait to see what it is! But I gotta go now," Kevin told her. "Grandma says breakfast is ready, and then I have my soccer game."

"Love you, honey. Have a great game."

"Love you too."

And then he was gone. Her heart squeezed from

missing him, but she also knew that spending time with his grandpa without her always hovering around was good for him.

"Sounds like he's having a good time," Nash noted with a smile.

"He is. I still wish he could have come to Vienna with me, but the truth is he's probably having a way better time eating pizza and going to the skate park and playing video games with Grandpa than he would walking through some old buildings."

"Your dad sounds pretty cool, doing all that stuff with his grandson."

"That's because my dad still thinks he's a kid some-times."

"Is your whole family like you and Brandon?"

"What do you mean?"

"Smart. Successful. Friendly."

It was an incredibly nice compliment. "Well, it's true that all my siblings have done well. And I've always liked working in the family business."

"Are you all in the hotel business?"

"No. My parents opened the Sullivan Café and Irish-themed retail store when we were little. Once I had Kevin and I wanted the flexibility to be accessible to my son, they offered me the job of managing both the café and store."

"Given how organized your sightseeing schedule is

and how much you clearly love spreadsheets, I suspect that wasn't the only reason they offered it to you. They must have known you'd do a great job."

"I worked in the back office throughout high school, so it was a good fit for all of us. We have great vendors, and our customers are fantastic, our staff is wonderful, and it's been really exciting helping to open up locations throughout Maine."

"But?"

She was surprised he'd heard the part she left out. No one else ever seemed to, not even the people she was closest to. "But I guess because I fell into the job due to my circumstances, there's always been a little part of me that's wondered what my life might have been like if I'd gone to college. I really do love my work," she said, wanting him to know, "it's just that I sometimes secretly find myself longing for a tiny bit more adventure."

While she spoke, his phone was buzzing like crazy. It had been doing that all day long inside his pocket.

"Do you need to answer any of those calls? It sounds like someone really wants to get hold of you."

"Everyone and everything else can wait. Today is about spending time with you."

His words made her heart flutter. As did the heat in his eyes. Throughout the day, she'd constantly thought about his kiss outside the hotel and longed for another one.

What, she suddenly found herself wondering, would he think if *she* kissed *him* this time?

Before she could act on her crazy impulse, her phone rang again. Unlike Nash, she couldn't ignore it. What if something had happened to Kevin?

Fortunately, it was only Brandon. "Hi, is the crowd gone outside the hotel?"

"They are. But I haven't been able to reach Nash. Do you have any idea where he is?"

"I do. He's right here with me."

"He is?" Her brother sounded more than a little incredulous at the idea that Nash would have wanted to spend the day with her.

"Yes, he is." Suddenly fed up with the fact that Brandon seemed to think so little of her desirability, even though she knew Nash was a million miles out of her league, she couldn't resist adding, "And we're having a *fantastic* time together."

Her brother growled in response. "Put him on," he demanded.

She rolled her eyes, even though Brandon couldn't see it. "I'm not going to hand the phone to him if you're going to be totally ridiculous and go ballistic." She wanted to remind her brother how he'd said earlier that he liked Nash, but she couldn't think of a way to tactfully say it in front of Nash. The last thing she wanted to do was hurt his feelings. Especially now that she'd had a window into his difficult childhood. It broke her heart thinking of him as, for all intents and purposes, a motherless child.

"Fine, I'll keep it together," Brandon reluctantly agreed. "Now will you put me on with him?"

She held her phone out to Nash. "As I'm sure you've guessed, it's Brandon. He says he needs to talk with you."

Nash took the phone, and she couldn't read his expression as he listened to what her brother had to say. Finally, he said, "Okay. I'll keep an eye out for a call from you later." He ended the call and handed the phone back to her.

She narrowed her eyes. "He said something rude to you, didn't he?"

"He wanted to let me know that there don't seem to be any available rooms in Vienna due to a major cultural festival taking place this weekend. He said he's still working on finding me one, but for the time being, my things are staying in your apartment."

But Ashley had been around enough men by this point in her life to know when they were leaving something out. "What else did he say? I know Brandon, so I'm positive there was more."

Nash grimaced slightly. "He also reminded me that if I don't keep my hands off you, he'll tear me to pieces."

"I knew it! If it's not Brandon trying to keep me locked up in an ivory tower with a chastity belt on, it's my father, or my other brothers."

"I'm sure it's just because they care about you."

"That excuse wears thin after hearing it so many times over the years. And this is the perfect example of Brandon not thinking straight. If he wasn't so intent on thinking he needs to protect me, he'd realize that the smartest thing is for you to stay with me, rather than trying to pull strings to find you another place. My rental apartment has two bedrooms, since that was the only option still available when I was booking the trip. I don't need all that space for myself."

"I would love to spend more time with you, Ash," Nash said, making her heart race again. "But if I take you up on your offer, I'm almost positive your brother will make good on his threat."

"Just because I got pregnant at seventeen doesn't mean I can't take care of myself at nearly thirty! And it sure as hell doesn't mean I'm not capable of making my own decisions. So if I want to take a hot guy back to my apartment on the Michaelerplatz and have sex with him all night long, that's exactly what I'll do. And no one in my family can stop me."

It wasn't until the words had spilled from her lips that she realized it sounded like she expected Nash to share *her* bedroom tonight, rather than sleep in the extra bedroom.

"That was the most embarrassingly mortifying thing I've ever said." She put her hands over her face, then spoke from behind them. "I didn't mean for that to sound like I think you want to be with me tonight as more than a friend. Not when I know it's the most ridiculous idea in the world."

She stopped speaking when she felt his hands move over hers. Gently, he drew them away from her face.

"It's not a ridiculous idea. In fact, I think it might be one of the *best* ideas I've ever heard. Because I *do* want you, Ash. More than I've ever wanted anyone else. I wasn't kidding when I told you in the hotel suite that you're gorgeous and that any guy who got to be with you would be a lucky bastard. And I meant it when I said how attracted I am to you. I'm *crazy* attracted to you."

Her mouth fell open. Actually dropped open. She'd never believed it could happen in real life. But now she knew it was a completely natural response to someone saying the very thing you least expected them to say.

Still stunned that he wanted her the way she wanted him, she told him, "You're so sweet to say that, Nash, but you don't have to let me down easy. I know what league I'm in—and it's not yours. Just because we've had a great time together today doesn't mean I think our day should end with us in bed together."

But he was smiling at her the whole time she was speaking. The sexiest smile she'd ever seen. "Being with you today hasn't been great, Ash, it's been *perfect*. The only thing that could possibly make it better would be to end it naked in bed with you."

Her heart was pounding like crazy. Completely out of control. She could hardly catch her breath.

Was this really happening?

Was Nash Hardwin actually saying he wanted to sleep with her?

Despite the secret fantasies she'd had about him over the years, never in a million years had she thought something like this could actually happen.

"Do you really mean what you're saying?"

"Why won't you believe that I find you attractive? Not just attractive, but hands down the sexiest woman I've ever been with. Why won't you believe that I want to be with you? Especially since you're a million times too good for me."

She was taken aback by the passion in his words. He didn't sound like he was just trying to be nice. He sounded like he wanted her. Really, truly wanted *her*.

But though warmth was starting to unfurl in her belly, she'd spent so many years feeling like the ultimate wallflower that she could barely believe it was true.

"I'm not too good for you, Nash."

"You sure as hell are, in a million ways. But the truth is, right now I want you too badly to give a damn."

The next thing she knew, his mouth was on hers, and they were kissing. His tongue slicked against hers, and a gasp of pleasure escaped her throat. She wanted to get closer. Closer to Nash than she had ever been with anyone else. She was practically wrapping herself around him when he drew back slightly, his breath coming in harsh pants.

"Now do you believe me? Now can you finally stop doubting that what's between us is wickedly hot?"

She couldn't deny it. Not after that kiss.

But though she didn't argue, she had to remind them both of something. "The only other time I had reckless, spur-of-the-moment sex, I got pregnant."

Shockingly, her frank reminder didn't deter Nash. "I'll do everything I can to ensure you don't get pregnant tonight. But if it did happen, I would never turn my back on you, or our kid, the way your ex did."

Yet again, she was having conversations with Nash that she simply couldn't imagine having with another man. Conversations where she put it all out there, leaving nothing out for fear of embarrassment.

Did that also mean she wouldn't have to hold back with him in bed? Could she give in to her wildest fantasies with him?

Oh my God. She was actually considering it.

Actually, she was more than just considering it.

She was going to *do* it.

"Okay," she said, the word barely above a whisper, "let's go back to my apartment." She swallowed hard before adding, "And let's leave the other bedroom empty."

His grin was huge. But then he seemed to check himself. "I don't want you to feel like I pushed you into this, Ash."

She thought about it. Really thought about it. There was no question that he had been very persuasive, both with his verbal arguments and with his kiss. But just as Nash had said earlier, she was strong. Strong enough to support her son, and buy her own home, and pay her own way to Vienna.

And a strong woman could make a spur-of-the-moment decision to sleep with a hot guy if she wanted to.

In fact, it suddenly occurred to her that walking away from him now would be the *opposite* of strong. Walking away would mean she didn't think she could handle any fallout after tonight. Walking away would mean she was worried about getting so attached to Nash that she'd never be able to let him go without her heart breaking.

But that could never happen, because Ashley knew without a shadow of a doubt that this was one night only. One glorious night in Nash's arms that would never be repeated.

So yes, she was going to do this. She was going to have a one-night stand with Nash Hardwin.

And she was going to enjoy every single second of it.

"I want this." She stood and held out her hand to him. "I want *you*."

CHAPTER SIX

Ashley swung back and forth between thinking that sleeping with Nash was crazy and feeling beyond desperate to be with him.

They'd only met this morning, and things were moving really fast. But what felt most daunting to Ashley was her inexperience. Apart from sleeping that one time with Josh, she was pretty much untouched. Whereas Nash was one of the world's most famous—and sexy—men. Which surely meant they were polar opposites on the experience front. He seemed to be as attracted to her as she was to him, but what if he ended up disappointed once her clothes were off, and they were actually in bed together?

Stop it! The voice inside her head spoke loudly enough to get her attention.

The voice was right. There was no point in going down a rabbit hole of insecurity. She was going to sleep with Nash Hardwin tonight, gosh darn it! She wanted to do it, he wanted to do it, and there was absolutely nothing wrong with two consenting adults making each other feel good. Even something as innocent as holding Nash's hand in the taxi that took them back to her apartment felt charged, potent, heavy with anticipation.

The taxi pulled up outside her apartment, and after she paid the driver, Ashley and Nash walked through the narrow pathway. She unlocked the front door to the building, and they had just stepped inside and were about to climb the stairs, when she felt his hands on her waist.

Gently, he turned her to face him. "Everything you're thinking is written on your face." He brushed a lock of hair from her cheek, and his fingertips against her skin sent tremors through her. "I don't have to come upstairs with you if you don't want me to."

Darn it, this was exactly what she didn't want to happen. She didn't want to be a wimp and forever remain on the perfectly safe life path she'd been on since the pregnancy test had displayed a double blue line in high school.

"I want you to come upstairs with me, Nash. I want to be with you."

He studied her face in the dim light of the hallway. "I know you are an honest person, so I'm going to take you at your word. But if at any time you want us to stop, or if you want me to leave, promise you'll tell me."

"I promise," she said, then led him up the stairs. She typed in the code on the electronic door lock, took a deep breath, then pulled him inside. Once the door was closed, he drew her against him.

"You are so beautiful, Ashley. Inside and out."

Certain that her looks couldn't possibly rate as high as most of the women he'd slept with over the years, instead of replying, she put her arms around his neck and lifted her mouth to his.

He let her lead the kiss, let her taste him, discover him. She ran her tongue over his lower lip, then slipped it inside his mouth to tangle with his. Their kiss was at once sweet and sensual, and all of her senses were quickly being taken over by intense desire.

As they continued to kiss, she ran her hands down his neck, over his broad shoulders, and down to his strong, muscular chest. It was gratifying to feel his heart beating so quickly against her palm. As quickly as hers was beating.

"You make me feel things," he said in a low voice against her mouth. "Things I don't normally feel."

"Me too," she said.

The next thing she knew, her back was against the door, and his hands were on either side of her face as he *devoured* her. Nash was kissing her like he couldn't get enough of her. Like he craved the very essence of her.

His lips moved to her throat, and the next thing she knew, he had torn open the ugly blouse. She helped him shove the remaining shreds of polyester off, leaving her only in her own bra and the beige, floral skirt.

Having sex with Kevin's father hadn't been anything like this. No one had ripped anybody else's clothes off, for one. They'd been two teenagers fumbling around in the dark.

But Nash was clearly a master of the sensual arts.

Who knew what she'd do with everything she was sure to learn from Nash tonight? Would she go back to Bar Harbor and be a wild woman? Even if she went back to living the same life she had before, she'd still know *more*.

More about pleasure. More about what it was like to be with a shockingly sexy man who wanted her. Truly wanted her in a way no other man ever had.

Wanting to strip away the layers of fabric between them, she grabbed his shirt in her hands and pulled. Unlike her shirt, his didn't tear open. A button didn't even pop off. Undaunted, she tried again, and when it still didn't work, she couldn't hold back her giggles. Soon, he was laughing too.

Kissing and laughing. It was a heady combination. And one she hadn't known existed.

That first time, there hadn't been laughter. On the

contrary, losing her virginity had been so serious, both she and Josh trying to pretend they knew what they were doing.

"How about I help you with that?" Nash finally said, the laughter in his voice layered with desire.

"Good idea. I clearly need to work on my tearing-clothes-off skills."

Together, they undid the buttons on his shirt, and as they revealed more and more of his broad, tanned, muscular chest, Ashley nearly gasped aloud at his male beauty.

She wanted to run her hands over every inch of him, discover his contours, his hollows, his every muscle and sinew. Acting on a combination of instinct and lust, she gave in to her desire, letting both her fingertips and her eyes appreciate him. Until she had to taste him, too, unable to stop herself from leaning forward to run her lips and tongue over his chest.

His groan of pleasure reverberated against her mouth. When she turned her head to look up at him, his eyes were blazing with heat.

"No fair," he said. "You're doing everything to me that I want to do to you."

She didn't know what made her so bold, but she found herself saying, "Then do it."

He captured her mouth again, his kiss deep and passionate. A few moments later, he hooked his thumbs beneath her bra straps and slid them off her shoulders, watching hungrily as the upper swells of her breasts above her bra cups rose and fell. He ran the pads of two fingers over her breasts.

Her head fell back against the door, and she swallowed convulsively.

"Do you like it when I touch you like this?" he asked.

She could barely speak, could manage only a simple, *"Yes."*

"All day long," he said in a voice made hoarse with need, "I've been wondering what you looked like under your god-awful clothes. I knew you'd be beautiful, but you're even better than my fantasies."

She loved what he was saying, but she also had to call him on it. Had to keep things completely honest between them. "You haven't known me long enough to have fantasies." Not the way he had been her secret late-night fantasy for years.

"Are you kidding me?" he countered. "I've spun out so many fantasies about you in the handful of hours we've spent together that even if we make love all night, we won't get through them all."

Wow. No one had ever talked dirty with her before. She wanted to talk dirty back, and he'd made her feel so comfortable from the start that if she didn't try with him, who would she ever feel comfortable enough to do it with?

"Tell me one of your fantasies." She licked her lips,

gratified to see his gaze immediately drop to her mouth. "And then we'll live it out. Right here, right now."

He looked like he could hardly believe his luck. But then she watched him check himself, just as he had before.

"I don't want to go too fast, Ashley. I don't want to ask you for too much. Or be too rough."

But didn't he see that she wanted to spend at least one night in her life with someone who wouldn't obey the rules? That she wanted to know what it was like to be with a man who would give in to desire completely and show her pleasure beyond her wildest imagination?

"That's exactly what I want," she told him. "I want you to go fast. I want you to ask me for more than anyone else ever has. And if you're a little rough... Well, I think I might just love it."

He closed his eyes as though he were in pain. "Don't say it if you don't mean it."

"You said earlier that you knew I'd never lie to you," she reminded him. "And you're right, I'm not a liar. I never have been, and I never will be. So that means I couldn't possibly be lying to you when I say that I want all those things." She paused a beat to let her words sink in. "So tell me one of your fantasies, Nash." She smiled a wicked little smile, feeling sexier than she ever had in her life. "And then we'll make it come true."

CHAPTER SEVEN

Nash tried to think straight, but how could he when Ashley was begging him to tell her his fantasies about her…and promising to turn them into reality?

She looked so delectable in her bra and skirt, her skin flushed with desire, her eyes dilated, her lips plump and well kissed. He'd never wanted anyone as much as he wanted her. But he'd never been with anyone as innocent as she was either.

He needed to go slow. No, the truth was that he needed to back away entirely. He needed to let go of her, leave her apartment, and let her return to her normal life. Ashley was a single mom who lived and worked in a small town. The last thing she should do was get involved with a musician who had a prison record. Granted, he hadn't been to jail since his early twenties, but he still wasn't good enough for her.

And yet…

He couldn't walk away. He couldn't let her go.

Not without tasting her. Not without taking her.

Not without giving her the best night of her life.

"I'll tell you my fantasy," he finally said in a low voice, "but only if you'll agree to do everything I say."

Her eyes grew big, and her chest rose and fell even faster. He could almost see the thoughts inside her head as the urge to retreat to her safe little world warred with the urge to be wicked.

At last, wicked won. "Okay. Start talking."

Beyond relieved that she wasn't kicking him out, he pressed another kiss to her sweet lips, then dropped his hands from her body and moved into the living room to sit in the middle of the couch.

"Step away from the door." She followed his instructions, walking to the center of the living room. "Stop there...and take off your skirt."

His voice was raspy with need. He was practically shaking from the strength of will required to keep from pouncing on her. But the longer he drew this out, the higher the anticipation would grow, and the better it would be. And not just for her. For both of them.

By the time they finally made love, they would both be ready to combust.

Her hands were remarkably steady, steadier than his would have been if he'd been the one pulling down the zipper at the side of the polyester skirt. Seconds later, the horrible fabric was falling to her feet. Her panties matched her bra, a light pink cotton. They might not have been silk or lace or satin, but they were still the sexiest thing he'd ever seen.

"Now what do you want me to do?" she asked in a soft voice.

"Just stand there. Let me look. You're so damned sexy. I don't ever want to forget how amazing you look right now."

Her cheeks grew even rosier, but she didn't move to cover herself. Instead, she lifted her chin slightly and tucked her shoulders back to stand proud and beautiful in front of him.

His chest squeezed as he drank her in. And suddenly, something that should have been purely sexual felt like so much more.

"Your bra." The two words sounded hoarse. "Take it all the way off."

She licked her lips again, making them look even more kissable. He gripped the back of the couch to keep from jumping up and taking her on the living room carpet.

Slowly, she undid the clasp at the front of her bra. His heart was beating out of control, and all he could hear was the blood rushing in his ears. He felt like he was thirteen years old and about to see his first naked girl.

Only this was so much better, because he wasn't thirteen. He was thirty-six years old and knew *exactly* how to give Ashley the ultimate pleasure.

At last, the bra sprang open, and she shrugged it off so that it joined the skirt on the floor. As his low groan reverberated through the living room, she held his gaze, as if silently saying that she would rise to every challenge he gave her tonight.

"Put your hands beneath your breasts. Cup them for me."

There was only the slightest pause before she lifted her hands to do as he'd asked.

"Is that all you want me to do for you?"

Sweet Lord, she was going to be the death of him. Ashley was not only rising to the occasion, she was teasing him as much as he was teasing her. Even more.

"Touch yourself the way I would."

Thankfully, she knew what he meant as she ran her fingertips over the soft swells of her breasts. Her eyes fluttered closed as she touched herself, and this time, the moan came from her.

"Your panties," he managed to grind out. "Take them off."

He watched her throat moving convulsively, her eyes slowly opening as she moved her hands from her breasts to her hips. Slowly, she slipped her fingers beneath the cotton fabric. And then she was shimmying her panties down legs that were so much longer than they had seemed when she was fully clothed.

Nash had seen more naked women than he could

count. He'd earned his playboy status. He'd lived every musician's fantasy.

But all of the women from his past paled in comparison to Ashley.

He felt like he was looking at a woman for the very first time. A real woman. A woman who was beautiful, not in spite of the faint stretch marks on her stomach, but *because* of them.

"Do you want me to touch myself again?"

She threw the words down as a softly spoken gauntlet. One that he knew would have him losing all control if she moved her fingers even one inch closer to her sex. But he wasn't ready for their game to end yet.

"Come here." She blinked at his gently spoken command, before moving slowly toward him.

It occurred to him that she might find their game sexist, because he was the one telling her what to do. But when she smiled with delight and pleasure, he understood that when she'd told him that she wanted to live out one of his fantasies, she'd meant it. Tonight, she'd set all rules aside, all taboos, all ideas of the roles they should and shouldn't be playing. Instead, she was willingly, and happily, giving herself completely over to being with him.

Of course, before tonight was done, he was going to make sure she also had her say. Hell yes, he was *dying* to know her fantasies.

"Climb onto my lap," he said next.

Without any hesitation, she moved over him. He cupped her hips, her bare skin warm beneath his callused fingertips.

"Kiss me."

She put her hands on his shoulders and pressed herself close as she lowered her mouth to his. Her kiss was soft, gentle, and sexier than any kiss he'd ever had.

He ran his fingertips and the flats of his palms from her hips to her waist to the press of her breasts against his bare chest. Little gasps came from her throat as she took their kiss deeper.

Of their own volition, her hips moved against his, his polyester-covered erection pressing up against her. This game they were playing as they brought one of his fantasies about her to life was the hottest one he'd ever played. Especially when she slid from his lap to kneel between his legs.

Putting her hands on the belt buckle of his Army green pants, she said, "This is the next part of your fantasy, isn't it?"

He couldn't speak, could manage only a nod.

Looking like the cat who'd gotten the cream, she undid his belt, then drew down the zipper. Moving his boxers and pants out of the way, she looked extremely pleased by what she saw.

"Let me guess what comes next," she said barely

above a whisper.

Before he could take his next breath, her lips were on him. She ran soft kisses from the head of his shaft, down to the base. He forgot to breathe as she licked him as though he were the tastiest ice cream cone she'd ever had.

That was when he realized he couldn't possibly play this game another second.

Putting his hands around her rib cage, he lifted her up from the carpet so that she was on the couch. Laying her back against the cushions, he levered over her.

"I have to have you, Ashley. *Now.*"

"I have to have you too." But then she frowned. "I wasn't expecting to come to Vienna and have sex with anyone. I don't have any protection. Do you?"

Hating to let go of her for one single second, he fumbled for his wallet in his pants on the floor. Thank God there was a condom in there.

He held it up triumphantly. "You know us musicians, we're always prepared."

He didn't realize until he'd spoken that she might not be thrilled by the reminder of how many women he'd slept with, or that he was always ready for action.

Thankfully, she smiled and said, "Thank God." Then she reached for the condom and tore the wrapper open. "Help me with this."

Together, they slid it on, the slightest touch of her hands on him making him nearly lose control. But though he was desperate to have her, he knew he couldn't go too fast. He needed to make sure she was ready for him. *Beyond* ready.

Forcing himself to go slow, he slid his hand into the vee between her legs. His breath left him in a rush as he felt how hot, how slick she was. As he stroked her, she instinctively opened her thighs wider for him. Her eyes closed, and her head fell back against the cushions at the same time that her hips rose to meet his hand.

He whispered against her ear, "Are you ready for me, Ash?"

She drew back to look at him, passion dilating her pupils so that her eyes were nearly black. *"Yes,"* she breathed. "I've never been so ready for anything, or anyone, in my entire life."

On a hungry groan, he moved into her, slowly stretching her to accommodate his hard heat. The last thing he wanted was to hurt her, so despite the desire rushing through him, he gently rocked in, then out, then in again, until her arousal paved the way for him to be seated fully inside her.

She gazed up at him, wonder in her eyes. "This feels so good. *You* feel so good."

He barely had the presence of mind to find the right words, but he needed to let her know how he felt.

"It's *never* felt this good, Ash. Only with you."

"Love me," she whispered against his lips. "Take me. Don't hold anything back." Then she lifted her hips, bucking up into him as if to prove that she meant exactly what she said.

Even if he had wanted to hold back, he couldn't have. Not anymore.

Not now that she was finally *his*.

Nash threaded his fingers into her hair as he kissed her, and as they moved together, they were complete equals, with neither taking the lead and both of them willing to follow the pleasure wherever it took them.

They were a perfect fit in every way. Already, Nash knew one night with Ashley could never be enough.

He felt her inner muscles tighten around him, and she shattered beneath him with sweet sounds of ecstasy erupting from her throat. As he looked into her eyes and followed her over the edge, the deepest pleasure imaginable took over every part of him. His body, his mind…and even his heart.

CHAPTER EIGHT

Ashley had just had the most glorious sex of her life! Every second of their lovemaking had been mind-blowing, from playing out Nash's fantasy to the final moments when he'd been staring into her eyes as she'd shattered into a million blissful pieces.

A warning bell went off inside her head. Just because he'd gazed into her eyes as they'd climaxed together—even if for a few magical moments, it had felt like more than just sex—didn't mean it had been lovemaking. It was just sex.

And, oh, what a wonderful thing *just sex* could be. How could she have gone her whole life without experiencing that? No wonder her sisters were always on her to date more. They must have known what she was missing all along.

For the first time in her life, she felt like a sexual woman. She wasn't just a mom, or a sister, or a daughter anymore. At long last, she was more than that.

All thanks to Nash.

He lifted his face from where he had been resting it against the top of her head. Smiling down at her, he said, "You just blew my mind, Ashley."

She smiled back, feeling like she was glowing from the inside out. "Not nearly as much as you blew mine."

He kissed her, and she wrapped her arms and legs tighter around him. It felt so good to kiss him while he was still inside of her, still hard and throbbing. But for safety's sake, if she didn't want to accidentally get pregnant again, she knew they needed to remove the condom immediately.

Obviously thinking along the same lines, he carefully moved away. When he got up to throw it away in the bathroom, she missed the weight of his body over hers.

He came back into the bedroom and held out his hand. "How does a shower sound?"

Her body instantly heated up again, as if her lust for him hadn't just been sated. She took his hand and let him pull her from the couch. "A shower sounds perfect."

"This time," he said in a low voice that rumbled over her skin like a heated caress, "you get to be in charge of the fantasy."

If only he knew how many fantasies she'd had about him over the years. And then it occurred to her—their relationship had been completely honest up until now, so why not tell him?

"I've had fantasies about you. Lots of them. And not just today."

He looked at her with great interest as they walked into the bathroom. "Do tell."

"Even though I wasn't with anyone all those years, I still had urges."

Heat jumped into his eyes at the word *urges*. "Tell me more."

Surprisingly, it was easy to tell him her biggest secret. Everything with Nash had been easy. Talking, laughing, loving. And now, confessing. "Late at night, alone in my bed, I would make up sexy stories inside my head. Fantasies where I was the focus of a very sexy man's desire. And he knew exactly how to touch me, exactly what I wanted."

"Are you saying that 'very sexy man' was me?" His voice was even deeper now.

"Yes," she admitted, her voice barely above a whisper. "I thought of you." She looked into his eyes, which were blazing with even more desire now than they had in her fantasies. "Always you."

He tugged her against him and kissed her until she was breathless.

When he finally let her mouth go, he said, "I'm hoping there were some shower scenes going on inside that big brain of yours."

"Of course there were. Lots and lots of X-rated shower scenes." She'd never seen anyone look so happy as he did just then. "I didn't think I'd actually get to live out any of my fantasies with you, though."

"I must have done something good at some point in my life to be rewarded by this night with you."

But before they got into the shower and gave in to passion again, she still needed to be practical about contraception. "Do you have another condom?"

"I'd better."

He went to look through his wallet again, leaving her in the bathroom to adjust the water temperature.

She got beneath the spray, and when she was joined by Nash, she was hugely relieved to see another condom in his hand. She wasn't sure how she would have been able to resist him. Now she didn't have to.

"Soap me up, Nash."

It was heady to watch his hands shake slightly as he reached for the gel soap. She still could barely believe that he wanted her as much as she wanted him.

Slowly, gently, he rubbed the gel over her skin, starting with her shoulders, then running his hands down her arms. He soaped up the fingers on her right hand and then her left, before running his hands back up her arms, then down her back, sending bubbles running across her torso. Putting more liquid soap into his hands, he moved them around to her stomach and her rib cage, sliding them directly beneath her breasts without actually touching them.

This had been exactly how her secret late-night fantasy had played out. The way he was teasing her. The way he was caressing her. The way he was looking at her, like he'd never seen anyone more beautiful. How did he know exactly what to do to give her such pleasure?

Touching her even more possessively now, he slid his hands over her hips, gently grazed his fingertips down her thighs, then lowered himself to one knee. As he stroked down her right leg, then her left, he pressed kisses to her stomach.

Ashley's legs felt so shaky that she had to steady herself on his shoulders. The shower was warm and steamy, but thrill bumps still rose over the surface of her skin.

He looked at her from beneath his long, wet lashes. "Is this what you imagined in your fantasies?"

"What you're doing to me is even *better* than my fantasies."

"Tell me, Ashley. Tell me exactly what you want from me."

Knowing her every wish was his command was extremely heady. And yet, because it was completely consensual, she didn't feel the slightest bit bad about momentarily having power over him. They both loved the game they were playing.

"My breasts." She licked her lips. "Taste me."

The words were barely out of her mouth before he brought his mouth to the tip of one breast and made a slow circle over the taut peak with his tongue. Moments later, he turned his attention to her other breast in the same shockingly delicious way.

Again and again, he tasted her, teased her, until she was practically sobbing with need. She clasped the back of his head and held him tightly to her, encouraging him to feast on her.

And feast he did.

His mouth, his hands were everywhere, and she couldn't get enough, even as she arched her back so that she could get closer to him.

"Tell me more, Ashley." His breath was coming fast and hard. "Tell me what you most desire."

With his thumbs moving across the aroused tips of her breasts as he spoke, it was impossible to think clearly. Fortunately, she didn't need her brain to work to know exactly what she wanted.

"Taste me. *All* of me. And don't stop."

Again, she was barely done speaking before he started to fulfill her fantasy. Crouching lower, he used his hands to widen her thighs so that he could put his mouth on her sex.

He tasted her. He teased her. He pleasured her. He

made her feel the kind of ecstasy that no one else ever had.

With his tongue over her aroused flesh, with the fingers of one hand moving inside of her, with his free hand on her breasts, he knew how to drive her completely insane.

He knew that a nibble here, a lick there would make her writhe and buck against him.

He knew that the heat, and the pleasure, would keep rising higher and higher inside of her until it finally burst into flames of joy, and wonder, and soul-deep pleasure.

She was on the verge of begging him for a moment to catch her breath, to get her brain working again, to try to remember something, anything about who she was and the life she'd led up until today. But then she heard him tearing open the condom wrapper, and she forgot about anything except having him inside of her.

"Do you think your legs can hold out just a little bit longer?"

"Please," was her answer. "Please take me, Nash."

He lifted one of her legs high enough so that her calf was wrapped around his hip, and then he cupped one large hand over her hip.

"I'll do all the work," he said against her lips, stealing a kiss. And then another. "All you need to do is hold on tight."

The next thing she knew, he was inside of her. Thrusting high and deep and rough and *perfect*.

She'd never known such bliss, or felt as happy as when Nash took her and made her his.

In this very moment, it wasn't just her body that was his. Her heart was too. Because he'd shown her, in the most glorious of ways, just how much more there was to life. To joy. To adventure.

She would never forget this perfect day.

She would never forget him.

And then there were no more thoughts, because all she could do was feel. Feel Nash inside of her, over her, holding her, kissing her, caressing her as warm water ran over and between their bodies. Feel another climax rip through her as he came apart in her arms, their combined pleasure tearing the old Ashley Sullivan apart so that she would have no choice but to wake from tonight a brand-new person, inside and out.

A short while later, he turned the water off, toweled them both dry, then carried her to the bed. The last thought she had before falling asleep was how wonderful it was to be held in Nash's strong arms while he spoke her name with wonder.

CHAPTER NINE

Ashley woke to the sound of pounding on the front door. She was momentarily disoriented. This wasn't her bed. This wasn't her house. And she had never woken up in a man's arms.

Seconds later, technicolor memories of the previous, wonderful day—and sinfully glorious night—came rushing back to her.

Nash wasn't yet stirring when she heard a voice from outside her door. "Ashley, are you in there?" It was her brother's voice.

Why was Brandon here? And why did he sound so worried?

Oh God, it had to be Kevin. She hadn't checked her phone for hours. Something must have happened to her son!

She jumped out of bed and only barely remembered to wrap a robe around herself before she yanked the door open. "Is Kevin okay? Did Mom and Dad call you to say that something is wrong?"

Brandon shook his head, clearly surprised by her

anxious questions. "As far as I know, everything's fine with Kevin. I haven't heard anything from Mom or Dad to the contrary."

Relief swept through her. But she still needed to know for sure. She looked around for her bag. Where had she left her phone last night?

Oh yes, there it was, in her bag on the floor by the door. Where she'd dropped it when she and Nash had started kissing.

She pulled out her phone, and her relief was complete as she saw a smiley face emoji from Kevin. Her mother had texted as well to say that everything was going great and that she hoped Ashley was having a wonderful time in Vienna.

If only her mom knew just how wonderful a time she'd been having with Nash...

Now that the adrenaline had left her body, she felt drained. Sinking onto the nearest seat, she looked up at her brother. "If it's not about Kevin, then why were you banging on the door, desperate to see me?"

"I tried to reach you late last night and then again early this morning, and when I didn't hear from you, I assumed the worst. This is the first time you've been in a foreign country. And given that I left you with Nash yesterday, who knows what kind of trouble he could have gotten you into?"

Of course, Nash picked that precise moment to

emerge from the bedroom. With only a towel wrapped around his waist.

Brandon's fists clenched tight as he made a beeline toward Nash. "I'm going to kill you."

She leaped between the two of them before Brandon could throw a punch. Or worse, since seeing Nash coming out of her bedroom might very well have primed her brother for murder.

"Brandon," she said in a firm voice, "this is none of your business. And you didn't need to worry about me. I was fine."

"Fine?" Steam was practically coming out of her brother's ears. "You call sleeping with this dirt bag *fine*?"

"He's not a dirt bag." She hated to hear anyone speaking about Nash with disrespect. He was a good man, and he didn't deserve it.

"He's been to prison, Ash! Multiple times! He isn't good enough to clean your shoes."

"I don't care what he did when he was younger," she growled at her brother. "So what if he made mistakes? Nash isn't the one acting like a dirt bag right now—you are. Get out of my apartment."

"Oh, no," her brother said, standing his ground, "I'm not leaving until I drag this sorry excuse for a human being outside with me. And then I'm going to tear him to shreds."

Ashley didn't often get furious. She tended more toward a slow simmer, rather than a boiling pot of rage. But her pot had just boiled over.

"How dare you?" she yelled at her brother. "I've never barged in on you and whomever you're sleeping with. I've never told your lovers they're dirt bags and that they should get out of your bed. So don't you dare think you can do the same with me! Okay, so I screwed up in high school. But I'm a fully grown woman now, and if I want to sleep with someone, by God I am going to sleep with him! And I'm going to enjoy the hell out of it too."

Throughout their exchange, Nash hadn't interjected, even when Brandon had made his threats. She appreciated that, instead of trying to defend her, he let her fight her own battles. But after growing increasingly tense with every word out of Brandon's mouth, it was clear that Nash was at the end of his rope.

"You heard your sister," Nash said to Brandon, his voice full of serious intent. "It's time for you to leave."

"Don't tell me what to do," Brandon said, squaring off against her lover.

"Both of you, stop it." Ashley looked her brother in the eye, square and unblinking. "Go back to your hotel, and we can talk once you've had a chance to cool down."

Brandon studied her face, seeing that she was dead

serious. "I'm not going to cool down anytime soon, but I still want you to call me the very second he leaves." He turned to Nash. "You don't need to play at the launch tonight. I no longer want you there."

Nash was in Vienna to drive Brandon's VIP hotel investors wild when he took the stage. And now Brandon wanted to call the whole thing off because she'd slept with Nash? No, she wouldn't let her brother do anything that stupid.

"The two of you are going to abide by the contract you signed," she insisted. "Whatever happened last night has nothing to do with the hotel launch. And I won't hear a word of argument about it from either of you." She had been a mother long enough to know how to make herself understood in a way that brooked no argument.

Her brother looked like he was about to break a molar, he was clenching his jaw so tightly. But thankfully, he knew better than to argue with her. "Sound check is at three." Brandon slammed the door behind him as he left.

Ashley didn't know how yesterday's perfection could have turned into such a complete and utter disaster so quickly this morning. What's more, she had a bad feeling that Brandon was going to blab to the rest of her family. Once he told them about her wild night with a superstar, they would probably all think the same thing. *Poor Ashley, she couldn't have known what she was getting herself into when she slept with Nash Hardwin. If only we had been there to protect her.*

But she *had* known exactly what she was getting herself into with Nash. She'd had a great night of super-hot sex with a very likable, extremely sexy man.

She wasn't going to apologize for it. Not to anyone.

But when she turned back to Nash, she wasn't sure she liked what she read in his eyes. "He got to you, didn't he? He made you feel guilty for being with me."

Nash didn't deny it. "I don't normally run into the brothers of the women I've spent the night with."

"Who cares what my brother thinks?"

Nash ran a hand over his face, his body language alone telling her plenty about how much he cared about what Brandon thought.

"Do you regret what happened between us last night?" she asked him, point-blank.

"No." But then he reconsidered. "I knew you deserved better. Better than me. Because I'm exactly what your brother says I am. I've been a dirt bag way too many times over the years. I don't settle down. I don't do more than a night."

"Who asked you to settle down? Who asked you for more than a night?" She was beginning to feel as livid with Nash as she was with Brandon. "I certainly haven't!"

"I know you haven't, but the way you were raised, and the way you live your life—"

"You mean as a spinster single mom? Little Miss Goody Two-shoes, who never does anything outside of the boundaries?" She laughed, but there was no humor in it. "I knew that was how you saw me at first, but I didn't care. Not after I thought we'd become friends."

"We are friends. And that's why I am feeling guilty. Because I wouldn't give up last night with you for anything."

She blinked, trying to process what he was saying, that he felt guilty but also that he was glad they'd had their time together.

"Ashley, last night with you... It was more than I ever expected. So much more. Because you're beautiful and sweet and good. Hell, you defended me to your brother in a way I don't think anyone else ever has. The very last thing I would ever want is to hurt you in any way."

"You haven't hurt me. At least, not until you started looking and acting all regretful."

"I swear to you, I don't have any regrets about being with you last night. Maybe I should, but I can't. Not when it felt so damned right. But that doesn't mean your brother is wrong. You deserve a hell of a lot better than me."

"Funny," she said, sarcasm dripping from the word,

"how everybody seems to think they know what I deserve better than I do. Although you're right about one thing—I deserve better than *this*. Better than waking up to my brother banging down the door because he thinks I can't handle myself in a foreign city. Better than you beating yourself up, thinking you somehow led me on." She wrapped the robe tighter around herself. "You haven't led me anywhere, Nash. Of course I know the score. What you and I had was one night only. I loved being with you. Every single second of it. I loved finally feeling like it's okay to be a sensual woman. You helped show me that. And that's a gift, Nash. A gift you gave me."

"Ashley—"

She held up her hands, her chest aching. "You should go now. Back to your life on the road, playing shows and recording albums and doing interviews and being a superstar. And I'll go back to mine, being a small-town single mom." She gave him a little smile, hoping she could keep her lips from wobbling. "Although I already know my life is going to be more than that from now on. More full, more contoured, more colorful than I've let myself live up until now."

He tried again. "Ashley—"

"Please, just leave me with the memories of our perfect twenty-four hours together. I'm going to take a shower now. By the time I'm done, I'd like you to be gone. And when I see you tonight at your show at the hotel, let's agree to pretend we were never more than friends. It will be easier that way."

Nash didn't speak for several long moments. Finally, he said, "I hate that things are ending this way."

Willing back tears, she took a deep, shaky breath. "Good-bye, Nash." Then she headed into the bathroom and locked the door behind her.

★ ★ ★

Nash quickly dressed in clean clothes from his bags that had been moved into Ashley's apartment, also donning a black baseball cap and dark sunglasses. Leaving was the last thing he wanted to do, but he wouldn't disrespect her request for him to go.

He wasn't going to bother with a disguise today. Frankly, he didn't care if people in Vienna recognized him now. The reason it had been fun to wear a disguise yesterday was because he'd done it with Ashley.

In any case, as soon as he finished his performance tonight at the hotel launch, he was booked to fly to Budapest, the first of the shows scheduled throughout Europe for the next six weeks.

Walking briskly to try to let off some steam—thankfully, the fans who clearly recognized him seemed to get the message that he wasn't in the mood to sign autographs—he headed for the river. Yesterday, for the first time, he'd gotten to be a normal guy spending time with a pretty girl, having fun exploring a new city.

He should have known better than to think he could be that guy.

And he should have known better than to think that he could keep his hands off Ashley.

Because she wasn't just a *pretty girl*. She was *extraordinary*. Not only beautiful, but also intelligent, and warm, and real.

Ashley was everything he couldn't let himself have. Her life would turn into a media circus if they became an item, not only because of his celebrity, but also because of his arrest and prison record. He couldn't do that to her or her son.

What's more, Nash wasn't a long-term-relationship guy. He'd never had the urge to settle down, to start a family. And even if that no longer felt quite true anymore, even if he'd begun to envy people on his staff with spouses and kids and houses with vegetable gardens, he had no idea what being part of a happy family actually looked like.

Growing up, there not only hadn't been money, there also hadn't been affection or love, dreams or hopes. There had only been, for both his mother and himself, an urge to escape. For his mom, via booze and drugs. For him, via the van he'd rebuilt.

Nash deliberately shook off thoughts of his past, silently reminding himself that he had everything now. Money. Any woman he wanted. Adoration of the masses.

What more could he possibly ask for?

He walked along the river until he found himself standing at the entrance to a huge amusement park that had been on Ashley's spreadsheet. *Prater.*

He'd never gotten the chance to go to an amusement park when he was a kid, because they hadn't had the spare money for it. Now, all he could think was what a good time he and Ashley would have on the rides. And her son too. This place was a kid's dream, with roller coasters and arcade games as far as the eye could see.

Nash had plenty of money now. He could ride every roller coaster at every amusement park ten times in a row if he wanted. Hell, he could pay the management to shut the entire park down for him for the day, and the cost wouldn't even be a blip in his bank account.

Instead, he turned and walked away from the amusement park. When people suddenly started running up to him to ask for autographs and pictures, it should have been a relief.

A relief to go back to what he knew. To the way his life had been for so many years. One where every day might be more of the same, but where the dreams he'd had as a kid had finally come true.

He should have been the happiest bastard alive, damn it. Because he had everything.

Everything but Ashley.

CHAPTER TEN

By the time Ashley got out of the shower, Nash was gone. Though his bags were still there, and likely would be until Brandon sent someone from the hotel to pick them up, it felt as though all of the life, and the joy, in the apartment had gone.

Her heart clenched, tight and aching, even though she knew it was for the best. One night was all they were ever going to get. She'd known all along that good-byes were coming in the morning.

Still, she wished it had ended differently, that there could have been smiles and hugs instead of harsh words.

Ashley had spent only twenty-four hours with Nash, but in that short period of time, she'd come to like him very much. Regardless of his brushes with the law, or if he'd done some things he shouldn't have in his past, she believed that, at his core, he was a good man.

Her belief in his goodness only made Nash's reaction to her brother's accusations sadder. Nash had actually *agreed* with Brandon that he wasn't good enough for her.

She wished Nash could see how wrong he was. The reason she could be with him for only one night wasn't because he wasn't good enough for her. It was simply because their lives were polar opposites. Ashley was a single mom with a normal job and a big family. She still lived in the town where she'd been born, whereas Nash didn't call anywhere home, his life one long string of hotel rooms and tour buses. And he didn't seem to have any family either.

She rubbed her hand over the ache in her chest as she thought about his childhood. At sixteen, he'd driven away from a mother he believed didn't love him.

Ashley couldn't imagine how that could possibly be true. She'd been drawn to him from the moment they'd started to talk with each other, and that had nothing to do with her fantasies about his music-star persona. He was indisputably sexy and charismatic, of course, but they'd become friends so quickly because he'd made her feel comfortable with being herself. She'd never had such an easy, open rapport with a man.

She walked to the French doors, opened them, and stepped on to the balcony. This morning, everyone and everything looked completely different.

She was completely different.

Being with Nash had changed her.

As soon as she'd made the decision to be with Nash, she had already begun to change as she took control of her life in a way she never had before.

Yes, she was in control of her career, and the way she parented, and the way she managed her money. But she'd never taken control of her sexuality, her femininity. Not after her first experience with sex had left her with the most massive consequence imaginable.

She'd told herself that living vicariously through her sisters was good enough. But it wasn't. She understand that now.

So even though her good-bye with Nash had gone terribly wrong this morning, she would never regret being with him. Nor would she regret opening up to him or holding nothing back in bed.

She hoped that when she left Vienna, she would be brave enough to be true to herself, to keep exploring, and to continue living her life to the fullest, the way she had during the past twenty-four hours.

She would be forever grateful to Nash for helping to show her that she could have *more*. It wouldn't be easy to watch him sing onstage tonight at the hotel. The thought of seeing him again made her heart flutter like mad. And her heart still felt raw from sending him away.

But as she took a deep breath of air scented with pastries and espresso, she refused to use those as excuses to waste her last day in Vienna moping. She still had a list of extraordinary places to visit. Who knew when she'd be able to explore an exotic city again?

Determined to enjoy herself, she quickly dressed and headed out. Hours later, when she returned to her apartment after traipsing through a half-dozen museums and gardens—a very long day in which she refused to admit that Vienna didn't seem quite as spectacular without Nash at her side—she wasn't surprised to see that his bags were gone.

She was surprised, however, to find a large box tied with a magenta bow on the coffee table. She opened the attached envelope to find a message from her brother: *I'm sorry.*

Inside the box was a dress and a pair of heels. The dress was stunning—the fabric a beautiful rose hue and embellished with just enough sequins to catch the light. Nearly floor-length, it had a square neckline and a fitted bodice, with an embellished waist and an A-line silhouette.

Everything fit perfectly, and Ashley guessed that Brandon must have gotten her measurements from Lola. She felt like a princess in the gorgeous dress, by far the nicest garment she'd ever worn.

On the one hand, Ashley didn't want to make it too easy for Brandon to get away with his overbearing behavior. At the same time, she knew there was no point in holding a grudge. Not when it would only make them both feel worse.

In any case, she was glad to have a lovely dress to wear tonight. The last thing she wanted was for Nash to see her from across the room and wonder how he could have wanted to be with her. Last night, he'd told her she was beautiful, and her female pride wanted him to remember her the same way.

Thirty minutes later, Brandon's driver pulled up outside. As she headed down the stairs, she could hardly believe that her whirlwind trip to Austria would be coming to a close tomorrow morning.

But first, she would attend a grand gala event, wearing a beautiful dress...while savoring her memories of her kisses and heady lovemaking with the sexiest man at the party.

She slid into the town car and steeled herself for what lay ahead tonight. She not only needed to retain her equanimity when she saw Nash on stage, but she also needed to resist the urge to slug her brother in front of his staff and guests.

Minutes later, she alighted from the car in front of the hotel. Music was playing through the outside speakers, and the hotel was beautifully lit both inside and out. She accepted a glass of champagne from one of the waitstaff as she walked into the lobby, which had been transformed for the celebration.

The hotel was full of people laughing and chatting and sipping champagne. Unable to find her brother in the crowd, she assumed he must be busy networking with local VIPs and government officials.

She hadn't eaten much today, and though the appetizers the waitstaff offered her looked delicious, she was far more interested in a second glass of champagne. Anything to take the edge off her nerves over seeing Nash again. The party guests were funneled into the ballroom. The space was exquisite, and it looked as though no expense had been spared.

Suddenly, the lighting changed, and a spotlight lit up the stage. Brandon stepped into the light with a smile. "Welcome! Thank you for coming to celebrate the opening of another jewel in the crown of the SLVN Hotel Group. Everyone in Vienna has been hugely welcoming to us, and we deeply appreciate it."

The crowd applauded, and Ashley felt so proud of her brother. Though she wished she could see him more often, she knew he had always wanted more than a small-town life. Looking around the magnificent hotel full of guests in their glittering best, she was happy for him. She hoped his life was everything he'd ever wanted it to be.

"And now," he continued, "for the moment I'm sure all of you have been waiting for. Tonight's special guest needs no introduction." Ashley thought she saw Brandon's smile turn to a scowl for a split second before he said, "Please welcome Nash Hardwin!"

The applause was deafening. It didn't matter how young or old people were, or what language they spoke, everyone around the world loved Nash.

Walking onstage with a guitar and without saying a word, he began to play an acoustic version of one of his biggest hits. The audience enthusiastically sang along, and over the next thirty minutes, the crowd went more and more wild with every song.

Only, Ashley was frozen where she stood, barely blinking or even breathing. Listening to him sing and watching his talented hands play across the strings of his guitar, she couldn't stop the sensual memories from flooding her. The way he'd whispered in her ear while they were making love. The feel of his hands on her skin while he'd played her passions like a maestro.

As she listened, all she wanted was to feel his hands on her again, his lips on hers, the wicked growl of his voice as he urged her to come apart for him. Thank God she was too far from the stage for Nash to see her.

After he'd played seven of his biggest hits, he finally spoke to the audience. "I'd like to play one more song before I go, one I haven't played for a very long time. Not until yesterday when a very special friend helped me to see things differently. This is for her."

And as the first notes of "Scarborough Fair" sounded, Ashley's heart shattered, breaking in a way that she had steadfastly not let it break until that very moment.

She turned and fled the room, accidentally knocking into a few people and spilling their drinks. Desperate to get away, she opened the nearest side door and launched herself into a service hallway. She tried to catch her breath, still her racing heart, calm her mind. But it was impossible when she could still hear Nash playing.

The applause at the end of the song reverberated down the dark and deserted hallway to where she was standing. Brandon's staff members were in the ballroom, cheering for Nash, celebrating his talent and artistry.

Knowing they would return to work now that the concert was over, she moved farther down the hallway, hoping to find an outside exit. She hadn't gotten far when she heard the door behind her open and close.

Without turning around, she instantly knew who had come into the hallway from the way every cell in her body came to attention.

Nash.

For the second time that night, she was rooted in

place. Unable to move. She didn't turn around until he put one hand over hers and gently turned her to face him.

Even in the dim light of the hallway, she could see that his eyes were blazing. Blazing with the same emotion she knew must be reflected in her eyes.

And then his mouth was on hers, and he was kissing her so passionately that her entire body and soul were swept up in him as they kissed and kissed and kissed and kissed.

"I needed to see you one more time," he said in a raw voice as he peppered her lips with more kisses. "I needed to kiss you one more time so that I can always remember how good it feels to hold you in my arms."

She looked up into his beautiful eyes and silently said good-bye. Then *she* kissed *him*. A soft, sweet kiss she hoped told him everything that was in her heart. That she thought he was a good man. A wonderful man.

And that maybe, in another life, they could have been together. But not in this one. Never in this one.

With one last intense look, he let her go, and then he turned and walked out of her life.

Forever.

CHAPTER ELEVEN

Waiting until she felt she had some control over her emotions, Ashley dried her eyes, then ducked into the nearest bathroom to make sure her mascara hadn't run. She didn't want anyone at the party to guess at her emotional upheaval. Especially her brother.

Speaking of Brandon, it was long past time to congratulate him on an exceptional hotel launch and thank him for the beautiful dress before she headed to her apartment to pack for her early-morning flight home.

Her brother spotted her as soon as she stepped out of the restroom, making his excuses to the couple he'd been speaking with. "Ash, there you are. Sorry I wasn't able to say hello earlier."

She smiled, a smile that felt totally fake but that she hoped he'd believe was real. "Your launch party was fantastic, Brandon, just like I knew it would be. Congratulations! You've done it again." Before he could look closely at her face, she added, "Thank you for the dress. It's beautiful. And for the apology. I appreciate it. And now, considering how early my flight is, I should probably head back to the apartment to pack and get some shut-eye."

Before she could dash away, he put his hand on the small of her back and propelled her into an office tucked behind a side door.

He closed the door behind them, then took a good look at her red, puffy eyes. "What happened between you and Nash after I left your apartment this morning? I would have pinned him down to ask him earlier, but I was run off my feet dealing with last-second emergencies and never got the chance to corner him."

"It's none of your business," she told her brother, squaring her shoulders and looking him in the eye.

But her bravado didn't fool him. "I knew I shouldn't have let him come to play tonight. Hell, I should never have let him near you, period." Brandon looked utterly furious. "If he's still in the building, I'm going to find him and *destroy* him."

She put her hand on her brother's chest to hold him in place, even though she knew Nash was already gone. Just as her apartment had felt empty without him, the hotel felt empty too.

"Nash hasn't done anything wrong, and neither have I. We're two people who made a decision to be together for one night only. He didn't take advantage of me. And I didn't take advantage of him."

"Then why have you been crying?"

"I didn't think I would," she replied honestly. "But even though I'm more emotional about having said good-bye to him than I thought I would be, it's nothing that you or anyone else needs to try to fix for me."

"Of course I need to fix it. If it wasn't for me, you never would have gotten involved with him in the first place."

Whirling away from her brother in frustration, she looked out the window at the lights of Vienna. It wasn't his fault that he couldn't see beyond her accidental high school pregnancy. Though she was tempted to keep her revelations to herself, she knew Brandon would never understand why her night with Nash had been so important if she didn't at least try to explain how the experience had changed her.

"For the first time since I was seventeen," she said as she turned back to face him, "I've finally reached beyond the boundaries I've put around my life. With Nash, I went into the world and had an adventure. A wonderful adventure with a good man. I know you might not think Nash is a good man," she said before her brother could argue, "but he is."

"Ashley—"

She put her arms around her brother before he started arguing with her, thinking he knew best. "Thank you for always caring. Thank you for always loving me." She stepped back. "But you have to let me live my life the way *I'm* going to live it. You can't protect me forever. None of you can, not Mom or Dad or the rest of our siblings. It's true that I did desperately need your help when I was barely eighteen and raising Kevin without a partner. But now, at long last, it's time for me to stand on my own two feet and have some adventures. Even if some of those adventures end in tears, I'm not going to regret them. Because I'm ready to live, Brandon. Beyond ready."

Her brother stared at her for several long moments. She could practically see his brain warring over whether he should do what she asked and let her deal with her own life on her own terms, or make good on his threat to avenge her honor with Nash, even though she'd told him there was nothing to avenge.

Finally, he nodded. "Okay, I'll back off. I'm not going to lie to you and say I'm happy about you and Nash, but I can see where you're coming from. After all, I'm the one who encouraged you to come to Vienna to live a little. But then when you went and actually did some of that living, I couldn't handle it. So I'm going to work on that, okay?"

"Please, just try to trust me."

"You usually do make smart decisions," he admitted. "Usually, anyway."

"Are you telling me you've never made any crazy split-second decisions?"

"Point taken," he said, suddenly looking a little shifty.

She frowned at his tone. "Is something going on with you?"

Brandon was a master at keeping his emotions and the intimate details of his life close to the vest. The fact that he was away from Bar Harbor more often than he was in town meant none of them had a great handle on what his life was like. Was he in and out of relationships? Or was there one person who meant something deeper to him?

"I'm good," he replied. "Everything is great."

His reply came a little too quickly. But right at this moment, she didn't have enough clearheadedness to probe any further. She made a mental note, however, to spend more time with him when he came home to Bar Harbor for Cassie and Flynn's wedding.

"I want to spend more time with you," she told him. "I don't get to see you nearly enough."

"I agree," he said as he pulled her into a hug.

Giving him a kiss on his cheek, she smiled at him. "Go back to your adoring crowd. And thank you again for inviting me to come to your opening. I've absolutely loved Vienna. It's been the trip of a lifetime."

They headed back out, and after he was swallowed up by the crowd, she made her way to the exit. She waved away the offer of the town car, wanting to walk to clear her head and to enjoy the beautiful evening.

She was a little cold in her dress, but she welcomed the rush of coolness over skin that still felt too heated from Nash's kiss.

It truly was a captivating city, with both locals and tourists eating and drinking, talking and laughing in the moonlight. One day, if she was ever lucky enough to come back to Vienna, she would vividly remember this whirlwind trip where her life had changed.

Where *she* had changed.

She wasn't going to lie and pretend that she wasn't hurting, that the wound from saying good-bye to Nash wasn't raw. At the same time, however, she felt more open to possibility and to all the wonders of a life well lived than she ever had before.

She wanted to take that wonder back to her normal life and give that same sense of adventure to her son. She wanted to tell him it was okay to take risks and that he didn't have to hold back either laughter or tears afterward.

Just then, a teenager rode by on a scooter, playing one of Nash's songs through a portable speaker. Hearing his soulful voice ring out into the moonlit Vienna night made her heart squeeze.

She would always be grateful to Nash for giving her the most wonderful weekend of her life.

CHAPTER TWELVE

Six weeks.

Ashley could hardly believe it had been a month and a half since her night with Nash. Sometimes, she found herself floating from the memories alone. Other times, her chest felt tight, achy.

Fortunately, Brandon hadn't spilled the news of her one-night stand to anyone else in the family. It also helped that since her return home, they had all been too focused on getting ready for Cassie and Flynn's wedding to have the time or energy to shine the spotlight on her.

There had been a couple of times when she'd nearly blurted out everything to her sisters and mom. But in the end, her memories of Nash were so precious that she wanted to keep them all to herself. The look in his eyes when he'd told her she was beautiful. The taste of his lips when he was passionately kissing her. The feel of his muscular body over hers.

As soon as she'd returned to Bar Harbor from Vienna, she had resumed her normal life. Getting Kevin ready for school in the morning. Taking him to soccer practice on weekday afternoons and games on the weekends. Helping him with his homework at night. Dealing with his father when Josh told Kevin yet another wildly inappropriate story. Running the Sullivan Cafés and stores throughout Maine. Attending family dinners on Friday nights. Going for lunchtime walks along the shore.

Those were the exact same things she had done before her trip. But one big thing *had* changed: She'd secretly signed up for a dating service. And tonight was her first date.

After dropping Kevin off at a friend's house for a sleepover, she came home and stood in front of her open closet doors to pick out an outfit for her date with a man named Oliver. She didn't want to look like she was trying too hard, but she also knew she should do better than jeans and a T-shirt.

Though she had found it nearly impossible to think beyond her time with Nash during the past six weeks, tonight she vowed to open herself up to the possibility that there might be someone special out there with whom she could build a life. So she knew she needed to at least make an effort with clothes and makeup.

She didn't plan on sleeping with her date tonight, however, no matter how great he was. Her spontaneous night of hot sex with Nash was something she

doubted she'd ever repeat with anyone else. She wasn't
sure that she could withstand the emotional aftermath
of another one-night stand. Not when saying good-bye
to Nash had been one of the hardest things she'd ever
done.

Thirty minutes later, she got into her car and headed toward the town of Trenton. She'd opted for a
restaurant outside of Bar Harbor where it was less
likely that she'd see someone she knew. The food was
always good at the Italian restaurant they'd agreed on,
so she knew she'd at least enjoy her meal.

As soon as she walked into the restaurant, she spotted her date standing at the end of the bar, a drink
already in his hand. He was as handsome as he'd been
in his picture. And his smile looked nice too. So why
did she feel nothing inside?

He came over, a wide smile on his face. "Are you
Ashley?" When she nodded, he said, "You're beautiful.
Even prettier than your picture online."

It was a nice compliment, and she smiled back as
she said, "Thank you." But her heart felt like it was
behind glass. Like nothing this guy did would be able
to penetrate it, no matter how amazing.

"Our table's ready," he said, breaking into her
thoughts. "Unless you'd like to have a drink first?"

She nearly said that they should go eat, simply to
get through their date more quickly. But it wasn't

Oliver's fault that he wasn't Nash, so she said instead, "Why don't we have a drink to get to know each other better before dinner?"

He looked pleased by her response and led her over to two empty barstools.

For the next thirty minutes, she learned about his career as a schoolteacher, where he'd been to school, and that he loved kids. She learned that he liked sports and music and was basically the perfect guy. He made her laugh a couple of times, and by the time they sat down to eat, she felt fairly relaxed.

The glass of wine had helped. She wouldn't have another so she'd be okay to drive home, but it had taken the edge off. Unfortunately, it hadn't gotten rid of that numb feeling. She still felt like she was watching her own date from a distance.

As they ate, she told him about where she'd grown up, what she did for a living, and a little bit about her family. Their conversation was perfectly pleasant, but they never dipped below the surface.

With Nash, by contrast, they'd both gone deep right away. She'd been simultaneously comfortable enough with him to spill the innermost contents of her heart, while also being breathlessly attracted and willing to shed her inhibitions.

After Oliver walked her out to her car after dinner, and she couldn't quite bring herself to agree to a second date, she realized that Nash truly had ruined her for other men. If even this perfect guy couldn't measure up to her one night with Nash, she was destined to be alone forever.

As she drove home, sadness finally broke through the numb barrier around her heart, spilling out as hot tears ran down her cheeks. Her life was great in so many ways, but she didn't have the kind of love, the kind of passion, that Lola had with Duncan, that Rory had with Zara, that Cassie had with Flynn. The same love and passion her parents still had with each other after more than three decades.

Ashley so badly wanted that passion, that intimacy, that connection.

But would she ever find it with anyone other than Nash Hardwin? The one man she could never have beyond one perfect night in Vienna.

* * *

Ashley tossed and turned for most of the night, and when she woke up, she decided it was time to come clean with her sisters. She couldn't go another day without telling somebody how she felt.

She sent a text asking if they could meet at Lola's studio in a half hour. When their affirmative responses came back immediately, it already helped knowing that she could spill her guts to them. Surely, they'd have some suggestions on how she could move on from Nash with a lighter, more positive heart.

Lola and Cassie were already at the studio when Ashley arrived with doughnuts and coffee in hand. It was an unspoken rule that whoever called the morning meeting brought the treats.

She had barely walked inside the door when she told them, "I joined a dating site, and I went on a date last night."

"Wow," Cassie said, looking surprised but pleased. "This is huge news."

"Why is this the first time you're telling us this?" Lola wanted to know.

"I wanted to see how it went first." Ashley let out a breath. "And also because I haven't been totally honest with either of you about what happened in Vienna."

"Something happened in Vienna?" Lola asked, her antenna poking up even higher now.

Ashley nodded, a flush spreading across her cheeks. "Something big."

"I thought you seemed different since your trip," Lola said, "but I've been so run off my feet with the growth of my business and wedding prep that I never found time to pull you aside and ask. I should have made the time."

Cassie looked guilty. "I should have too, Ash. I've been so wrapped up in the wedding, but that's no excuse."

"Neither of you has anything to apologize for," Ashley insisted. "Especially since I wasn't ready to talk about any of it until today."

Lola pinned her with an intense gaze. "I'm guessing *it* has something to do with a man?"

Ashley smiled—she couldn't help it. Thinking of Nash made her smile. But it also made her ache. "You know how Brandon always brings in a celebrity for his hotel launches to ensure they're the hottest ticket in town? Nash Hardwin was Brandon's guest of honor at the hotel gala."

"You slept with him, didn't you?" Lola asked, sitting on the edge of her seat as she waited for confirmation.

Again, Ashley couldn't hold back her smile. "I did."

Lola looked immensely impressed. "You have to tell us *everything!*"

Of course, Ashley wasn't going to tell her sisters the intimate details that would forever be only between her and Nash. But she needed to tell them enough of what had happened so that they'd understand how she was feeling.

"I was planning to be a solo tourist for a couple of days. But then it turned out that Nash was staying at the new hotel, and when the streets became mobbed, and the local authorities were brought in to send the crowd home, Brandon needed a way to get Nash out of the building without anyone noticing. Somehow, I ended up an integral part of the plan. Both Nash and I put on disguises and pretended to be a couple. Amazingly, it worked, and we got out of the hotel undetected."

"Weren't you awestruck by Nash? Or nervous to be around him?" Cassie asked. "I know I would have been. I've loved his music for so long."

"I love his music too," Lola said. "Almost as much as I love looking at him," she added with a smile. "But something tells me you weren't nervous at all, were you, Ash?"

"Strangely, I was really comfortable with him from the very beginning. Probably because he was so far out of my league that I would never register on his radar. Before I knew it, we had spent the whole day together. And because I was never going to see him again, I was able to be open with him in a way I would never be with anyone else on a first date. He said he felt the same, that being a tourist with me for the day was the perfect escape from his rock-star life." She took a breath before telling them the rest. "And then I boldly invited him back to my apartment and had the best night of my entire life." She closed her eyes as she remembered, warmth running through her. "It was just *perfect*. Completely incredible in every single way."

Lola fanned herself with her hand. "This might be the hottest story I've ever heard."

"I agree," Cassie said. "Although it doesn't sound like the story is over quite yet, is it?"

"There's definitely more," Ashley confirmed. "Brandon came to my apartment the next day and went through the roof when Nash walked out of the bedroom wearing only a towel."

"Only a towel?" Lola said on a gasp. "I can't believe Brandon didn't tell us."

"I'm glad he didn't," Ashley said. "He wanted to challenge Nash to a duel, until I pointed out that he's probably had a dozen one-night stands, so he shouldn't be such a hypocrite."

"You're right," Lola agreed. "He has no right to judge you or Nash for spending the night together."

"You know how they are," Cassie said, referring to their brothers and their father. "*Way* too protective."

"I told Brandon to mind his own business," Ashley said. "But Brandon's unexpected appearance meant that the good-bye Nash and I had planned on making that morning wasn't nearly as straightforward as I'd hoped. Nash and I got into a disagreement, and then I asked him to leave." She blew out a harsh breath. "We did end up sharing one more stolen kiss that night, after his show." A kiss that haunted her dreams every single night. "I haven't seen or heard from him since, and I don't expect I will."

"Oh, Ash." Cassie put a hand on her knee. "I can't believe you've been holding this in for over a month."

"I should have told you guys sooner," Ashley agreed. "But the reason I finally had to come clean is because I'm worried no mere mortal will ever live up to Nash. Take the guy I went out with last night. He's nice. He's handsome. He's smart. He has a good job. He likes kids. And I felt *nothing*."

"Maybe that's because there was no chemistry between you and your blind date," Cassie suggested. "Someone can be great on paper, but that doesn't mean that you're going to fit together like puzzle pieces."

"And maybe," Lola said, "it means you should spend more nights with Nash. From everything you've said, it sounds like he had as good a time with you as you had with him. Are you sure one night is all you can ever have with him?"

"Can you imagine Nash Hardwin living in Bar Harbor?" Ashley asked her sisters. "First of all, he's always lived on the road, so I can't imagine him wanting to settle in a small town. And even if he miraculously *did* want to move here, people in town would talk about his past."

"What about his past?" Cassie asked.

"He spent some time in jail when he was younger.

It's not because he's a bad person," she said, needing her sisters to know. "He was just lashing out at the world because—" No, she couldn't share his secrets with her sisters. All she could say was, "He had a difficult upbringing, and I think it took him a while to make peace with it all. But if Nash and I were together, the sad truth is that gossip and conjecture about his past could end up hurting Kevin. And that's something I can never allow to happen." She gave a firm shake of her head. "I'm happy savoring the memories of our amazing and magical twenty-four hours together. But at the same time…" Ashley let out a big sigh. "When I was in Vienna, I told myself I was being brave and turning over a new leaf by being with Nash. I vowed to be a woman of adventure and embrace my sexuality when I came home. But even though we were only together for twenty-four hours, I miss him. It wasn't just that the sex was hot, it was also that it felt like we became friends."

Lola put her arm around Ashley. "I hear what you're saying about gossip affecting Kevin—although I'm not convinced that's an unsurmountable problem—but are you absolutely sure you won't see each other again?"

"I'm sure." That was why their good-bye had been so painful. Because they both knew it was the last time. "And it's for the best, since it would be impossible to fit into each other's lives when he's always on the road, and I need to be here until Kevin is eighteen and heads off to college. But at the same time, I'll never regret being with him, because Nash helped me finally see that my life can be bigger, better, and more full of pleasure than I've let it be all these years."

"I'm really proud of you, Ash," Lola said. "I know that might sound weird—that I'm proud of you for sleeping with a rock star. But it's a big deal that you finally let yourself have a good time."

"The *best* time," Ashley said. But now that she'd shared so much with her sisters, she was ready to get out of the spotlight again. Turning to Cassie, she asked, "How are you feeling about the wedding? Is there anything more I can do to help?"

Cassie looked radiant. "I can't wait to marry Flynn! I know saying our vows to each other shouldn't change anything when we already live together and are raising Ruby, but it still feels like it will."

"Of course it will," Ashley agreed. "Promising forever to the person you love most in the whole world, in good times and bad, in sickness and in health, for better or for worse? It's the best kind of miracle! I know you and Flynn have already pledged yourselves to each other in private, but it will be such an honor to be present as you say your vows in front of everyone who loves you."

Cassie threw her arms around Ashley. "You said exactly what I've been feeling."

Lola put her arms around both of them, and just as they had so many times before, the three sisters held on tight and didn't let go.

CHAPTER THIRTEEN

Josh barged into Ashley's office in the back of the café kitchen fifteen minutes after she arrived at work.

"How do you expect me to be able to take Kevin for a big trip on spring break on my salary?" he accused. "Not everyone has a rich family like yours handing us everything on a silver platter."

She tried not to grit her teeth. This was one of Josh's favorite arguments, that her family had handed her career and savings account to her because her last name was Sullivan, rather than because she worked hard and had great ideas and followed through.

"Maybe if *my* family was full of movie stars or married to rock stars and billionaires," Josh continued, "I would have no problem giving our kid everything he wants, just like you do."

There were so many things she wanted to say to her ex right then. That he'd have more money if he learned to hold down a job, rather than showing up late and mouthing off to his bosses. That he'd be doing better if he had paid attention in school instead of cutting class to go off with his friends. But she'd made those arguments before, and they'd only served to make him feel like his failures truly were everyone else's fault but his and that he'd been dealt a bad hand.

Even worse, after having been absent from Kevin's life for the first eight years, he now expected her unending gratitude for finally being a part of their son's life. Simply because he was willing to occasionally play the "father" role, he believed she should shower him with praise.

As it was, nine times out of ten she wished he wasn't in the picture. Okay, sometimes he was a good dad when he momentarily forgot about his ego and played ball with Kevin, or went for a bike ride. But the majority of the time, he was either ignoring Kevin, or introducing him to things that were totally inappropriate for his age, like violent movies and video games.

The worst was when he promised to show up and then didn't. It was heartbreaking to see how abandoned her son felt. Of course she understood that Kevin wanted a relationship with his father. What kid wouldn't? And yet, theirs was a relationship that forever remained on Josh's selfish terms.

"Surely," she said in as measured a voice as she could manage, given how frustrated she was with hearing the same excuses over and over again, "you've been saving for your camping trip with Kevin." How expensive could it possibly be to go camping? Cooking over a fire. Sleeping in a tent. Apart from renting a couple of fishing poles and making campground reservations, there wasn't a ton to spend money on.

"You know my back isn't great," Josh whined. "If I sleep in a tent on the ground, I'll be in too much pain to do my job at the airport when I get back."

Josh was a baggage handler at Bangor International Airport. He'd been in the job for about four months, and while Ashley hoped he'd be able to actually keep this job, he'd made enough comments about how neither the staff nor the customers appreciated him that she sensed he wasn't going to be working there too much longer.

"I've rented an RV," he announced, "but the rental company told me I need to pay in full before me and Kevin head out on our trip."

She didn't know why she was even the slightest bit surprised by this turn of events. Of course Josh would take something as simple as pitching a tent and cooking over a campfire and turn it into what she could easily guess was a top-of-the-line RV rental, with all the bells and whistles.

Again, there was plenty she wanted to say to him. Swallowing it the way she usually did, she said, "How much do you need?"

His eyes lit with victory. He'd gotten exactly what

he wanted. Again. He'd known that he would, because she would do anything for her son. Even put up with being bled dry by Josh.

"Fifteen hundred should do it."

She swallowed hard—$1,500 was a lot of money. After taking her own trip abroad, it was far more than she could spare.

As though he could read her mind, Josh added, "You were the big spender taking that trip to Europe. You must be rolling in it to fly over for the weekend."

"I'm not an endless pool of money. This is the last time I'm going to bail you out."

Ignoring her threat, he said, "I need the money by tonight, or I lose my reservation."

Just then, there was a knock on her office door, and Annie, the hostess for the café, poked her head in.

"Ashley, there's somebody here to see you." Annie was flushed and looked hugely excited. Even more excited than she'd been when Ashley's movie-star cousin Smith Sullivan had been in town with his wife, Valentina, for their honeymoon.

Ashley didn't know why her sixth sense was suddenly speaking so loudly, but she had the craziest thought. Surely it couldn't be—

"Nash Hardwin!" Annie exclaimed. "He's here! And he's asking for you, Ashley."

Ashley's brain and heart and body instantly went

haywire. She honestly didn't know if she was thrilled or upset. Excited or horrified. She felt like she was spinning round and round until she no longer knew which way was up and which way was down. There was a roaring inside her ears, her heart was pounding, and she was sweating. It felt like everything was firing at once.

Everything except the ability to move her feet or her mouth. She felt completely stuck and mute.

"Nash Hardwin?" Josh spluttered. "What could he possibly want with *you*?"

Josh's wholehearted disbelief that a superstar like Nash could have any interest whatsoever in Ashley finally snapped her back to life. She narrowed her eyes at her ex. "I'll get the money to you later tonight."

Josh followed her out of her office, and after swallowing everything she'd wanted to say to him for so long, she found herself possessed by a devil on her shoulder. A devil who was encouraging her to show Josh that she could do *way* better than him. More than once over the years, he'd suggested that she'd been pining for him since high school, simply because she had never been with anybody else. It had never occurred to him that she'd been busy raising their son. Or that being with him had taught her to have far higher standards in the future, so she was holding out for the best of men. Ashley had *never* pined for Josh, and now she finally had the chance to prove it to him.

She pushed through the door into the café to find Nash standing in a beam of light that seemed to be coming through the window solely to illuminate him. Though everyone eating in the café was clearly in awe, the regulars knew better than to invade his privacy.

As soon as he set eyes on her, heat leaped into his eyes. The same intense flames of desire—and connection—that had been between them the last time they'd kissed in the back hallway of the Austrian hotel.

The devil pushed her, shoved her, taunted her. Whispered in her ear. *Do it. Kiss him.*

Her feet propelled her forward. Straight into Nash's arms. Strong arms that opened for her, then held her tight. She lifted her hands to cup his jaw, feeling the bristles there, breathing in his utterly delicious scent.

And then she pressed her lips to his.

CHAPTER FOURTEEN

Though the devil had made her do it, as soon as their lips met, Ashley forgot about anything except how much she wanted Nash. And how much she'd missed him.

She could faintly hear people talking behind them, throats clearing, forks scraping across plates, the bell over the door ringing, but she was so lost in Nash's kisses that she never wanted to let go. It wasn't until a plate dropped and shattered that she came back to the real world.

Still holding him close, she drew back to look into his eyes. "Hi, Nash."

His lips curved into a smile. That beautifully sensual smile felt as though it was just for her.

"Hello, Ash." He bent his head to kiss her again, and she let herself have one more lingering taste of him before finally letting him go.

"What the hell?" Josh exclaimed. "How do you guys know each other?"

Josh looked stunned by what he'd just witnessed,

and Ashley wasn't going to lie and say that she wasn't pleased. She was sick and tired of letting him think that she couldn't do any better than him.

"Ashley and I are close friends," Nash said before she could reply, which only served to make Josh's eyes widen.

"That's crazy. I mean, she's never even mentioned you." Josh was starstruck enough, however, that even his continued confusion over how Ashley could have Nash Hardwin as a close friend—close enough to passionately kiss—couldn't overcome his need for an autograph. "Dude, would you sign something for me?"

Nash looked from Josh to Ashley, obviously guessing that Josh wasn't any random fan.

"Nash, this is Kevin's father, Josh."

Josh held out his hand, and though Nash paused a beat, he shook it.

"No problem," Nash said. "What would you like me to sign?"

On the surface, Nash was perfectly polite, but Ashley could hear the vibration of distaste under his voice. Likely because she'd told Nash that Josh was a constant disappointment to their son.

"Hey, Ash," Josh said, "you got something I could have Nash sign?"

She barely kept from rolling her eyes. More free stuff, that was her ex's game.

She went into the store and came back with a T-shirt that said *Irish Do It Better*.

Josh hated the way her family celebrated their Irish heritage. But she also guessed that he would try to show at least some modicum of good behavior in front of a celebrity.

Nash took the T-shirt and quickly scrawled his name in permanent black marker. He handed it to Josh. "Here you go."

Once Josh had his signature, he turned to Ashley. "Remember our agreement. I'd hate to have to bail on Kevin."

"I'm this close to going after him and tackling him," Nash muttered as they watched her ex walk away. "I'm guessing that if I knew the details about what he's pulling this time, I wouldn't bother holding myself back."

She blew out a breath. "It's the same nonsense as always."

But she didn't want to talk about her ex. That would be a waste of breath. Especially when she still couldn't believe Nash was here.

"What are you doing in Bar Harbor? I thought you were going to record a new album after your tour."

"I was, but it wasn't working out. Which is why I'm here to see a guy about buying a van instead."

Of everything she'd thought he might say, this was

nowhere on the list. She couldn't make sense of it.

"You're here to buy a van?"

"Can you spare a few minutes to talk in private so I can do a better job of explaining?"

She turned to let Annie know. "I'm going to take an early lunch, okay?"

Annie nodded, still looking stunned by seeing Ashley kiss Nash. Tongues were going to be wagging all over town, if they weren't already.

She supposed it wouldn't do her nonexistent street cred too much harm to be caught kissing a beloved superstar like Nash. Although she didn't want to be the center of local gossip for any longer than strictly necessary, especially if it might negatively affect Kevin. "It's probably best if we go back to my place. Anywhere else, there's a chance you might be mobbed, since I can pretty much guarantee word is already out that you're in Bar Harbor."

"Your place sounds good to me."

They headed outside into a perfect Maine day. The sky was clear. Everything was in bloom. And the air smelled like sea and sand.

She took a deep breath to try to steady herself. But it was impossible to feel even slightly steady after those kisses.

Kissing Nash was one of the very best things in the entire world. Making love with him was also on the list, of course, but just kissing him? *Mmmm.* It was wonderful.

She wanted to do it again and again and again. But she couldn't. While the devil on her shoulder had sent her into Nash's arms—and she had loved every single second of it—she couldn't keep blaming kissing him on crazy impulses or further retaliation against her ex. Even the few kisses they'd just shared had muddied the waters. More kisses would only complicate things further.

"I don't live far from here, only a couple of blocks. Hopefully, we can make it to my house without pandemonium striking."

He grinned at her. "I have a newfound appreciation for pandemonium. It brought you into my life." His eyes were full of such warmth. Warmth that seemed to be about more than desire. "I had a great time with you in Vienna, Ash. Really great."

She'd never felt like this with anyone else, simultaneously wanting to jump his bones, while also feeling safe and comforted.

"I had a really good time with you too," she told him. "Although I'm stunned that you're here. I didn't think I'd see you again."

He held her gaze for a moment before saying softly, "I didn't think so either."

Her heart was racing by the time they turned from

the main street onto her street of neighborhood homes.

"Bar Harbor is beautiful," he said, temporarily moving on to safer subjects. "It seems so peaceful."

"It will only seem that way as long as you stay in hiding," she joked.

But he didn't seem to think it was any laughing matter. "You don't think I could keep a low profile in town for a while? No one rushed up to me in the café and asked for an autograph," he pointed out. "Except for your ex."

"Actually, people in Bar Harbor are pretty great about giving celebrities space. Maybe it's because my cousin Smith has been here several times over the years for family gatherings, and he and his wife, Valentina, also honeymooned here." His question about keeping a low profile in Bar Harbor only made her more curious about why he was here. "You said you were here about a van. Are you thinking of staying in town longer than it would take to buy it?"

She tried not to let her heart race at the thought of seeing more of him. Especially when she knew nothing could come of it other than losing *more* of her heart to him, meaning she'd feel more crushed when he said good-bye again and hit the road.

"When we talked in Vienna," he explained, "I re-membered how great it felt to build that van when I was sixteen. It felt like I was finally taking control of my life and paving a path for my future. In the past several weeks, I learned about something called Van Life. Have you heard of it?"

She nodded. "I've seen pictures online of people who sell everything to live and travel in a converted van or a school bus. Some of the vehicles look pretty luxurious."

"The designs people have come up with, and the innovations, are incredible," he said enthusiastically. "A million miles past my simple build as a teenager." He was talking with his hands now, the way he had in Vienna when he'd been excited about his subject. "I could hire someone to build out a van for me. And I already live in a tour bus half the time. But the idea of building my own custom-designed van to take out wherever I want to go—into the woods, or to a lake, or to explore Route 66—and doing it with my own hands? It's what got me to the end of my tour. I looked online for a van for weeks. Not something new and flashy, but the same model I had as a kid. A VW van with a pop-up top. Turns out they're hard to come by, probably because van life is so popular right now. But I got lucky a few days ago, and one finally popped up online. Here. In Bar Harbor."

They arrived at her cottage, and as she opened the door to let Nash in, she wished she could have had the chance to clean up a bit first. Kevin's stuff was all over the place. The gaming console his father had given him against her will (but with her money, of course) last Christmas. School books. Snack wrappers. His cereal bowl from breakfast, which rarely made it into the sink or the dishwasher unless she put it there. Ashley's things were there too. Her books, the half-done blanket she'd been knitting for the past year. A nail polish bottle on the coffee table. Dozens of pictures of her and Kevin and her family. And the flowers she'd cut from her tiny garden and put into vases.

"You've got a great place," he said with a smile after he took it all in.

"I love that it's mine and Kevin's. It's our safe space."

"Thank you for inviting me into your safe space."

Calling on every ounce of her self-control to keep from kissing him again, she asked, "What can I get you to drink? Tea, coffee, sparkling water?"

"Coffee would be great. Jet lag is always roughest when I fly west."

"I don't know how you handle all that traveling," she said as she began to brew his coffee. But she couldn't do small talk with him. Not when they'd shared so much right from the start. And not when she still couldn't quite wrap her head around his being in Bar Harbor. "Surely you could have found another VW van somewhere else. Why here?"

He sat on one of the barstools in her open-plan kitchen and living room. "Do you really need to ask why? Don't you already know? Just like you, I thought it was good-bye in Vienna. But I couldn't stay away, Ash."

She licked her lips, her heart thudding hard behind her breastbone. "I shouldn't have kissed you at the café. Josh had pushed all my buttons, and I was trying to prove to him that I'm not the pathetic spinster he thinks I am. I'm so sorry. I shouldn't have used you to prove a point."

"You don't need to apologize for anything. I don't care why you kissed me. I'm just glad you did. And you should know that if you hadn't made the first move, I would have kissed you."

"*Nash.*" His name came out a little breathy. It was so hard to keep it together around him. "We can't be together. I thought we agreed on that in Vienna. I thought we both understood that the rock star and the small-town single mom could never work. Not in the real world. Not outside of a blip in time where we got to be different people for twenty-four hours in an exotic locale." Especially when gossip about Nash's past was sure to surface as quickly as gossip about their kiss.

"I hear what you're saying. Of course I do." He

paused before asking, "But have you missed me, Ash? Have you thought about me at all during these past six weeks, the way I've thought about you?"

The last vestige of self-preservation had her backing away from him, pressing herself into the corner of the kitchen counter to put more space between them.

"Of course I did," she admitted, barely above a whisper. "How could I not? But that doesn't mean—"

"I don't know what it means either, Ash." He came toward her. "All I know is that I haven't stopped thinking about you. Not from the second that we said good-bye. Every moment of every day and all through each night, you've been inside my head. I've thought of you again and again and again." He took another step closer. "You're right that I probably could have found a van somewhere else. But when I found one in your town, it felt like a sign. A sign I needed to follow. I couldn't stay away. I had to come." He moved to stand directly in front of her. "And I have to do this."

A heartbeat later, his mouth was on hers.

As it hit her, yet again, just how beautiful and glorious it was to be in Nash's arms, Ashley temporarily forgot all the reasons *why not*.

CHAPTER FIFTEEN

Nash relished having Ashley in his arms, her lips beneath his, her hands in his hair as she drew him closer.

Everything he'd said about how he couldn't get her out of his head, out of his body, out of his heart, was true. Though he'd spent only twenty-four hours with her in Vienna, he'd missed her like hell during the past six weeks.

At first, he'd tried to convince himself that his connection with Ashley was simply physical, an itch he had to scratch until she was out of his system. But she was different from any woman he'd ever been with. He'd never *liked* anyone as much as he liked her. He'd never been friends with any other woman he'd slept with. And he'd certainly never felt such a strong connection with any woman but Ashley.

The only thing he knew for sure was that she was irresistible, and his need for her was unstoppable. Even when a future together didn't make any sense, their desperate need for each other was undeniable. And if he was being completely honest with himself, the depth of his desire to be with her—to make love to her and to laugh with her too—shook him to the core.

Lifting her into his arms, he carried her down the hall to what he hoped was her bedroom. Thankfully, he found it on his first try. As he lay her back on her bed and covered her body with his, he kept his lips on hers. She wrapped her legs around him as though she never wanted to let him go.

He hadn't intended for this to happen, for the two of them to end up in bed together again. But he'd been unable to do anything but give in to his desperate need to see her again. Despite any and all rational thoughts about how she probably wouldn't appreciate his intrusion into her real life, he'd used the van as the perfect excuse. An excuse that she'd seen through inside of thirty minutes.

He continued to taste her, to tease her with his lips and tongue and teeth, nipping and stroking over her skin as he untucked her T-shirt and pulled it up over her stomach. They momentarily had to stop kissing so that he could pull the shirt up over her head and toss it across the room. Then he dived back in, devouring her again.

He'd dreamed of being with her this way every single night they'd been apart. Dreamed of touching her. Kissing her. Loving her. Dreamed of the sounds she made when he kissed her. Dreamed of feeling her skin beneath his hands, his mouth. Dreamed of the sweet scent of her arousal.

He'd been so hungry for her the past six weeks, and now that she was in his arms again, he was even *hungrier*. Greed for more of her, for *all* of her, was taking him over and driving him beyond all rational thought.

Desperate to get her naked, he was rough with the button and the zipper of her pants, shoving the denim off her legs, pushing off her shoes too. When he took off her bra, desire made him clumsy as he tore at the clasp.

She gasped as the cotton gave way, and her breasts sprang free into his waiting hands. He found cotton so much sexier than silk or lace had ever been. Because it seemed real, honest, genuine.

Real like Ashley. Beautiful like Ashley. Steady like Ashley.

She was a miracle in every way.

He moved his mouth from her lips, across her cheekbones and then her neck so that he could kiss the sensitive spot behind her ear. Then the hollow of her throat and over the swells of her breasts.

She was so soft, so perfect as he laved his tongue over the aroused tips of her breasts and all of the delicious skin that surrounded them.

She cried out his name. A cry that sounded like a plea for *more*.

He wanted to give her everything. If only he had more to give to her. If only he understood what love was, because something told him that if he did, he would have declared himself to her in that very moment.

But Nash knew he couldn't give her any of those things. All he knew how to give her was pleasure.

So. Much. Pleasure.

He moved his sensual attention to her other breast, teasing, tasting, stroking. He loved the sounds she made, the abandon with which she expressed her pleasure. He continued lower, raining kisses over her belly.

She was so beautiful. Curvy in all the right places. A million times sexier than any supermodel would ever be.

He never wanted to hurt her. And yet, if she asked him to leave right now, he wasn't sure he would be able to make himself go. Not when she was begging him like this, begging him to strip her bare and taste her the way he had in the shower in Vienna.

Without any finesse, he yanked her panties down...and devoured her. Delving deep into the core of her with his tongue. Teasing and caressing the very center of her arousal.

His name erupted from her lips in a cry of raw, animal pleasure as he drove his fingers into her at the same time that he swirled his tongue over the apex of her pleasure.

As her climax rippled through her, he would have drawn it out forever if he could. Just kept making her come and come and come for him, over and over again.

At last, she stilled beneath him. Slowly, he moved up her body, digging out a condom from his wallet with one hand, then tossing the wallet to the side.

Damn it, he still had his clothes on. But he needed to be inside of Ashley *now*. Hell, he'd needed to be inside of her for every moment of the past six weeks.

As if she could read his mind, she tore at his clothes, ripped his shirt over his head, then yanked his jeans down his hips and legs. Together, they rolled the condom over him.

Where he'd been so careful in Vienna, cognizant of how little experience she had, today all that mattered was making her his in one hard plunge of possession.

She breathlessly urged him forward with her hands on his hips, pulling him in harder, deeper. Again and again, they rocked together, chasing the kind of bliss he'd only ever known with her. Feeling sensations so much bigger and brighter than he'd ever thought possible.

Stilling above her, he stared into her eyes. There was a wildness in her gaze, a desperation he knew must be mirrored in his own.

"Ashley."

There were so many things he wanted to say. So many things he didn't know how to say.

Wordlessly, she reached up to his face, brushed the pad of her thumb over his lips, then rested her hand on his jaw. He could easily read the wonder in her eyes.

And then she kissed him. Her lips were soft—so very soft and sweet—despite the wildness of their passion. She wrapped her arms around him and held him close, closer than he'd ever been held before.

On a groan, he lost himself in her. And as both of their releases spiraled out together, he felt the most beautiful sensation in the center of his chest. Right in the middle of the heart that he'd always felt was lacking, that he'd always believed could never truly know love.

But right here, right now, holding Ashley tight, he almost thought he understood.

CHAPTER SIXTEEN

Ashley never wanted to leave Nash's arms. But despite the glow of their lovemaking, she knew she couldn't keep living in a fantasy world for another second. Not when they were in her bed in her Bar Harbor home. And judging by the clock on her bedside table, Kevin would be home from school any second now.

After they'd made love, Nash had curled her close, and she had fallen asleep against his broad chest. She'd been so overwhelmed by the pleasure of being with him again that she hadn't been able to muster up the will to tell him they couldn't do this, or that he needed to leave immediately. Instead, she'd given in to the warmth and the joy of being with him.

"Nash," she said in an anxious tone, "you've got to go. Now!"

Still half asleep, he reached for her again, but because she knew Kevin would be walking in the door soon, she was finally able to muster up the strength to push him away.

"Kevin will be home any second!"

Thankfully, that was all it took for Nash to spring to life. The speed with which he hopped off the bed and put on his jeans and shirt showed her how much he respected her wishes when it came to her son.

She'd never seen anyone move so fast...or conversely been so upset at how quickly he'd covered up his physical beauty. She would have liked to stare at Nash for hours. Maybe even learn to sculpt so that she could make a statue of him to gaze at once he was gone again. But she wasn't an artist like so many of her family members. Ashley was good at spreadsheets and organization. She was good at putting a business plan together and making sure her plans stayed on track.

It turned out that she was also good at sleeping with Nash. *Really* good at it, she thought as she yanked her own clothes back on, her fingers fumbling slightly in her haste.

"We need to talk, Ash. About what just happened. About *us*."

"Okay. But not now. Call me later, and we'll figure out a time and place to talk things through."

Though Nash looked a little disgruntled at being thrown out of her house like this, he didn't argue. "What's your phone number?"

It was crazy how they knew so much about each other's lives and bodies, but didn't have each other's phone numbers. She called out the numbers as she led the way down the hall and into the living room.

But they were too late, because the front door was already opening.

"Mom?" Kevin called.

Ashley always made sure to be home by the time Kevin was done with school. She supposed Josh was right that working for the family business gave her some extra flexibility with her hours. But she'd more than earned that perk. She worked evenings and weekends, often putting in an hour or two at night after Kevin went to sleep. When he'd been a baby, she'd worked during his nap times. All her adult life, she'd been determined to prove herself to her parents, that sympathy for her predicament shouldn't be the reason they kept her employed.

Ashley was proud of the work that she'd done for the Sullivan Cafés and stores throughout Maine. She'd helped grow the business a great deal since she'd taken over the management so that her father could pursue other interests, and her mother could remain happily entrenched in the café kitchens.

Now, for the first time in Kevin's life, she needed to explain why a man he'd never met before was in their house.

She started with the basics. "Kevin, this is my friend Nash."

Kevin nodded. "Hey."

Nash shook her son's hand. Kevin seemed to like that, being treated like an adult by another guy. Eleven could be such a strange in-between age. Not nearly an adult, not quite a teenager, but not a kid anymore either.

It was something she regularly struggled with as a parent. How far to let him explore? How much to let him experiment with things? How tightly to rein him in to keep him safe?

Thus far, she'd erred on the side of safety. But what mom didn't? Especially when she didn't have a husband or true co-parent to help.

"Why don't you get your things together for soccer practice while I say good-bye to Nash?" she suggested.

As soon as Kevin headed into his room, not seeming the least bit dismayed by Nash's presence, she grabbed Nash's hand and tugged him out to the front porch.

"I don't know what came over me today, jumping into bed with you like that," she said in a low voice, even though she knew *exactly* what had come over her. "But—"

"Let's wait to talk about this until we don't have to whisper," he cut in. "I'll call you to find a time that makes sense."

For a moment, she thought he might kiss her good-bye. Instead, he squeezed her hand, then walked away, leaving her standing there on the porch, her legs barely steady, her skin, her blood, her body still pulsing from the pleasure of being with him.

But then, a beat later, he was back up on the porch, and his mouth was on hers again. Giving her a fast, fierce kiss that stole her breath.

Leaving her breathless long after he walked away.

★ ★ ★

Ashley wasn't exactly sure how she and Kevin got to soccer practice, considering she barely remembered getting into the car and driving to the field. Especially given that Nash both called and texted her to set up a private time to talk immediately after he left her house.

It was unbearably tempting to call him back simply to hear his voice. But she knew better. Knew that she needed to nip her addiction to him in the bud, rather than give in to it. Because it turned out that the more she had of Nash, the more she wanted. *More. More. More.*

Oh God...she could barely think of anything but him. Barely focus on getting her car between the white lines of the parking space in front of the soccer field.

Once they got out of the car, she realized she'd forgotten that she was in charge of snacks for the day and had left the container of cut-up orange wedges in her fridge. Fortunately, one of the parents had a bag of tangerines from a recent trip to the grocery store, so they planned to pass those out to the kids instead.

Ashley chatted with the other parents like she normally did, but all the while, she felt like she was barely keeping it together. Especially when one of the other moms, a cool blonde named Belinda with whom she had never been particularly close, said, "Is it true that you know Nash Hardwin? My cousin just texted me saying she heard you were with him at the café today. I told her I'd ask you because you're standing right here."

This was exactly the kind of gossip that solidified Ashley's belief that she and Nash could never make a relationship work. Especially not if her son ended up caught in the middle of it all.

Ashley knew she never should have kissed him at the café! But since she had, she needed to put her game face on and figure out how to spin things in a positive way. After all, the sheer fact that Nash was even in Bar Harbor was already big enough news. But the fact that Ashley Sullivan, the single-mom-slash-spinster, had made out in public with an ex-felon rock star?

She couldn't imagine much bigger news.

And if anyone had known precisely what had gone on between her and Nash in her bedroom after their kiss at the café…

The memories of their lovemaking made her skin

heat up, even as she tried to remain calm and collected in front of the other parents.

Focus! She needed to focus on shutting Belinda's gossipy question down—and quick. But how? Because everything Belinda's cousin had texted her was true...and then some.

What's more, it had taken Ashley years to live down her reputation as the girl who had gotten pregnant in high school. Actually, if she was being completely honest with herself, she wasn't sure she had ever truly lived it down. And now she was all but certain her very public kiss with Nash would revive her own past mistakes. She could imagine what people would say. *What can you expect from someone who had a baby in high school?* And, *Ashley Sullivan always manages to find trouble, doesn't she?*

Just then, as though some force in the universe was looking down on her with pity, a soccer ball flew toward the sidelines and hit one of the dads in the jaw. As Ashley was in charge of the first aid kit, she immediately rushed to his side to see if he needed help, rather than answering Belinda's question.

It was the coward's way out. She knew that. But despite the fact that in Vienna she'd vowed not to be a coward anymore, without a foolproof plan to circumvent gossip, she didn't know what else to do.

While getting pregnant at seventeen hadn't been

anywhere in her plans, she'd become a master planner in the years since. Everything in her life was done on track with her well-organized spreadsheets.

Until she'd had the best day, and night, in Vienna with Nash.

Until she'd kissed him at the café today.

Until they'd made love in her bedroom this afternoon, and then she'd fallen asleep in his arms.

Suddenly, it felt as though all her carefully laid life plans had gone out the window.

And now she was forced to scramble again, just as she had in high school.

CHAPTER SEVENTEEN

By the time Ashley put the first aid kit away, she had come to the conclusion that the other parents were bound to talk about her and Nash whether she wanted them to or not. So it was in her best interests to try to direct the narrative as best she could.

Putting a smile on her face, she headed back to the group of parents. As though she'd meant to answer Belinda all along, she said, "You can tell your cousin that it's true—Nash is a friend of mine. I was delighted to see him when he dropped by the café today. I wasn't expecting to see him again so soon." *Or ever again*, she added silently.

"Didn't he spend some time in jail?" Belinda asked, not bothering to cover up her nasty nosiness this time.

Ashley smiled so hard at the other woman she thought her face would crack. "I don't waste my time reading gossip magazines or websites, so I wouldn't know what they've said about him. All I know," she said, knowing she shouldn't stoop to Belinda's level, but she couldn't help herself, "is that millions of fans all over the world certainly don't seem to care about anything other than what a brilliant musician he is."

Fortunately, one of the other moms, a gentle soul, spoke up next.

"You're so right about that. I'm his biggest fan! Is he planning to do a show nearby? Because I thought he just finished a European tour."

"I'm not sure, but I think he might be here to take a bit of a break. He knows my cousin Smith and has heard how great everyone in Bar Harbor is about giving celebrities some space." Though she gave the warning lightly, she hoped the other parents would not only take her words to heart, but also let their friends and family know to respect Nash's privacy. "I've assured him that people here will be more than happy to leave him alone," she added with another big smile. And hopefully, if they all left Nash alone, that meant they'd also keep their noses out of *her* business.

At last, practice ended, and the kids ran toward them, sweaty and stinky, like they always were after practice.

"Mom, did you see me do that awesome bait-and-take?" Kevin asked her.

"I sure did." Thankfully, she had noticed him do the maneuver at the beginning of practice. "You're a superstar."

He grabbed a tangerine, and after he wolfed it

down, she gave him a granola bar stashed in her purse, then waved good-bye to the other parents.

She was just breathing a sigh of relief as they got into her car when Kevin said, "Sammy said his grandma saw you kissing Nash at the café today."

Ashley turned to look at her son with horror. Oh God, this was a million times worse than dealing with Belinda.

"I told him you guys were friends, 'cause that's what you said back at the house," Kevin added before she could come up with a response. "But how come I've never heard about him before?"

"Well..." she said slowly. "He's a fairly new friend. I met him in Vienna, at Uncle Brandon's hotel."

Kevin processed that information. "Sammy said Nash is super famous. Like, Uncle Smith famous." Even though Smith was more like a cousin once removed, Kevin referred to everyone in the extended Sullivan family as an uncle or aunt, because they were all so close.

"It's true," she replied. "Nash is really famous like Smith. Only, he's a musician instead of an actor."

"Is he as nice as Smith? 'Cause Sammy said he's been to jail."

"First of all, just because someone has made mistakes in their past doesn't mean he's a bad person. People can act badly for lots of reasons. And then they hopefully learn from their mistakes." She should have guessed that Kevin would learn about Nash's past. She just hadn't figured one kiss at the café would be all it took to send gossip spiraling around her son. "So yes, Nash is a really nice person. I wouldn't spend time with him if he wasn't, I promise."

Kevin thought about it for a minute. "Okay, that's cool. I wouldn't want you hanging out with some guy who's mean."

It was so sweet that she had to lean over at a stop sign and give her son a one-armed hug. "Thank you for looking out for me, honey."

With that, Kevin seemed content to finish his granola bar and turn on the radio, scanning through stations to find a good song.

First thing tomorrow, as soon as Kevin was off to school, Ashley needed to meet with Nash to tell him that they absolutely had to end things once and for all. This was too much upheaval, too fast. Wham bam, best sex ever...and now her kid and everyone else in town was asking questions. If only she could call Nash tonight to get it over with, but her cottage was too small to find a private place where Kevin wouldn't overhear her conversation. Which meant she somehow needed to keep it together until tomorrow.

Trying to act as normal as possible around her son, she asked, "Are you going to need help with your homework tonight?"

"I only have math. Should be easy."

"Okay, great. I'm going to make spaghetti for dinner. Sound good?"

"Yup."

For Kevin, everything was back to normal. He'd quizzed her about the stranger, then he'd immediately gone back into his regular world. But throughout the rest of the evening, as she coaxed him into the shower, then started a load of laundry, then browned ground meat and boiled spaghetti noodles, then sat down at the dinner table to eat dinner, Ashley felt wired. On edge.

She couldn't settle. Not until she put an end to things with Nash. Yes, she had wanted to make some changes in her life, to live more boldly and adventurously, but this was too fast. Way too much change all at once.

First of all, she was a responsible mother who needed to guard her son's heart. She couldn't let Kevin think she let men come in and out of her life willy-nilly.

Okay, so it wasn't like she was lining up random guys to have affairs with. Only Nash had ever made it past her bedroom door. But still, she didn't dare embark on a relationship with a road-warrior rock star when it was bound to fail from the start—not if there was any chance that it might have a bad impact on

Kevin.

With Nash, there was *every* chance that things would end badly. He was a superstar who lived a superstar's life. He'd never given her any indication that he was ready to settle down. In fact, hadn't he said that part of the allure of building out the VW van was so he could head off at a moment's notice?

And then, on top of everything else, she'd already had to defend Nash's past twice. Though she'd meant what she'd said to Kevin about how everyone should be given the chance to change for the better, that didn't mean she was willing to let the repercussions of Nash's past cast a shadow over Kevin's life here in Bar Harbor.

It didn't help her peace of mind that by that evening, word had spread to her family like an out-of-control wildfire. The texts from her brothers came in fast and furious.

> Turner: *When did you meet Nash Hardwin? I heard you were kissing him in the café, but that can't be true, is it?*
>
> Hudson: *Been hearing some crazy things about you and Nash Hardwin! Have you been keeping secrets from all of us?*
>
> Rory: *I've been deflecting rumors about you and Nash Hardwin (!) all afternoon. It would help to know what the truth is.*

Brandon: *I know you want me to stay out of your life, but what the hell is going on in Bar Harbor? I just got a text from an acquaintance in town telling me that you and Nash Hardwin were seen kissing today! I thought you said things were over between you. Text me back as soon as you get this, even if it's the middle of the night in Europe. I'll be waiting to hear from you.*

Only her parents, who were out of town for the next couple of days, remained silent. Furious with her brothers, she deliberately ignored their texts. As she'd said to Brandon in Vienna, they had no business weighing in on her personal life.

Her sisters, on the other hand, were precisely the people she needed to talk to right now. She initiated a group text among the three of them.

Ashley: *You've both probably already heard by now that Nash is in town. And that I kissed him at the café. You can't imagine the ridiculous texts our brothers have sent me already!*

Cassie: *We did hear that Nash was here, but we figured you'd reach out when you were ready to tell us. And of course we can imagine all the texts they're sending you! They should know by now that we hate it when they act like that.*

Lola: *Seriously, Ash, don't worry about them for*

another second. Cassie and I will make sure they stay out of your business from now on.

Ashley: *Thank you. Every time I look at their messages, steam comes out of my ears.*

Lola: *Speaking of steam… How are things going with Nash? I thought you said there was no chance of seeing him again.*

Ashley: *I swear I had no idea he was coming! And when I saw him unexpectedly standing there in the café, momentary insanity took over, and I couldn't stop myself from kissing him!*

Lola: *Wow, that sounds seriously hot.*

Ashley: *It was. But then Kevin almost caught us together, and the other parents in town are already gossiping about us, so tomorrow morning I'm going to tell Nash that we have to stop seeing each other for good.*

Lola: *Explain again why you have to call things off with Nash. Sounds like you both find each other irresistible…*

Ashley: *People in town are already bringing up Nash's time in jail. I have Kevin's well-being to think about.*

Lola: *You also have your own well-being to think about! For eleven years, you've given everything you are to Kevin. I know you'd do it all again in a heart-*

beat, but he's growing up. Your heart, your needs are important too!

Ashley had always appreciated Lola's passion and intensity. But right now it was too much for her to deal with when she already felt so topsy-turvy after seeing Nash. As though her sister could read her mind, Lola texted again before Ashley could reply.

Lola: *Sorry, Ash, I don't mean to make things harder for you. Even though I can't lie and say I'm not still hoping it could all end up magically working out for the two of you.*

Cassie: *We love you, and we're here for you, no matter what happens. And don't worry for even one second about the boys. We'll take care of their nonsense.*

More exhausted than ever, Ashley turned off the ringer on her phone and plugged it into the charging station in the kitchen, far away from her bedroom. She was tempted to bury it in a hole under the house at this point. Partly to avoid more messages from her family, but mostly because it was nearly impossible not to give in to the urge to text or call Nash and beg him to come over.

Ashley got into bed, only to toss and turn for another several hours. She counted sheep, one to a hundred, over and over and over, until she belatedly realized that she hadn't given Josh the money for his camping trip with Kevin.

Shoving off the covers, she went to the kitchen and opened her laptop to send the money to his bank account. When that was done, she didn't bother trying to go to sleep. Instead, she took care of the work that she hadn't gotten to yesterday afternoon at the café when she'd been too busy having sex with Nash.

But since she lived in the real world and not the fantasy world she'd dipped into twice with him, she corralled her focus and ticked her way through the emails in her inbox until Kevin's alarm clock went off.

Thus began another day in Ashley's life that should otherwise have been the same as always. School for Kevin. Work at the café. Soccer practice. Homework. Dinner. Bedtime.

But there was one big difference today: She'd need to find the strength to tell Nash that they could never be together again as anything more than friends.

And this time, they needed to stick to it.

No matter what.

CHAPTER EIGHTEEN

Nash wasn't used to staring at his phone, waiting to hear back from a woman. And he sure as hell wasn't used to having to stop himself from texting or calling someone again. He had always been the pursued, not the pursuer. Until Ashley.

He was amazed by how easily she broke apart his self-control, especially when they were in bed together. He couldn't wait to have her. And then when they were together, he couldn't get enough.

Ashley's kiss at the café had been the best surprise in the entire world. And making love with her again?

It had been the best damned thing he'd ever done in his life.

After jumping out of her bed and meeting her son, who looked like a really good kid, Nash had taken a taxi to his rental property to pick up the keys from his new landlady. It was a short-term rental, two weeks in a cottage in the woods on the outskirts of Bar Harbor. He'd chosen it because it had a secure fence around the property, in case word got out that he was here. He had deliberately opted not to stay anywhere five-star. He'd had enough five-star lodgings to last him a lifetime. He was craving something that felt more like home.

Not that he knew what *home* felt like. The apartment he'd lived in with his mom in Raleigh hadn't had any family pictures on the walls, no knitting in a basket, or books to read on a coffee table in front of a fire, or flowers on the kitchen table, or knitted throws on a couch.

His childhood home had been the polar opposite of the one Ashley had created for her son. The moment he'd stepped inside their house, he'd been filled with a longing that had surprised him. He had his every need catered to by hotel staff. People always said they wished they could change places with him.

So why did he suddenly want to make his own meals and do his own laundry?

It had been nearly twenty years since he'd had to do either of those things. He hadn't held a hammer or a saw for just as long. Though he usually loved writing songs, recording, and performing, when inspiration refused to strike after his European tour, he had canceled his plans to record the new album at the studio and come to Bar Harbor instead. Hopefully, he'd find some inspiration here.

Selma, his landlady, looked to be in her seventies

and, thankfully, had no idea who he was. She laid down strict rules about how she expected him to take care of her rental property, and he appreciated that she treated him without kid gloves. She didn't want anything from him. She didn't worship him. Selma treated him like she would any other short-term renter—with suspicion.

But grocery shopping and cooking a meal on the old stove top in the kitchen would have to wait. He was too wrecked from his six weeks of nonstop touring and then his transatlantic flight to do more than take one last look at his phone to see if Ashley had contacted him, then crawl into bed as the sun set.

Nash dreamed of Ashley all night long. Dreamed of living with her in her cottage. Dreamed about Kevin being his son. Dreamed of a life he'd only ever seen on TV or read about in books, one with parent-teacher meetings and dinner as a family and evenings on the couch in front of the TV.

What had once seemed boring to him now seemed like an out-of-reach fantasy.

Nash had gone from rags to riches, from being disdained to worshiped, from having no one who cared about him to millions of strangers professing their love. By the time he was eighteen, he'd signed a record deal. His first release had landed at number one six months later. Nearly two decades after that, the world was his oyster.

Only, he'd never suspected how lonely it could be at the top. Or how easily a pretty single mom from Maine would get beneath his defenses and make him wonder if the "dream life" he was living was the life he actually wanted.

In the morning, he found a bag of bagels in the kitchen cupboard that the landlady had left for him. Or maybe it was the previous tenant?

He burned the first bagel to a crisp before figuring out he needed to set the toaster dial lower or risk setting the house on fire. It was surprisingly satisfying to get his second bagel-toasting attempt exactly right.

When he was done eating breakfast and had cleaned up the kitchen—yet another thing he hadn't done for the past twenty years—he pulled out his phone again to make sure he had a signal. Or maybe the problem was that she'd entered his number wrong into her phone?

He almost had to laugh at himself, thinking that the only reason Ashley wouldn't have gotten back to him was because his phone was broken or the number was wrong, rather than because she'd thought better of ever seeing or speaking to him again.

Honestly, he wouldn't blame her for wanting to keep her life on the path it was on before he'd stormed his way into her life. Hell, if he could manage to be even the slightest bit selfless, he'd leave town without bothering her again. Lord knew Ashley didn't deserve to have her safe, steady world tangled up with his celebrity ridiculousness.

But he wanted her too much to be selfless, or to allow himself to think about the future.

Just then, his phone beeped. His heart leaped when he saw her name on the screen. He almost felt as though he had conjured her from the sheer force of his desire to hear from her.

I'll be free by 5:30. If you can come back to my cottage tonight, we can talk then.

He'd never been so glad to hear from anyone. So even though he was almost positive she was going to tell him to take a flying leap tonight, the knowledge that he would soon see her face again put a new spring in his step as he headed off to pick up his van.

Luck was on his side again when the man selling him the van didn't have the first clue who he was, just like his landlady. All the guy wanted was to make the transaction and get on with his day.

Nash put the keys for the old VW van onto the Empress Sisi key chain Ashley had bought him in Vienna. He could have easily purchased a new tricked-out van for six figures. But new and shiny wasn't what he was after.

The engine barely turned over, and all of the upholstery needed to be yanked out and taken to the dump. Fixing this vehicle up and turning it into something enjoyable not just to drive, but also to camp in overnight, would be a labor of love.

Love.

It was funny how often that word popped into his head lately.

He'd written love songs before, but they'd always been about other people's lives. Never about his own.

Many of his songs were, at their core, about feeling like a man on an island, alone and searching for something he couldn't quite explain. He'd long thought that was why so many people related to his music. Everybody felt like a man or a woman on an island at some point in their lives. Of course, he'd also written plenty of songs about having a good time, and fans around the world loved to sing and dance to those songs.

But a love song that came from his own heart?

No, he hadn't written one of those.

Shoving away the uncomfortable thoughts, Nash refocused his attention on the van. He needed to head to a hardware store and buy tools.

An hour later, he had made the local hardware store owner's day by buying up what seemed like half his inventory. Jim had known who he was, unlike the seller of the van and his landlady. But the guy had been cool about it. He hadn't asked Nash for an autograph. Instead, he'd told Nash to let him know if there was something else he needed once he got to work on the van.

Nash had a feeling the two of them were going to get to know each other very well during the next two weeks. He could still remember how many times at sixteen he'd been in the middle of working on something in his van and suddenly realized he needed a different size of screw or drill bit or plumbing tube.

Hungry again, he stopped off at a seaside restaurant that was little more than a waterside stand selling lobster rolls. Yet again, the person behind the counter took Nash's presence in stride. He hadn't felt this free since Vienna, and he didn't have to wear a disguise here.

He ordered two lobster rolls and enjoyed them more than he'd enjoyed anything he'd eaten in a very long time. They tasted better than the Michelin-starred meal he'd had in Switzerland three days ago.

And that was when Nash suddenly had to wonder—did the people who lived in Bar Harbor have it better than a worldwide superstar with money to burn and the entire world at his feet?

CHAPTER NINETEEN

When Nash pulled up in front of Ashley's cottage at 5:25 p.m., he was surprised to see Ashley and Kevin standing on the front porch, a duffel bag and backpack lying on the wooden floor between them. She was on her cell phone, and she looked upset.

Nash's gut tightened. He hated seeing her upset. And when he looked more closely at Kevin and realized the boy was barely holding back tears, Nash's gut clenched even tighter.

It didn't take a rocket scientist to guess who was causing the problem. Kevin's crap father.

Josh.

Nash got out of the van and caught the tail end of Ashley's message. "Call me as soon as you get this message, Josh. Kevin has been really looking forward to this trip."

She shoved her cell into her pocket as Nash walked up the porch steps. "Hi, Nash," she said in a distracted voice. "I know we were supposed to meet tonight, but we've got a bit of a problem here."

"Hi, Ashley. Hi, Kevin." He looked between their downcast faces, wanting to make them feel better any way he could. "Is there anything I can do to help?"

"My dad was supposed to take me camping for spring break," Kevin explained in a morose voice. "But he bailed. He left Mom a message saying he didn't have enough money to take me anywhere, so I'd have to stay home."

To say that Ashley looked furious was a massive understatement. She looked like she could happily stab Josh in the heart, if she could only locate him.

"He had enough money," was all she said through gritted teeth.

"What am I going to do for the next five days, Mom? Everyone else already has plans, and you have to work."

Her expression shifted from rage to heartbreak. "I'll figure something out," she promised. "I'll juggle my vacation days with someone at the café, and we'll find something fun to do together, okay?"

"I have an idea." Nash didn't mean to butt in, but Ashley was looking increasingly desperate. It didn't sound to him like it would be easy to "juggle" vacation days with a coworker at the last second. "See that van?" he said, pointing to where he'd parked it at the curb. "I just bought it."

Both Ashley and Kevin looked at it skeptically. He

didn't blame them. It was a piece of junk in its present incarnation. But he knew what it could be transformed into with a little love and attention.

"I'm going to fix it up, inside and out, starting tomorrow morning. I just came from the hardware store." He looked at Kevin. "You ever build anything?"

Kevin nodded. "Last month, we built birdhouses in school. We got to design them, and after they sawed the wood up for us, we put them together with hammers and nails. Then we painted them." He pointed toward a nearby tree. "That's the one I made. Mom said it's better than anything she could have bought at a store. She said if I wanted to make another one, she could sell it to a tourist at the store next to the café."

Nash admired the birdhouse. It wasn't perfect, but it had some serious charm. Especially with the purple and green paint combination.

"She's right. It's awesome." He smiled at Kevin. "I didn't know you had all that experience. Sounds like you could be a big help for me."

Kevin's eyes widened. "Really?"

Nash nodded. "It'll be a big job working to bring this classic van back to life. I'm planning to put in a bathroom with a shower, plus a kitchen and a convertible bed. I'm also going to trim out the walls and the floor with wood planks and put in a heater and air conditioner." He was glad to see sparks of interest in

Kevin's eyes. "You wouldn't happen to have any interest in helping me do that, would you?"

"Yeah," Kevin said. "That'd be super cool!" He turned to Ashley. "Mom? Can I? Can I help Nash build his van?"

She looked at a loss for words. Nash understood why she would be stunned by this sudden development, but as soon as he'd seen how upset they were about Kevin's deadbeat dad blowing Kevin off, Nash had felt compelled to step in.

After all, he knew *exactly* what it was like to have a deadbeat parent. It sucked. And it left you feeling unworthy and unwanted.

Even once you were in your thirties, and millions of people around the world professed to adore you, it still was hard to shake that sense that you weren't enough. That you would *never* be enough.

Realizing he needed to do a better job of selling Ashley on the idea, Nash said, "Kevin would be a great help to me, Ash. Working on this van is a big job for one person. Two would be much better."

Though she still looked conflicted, she finally nodded. "Okay. But you need to promise me," she said to Kevin, "that you're going to listen to everything Nash says about being smart and safe while working with the tools." She turned to Nash next. "And *you* need to promise me that you won't let Kevin work with anything dangerous where he could hurt himself."

"*Mom.*" Kevin rolled his eyes. "You've got to let me work with the saws and the hammers and stuff. I won't hurt myself. I'll be really careful."

She smiled at her son. "I know you will. But you also know I can't help but worry about you. That's just what moms do."

Nash got a sense this was a conversation the two of them had a lot. Not specifically about Kevin using hammers and saws, but about her son wanting to take chances and do things that had the potential to be dangerous—and her worrying about him.

"So I can do it?" Kevin asked, practically bouncing on the tips of his toes from excitement.

"Okay, you can do it." She turned to Nash. "In fact, I think I might know the perfect place for you to work. My brother Rory has a studio in an artist collective warehouse. I'll call him right now to see if you can work in his parking lot for a couple of weeks. He's got access to water and electricity, so hopefully you'd have everything you needed."

"That'd be great. Thanks, Ash." He grinned down at Kevin. "While your mom's making that call, why don't you come take a closer look at the van and the tools I just bought?"

As Kevin happily ran toward the van, his deadbeat dad and the spring break camping trip seemed to be forgotten. They talked about Nash's ideas for retrofitting the van, and Kevin had good suggestions about how Nash could create a removable bunk bed above the convertible couch to sleep a third person.

"Maybe you could draw that out for me," Nash suggested, "and then tomorrow, we'll have a game plan before we start taking measurements."

"I'm pretty good at drawing, so I'll do that when we all go inside for dinner."

Nash appreciated how Kevin automatically assumed Nash was staying for dinner. Kids were so accepting. So good at rolling with life.

Just that quickly, the crazy urge to have a family of his own hit him again, right in the solar plexus.

Ashley came out to the sidewalk to give them an update. "Okay, guys, everything is a go." After Kevin whooped with excitement, Ashley turned to tell Nash, "Tomorrow morning, I'll introduce you to Rory, and he'll show you where you can hook up to electricity and water."

"Sounds great, thanks." She was so beautiful, so good and sweet, that his chest ached just looking at her.

"Mom," Kevin said, "I need to draw something for Nash, because I had a really good idea about how to set up an extra bunk bed. Can I work on it while you make dinner?"

"Works for me," she said, clearly happy to see Kevin looking cheerful again.

After Kevin had run inside, Nash said to Ashley in a low voice, "I'm sorry his father bailed on him."

"I am too. He's such a bastard. I can't believe he said he didn't have the money for their trip. Especially after I gave—" She shook her head. "Never mind."

"Wait. You gave him the money for the trip with Kevin? And then he blew him off anyway?" Nash felt extremely protective of Ashley and her son. It didn't matter how long he'd known them. They deserved better.

"I did," she admitted. "And I feel so stupid to have fallen for his lies yet again. He's probably off gambling with his friends. Yesterday, he fed me a line about needing the money to rent an RV, but instead of sending the money to the rental company, I sent it to him. I knew better, damn it."

Nash reached for her hands, stilling her self-recriminations. "It's his fault, not yours."

"Thank you for coming to the rescue, Nash. But if it's going to be too much of a distraction to have Kevin working on the van with you—"

"No way am I going to back out on him the way Josh did," Nash interrupted before she could finish. "The two of us are going to have a great time working together on the van. He's a bright and capable kid. And you're a great mom, just like I knew you must be after spending time with you in Vienna. Although I probably shouldn't have asked him to work with me without asking you first. I know my being here is complicating your life, but when I realized what had happened with Josh not showing up for their trip, I didn't stop to think that stepping in might cause even more problems."

"Normally, I would have wanted more time to think the whole thing over," she agreed. "But right now, seeing how quickly Kevin went from sad to excited is outweighing anything else. And I know you and I still need to talk about…other things." Though her cheeks flushed as she said *other things*, her expression was far too grim for his liking. "But it will have to be later. After Kevin is in bed."

His chest tightened at what he figured she was planning to say to him. That she didn't want any more of his kisses, or lovemaking, because getting closer to him would only complicate her life more than it likely already had.

"Why don't you let me help you with dinner?" he said in as easy a voice as he could manage. "We can work out everything else later."

At the very least, he thought as he picked up Kevin's bags and carried them into the house, working with Kevin on the van meant he'd get to see Ashley for a little while every day.

He wanted to spend *all* of his time with her. But at this point, he'd take anything he could get, any smiles, any laughter, any chances to touch her again. Even if it was only five minutes in the morning and five minutes at night when she dropped off Kevin and then picked him up, they'd still be the best ten minutes of Nash's day.

CHAPTER TWENTY

Ashley wasn't surprised that Josh had blown off his son yet again. What *had* surprised her, though, was how Nash immediately stepped up to the plate and helped make Kevin smile. If she hadn't already been filled with warm feelings about Nash, this alone would have convinced her that he was a good man. A *really* good man.

Unlike her ex, who'd stolen money meant for a trip with his son to gamble it away with his friends, which she'd verified by looking at a picture he'd posted on social media. The jerk.

Enough was enough. There was no way she could let this slide. Josh had pushed her too far.

She was clearing the kitchen counter so that they could start cooking dinner when she saw Nash's key chain. "This is the Sisi key chain I bought for you in Vienna."

"It's the best gift anyone ever gave me."

"Kevin and I have been playing crazy eights with the card deck I bought."

"Hey, Nash," Kevin called from the dining room table. "We could play after dinner, if you want."

Nash gave her son a thumbs-up, and she felt a little bit of the tension in her shoulders dissipate, thankful that Kevin was smiling with Nash instead of crying over his father's desertion.

Sighing at the thought of Josh, she was surprised when Nash put his hands on her shoulders and began to knead the tight muscles. She'd never had a partner to share her problems with, so being able to lean into him, even if only for a few seconds, meant a great deal to her.

Of course, she understood that they had no realistic future together. But for a few precious minutes, she allowed herself to appreciate that Nash was here, helping her with the kind of issue she always had to deal with on her own.

"I'm afraid I don't have too many kitchen skills," he said in a low voice that thrummed over her skin, heating her up all over. "But if you tell me what to do, I can follow your directions."

She fought back a shiver as she remembered just how good he'd been at following her directions in the shower in Vienna.

Every cell in her body longed to be with him again. To turn in the circle of his arms and kiss him. But with Kevin sitting at the dining table drawing—and the fact that she and Nash were mere hours away from having their we-can-never-kiss-or-touch-each-other-again conversation—she said, "Why don't you help chop carrots? We can make vegetable soup."

"I can do that."

"On second thought," she said, "I wouldn't want to be responsible for you harming your guitar-playing fingers."

He finished his massage by brushing the hair away from her shoulders. For a moment, she thought he might press a kiss to her bare skin. Instead, he stepped away and said, "I'll take good care not to cut anything off."

She got Nash set up with a knife, a cutting board, and a pile of carrots, then began chopping potatoes and onions. They worked in companionable silence until she asked, "How long do you think it'll take you to build out the van?" She held her breath as she waited for his reply. She would miss him terribly if he left as soon as Kevin's four days with him were up. On the other hand, the longer he stayed, the harder it would be to say good-bye.

"I rented a place not far from here for two weeks."

She had to put the knife down or risk cutting off her own finger. "Two weeks?"

"Building out a van has the potential to be a big job. I'm not sure how long it will take, but I figure two weeks is a good window of time to start with."

To start with? Did that mean he might stay even longer?

Her heart was racing as she asked, "And then what's your plan once the van is done?"

"I don't have a firm plan right now. But I'm thinking I'll hit the road to see what I find. Or what finds me."

Her heart sank all the way to her toes. Of course he was going to leave when he was done. It wasn't a surprise. But hearing him confirm his future departure from her life stung.

Ashley had to face facts. Despite her efforts to be realistic, she *had* created a fantasy narrative about them. A fairytale ending where Nash would realize she was everything he was missing in his life. A story where he would decide that he wanted to bring her son into his life too. A perfect romance where he would be so in love with her that he would give up his nomadic rock-star life to move permanently to Bar Harbor.

Life wasn't a fairy tale, though. Not for her, anyway.

Fortunately, she loved her life in Bar Harbor with her son and family. What's more, she knew it would be a waste to mourn the idea of Nash leaving when he was here now. She should focus on enjoying being with him.

She scooped up the chopped veggies and threw them into a large pot along with vegetable stock and corn cut from the cob. Spices went in next—cumin, coriander, garlic, salt, and pepper, and paprika to give it a kick.

After she covered the pot to let it simmer, she asked Nash, "Do you want to help me make cookies? Because tonight definitely feels like a cookie night." Not only to help give Kevin some chocolatey-sugary comfort after being let down by his father, but to soothe herself too.

"I've never made cookies before," Nash told her.

She felt that pain in her chest again at the reminder of his awful childhood. "After tonight," she said in a gentle voice, "you'll be a pro."

Ashley got out flour, sugar, butter, and chocolate chips, then showed Nash how to measure and mix them. He was a quick learner, and she suspected they were going to be some of the best chocolate chip cookies ever made in her kitchen.

Once they were in the oven, he said, "Thank you for showing me how to make cookies. It's one of the things most people learn to do at some point in their life, but I haven't."

"There are so many things you can do that most other people could never even aspire to do," she reminded him. "You have exceptional talents, Nash.

You don't have to know how to do everything. None of us can. For instance, I've accepted that I'm brilliant with spreadsheets, but terrible at hitting a tennis ball."

"Mom," Kevin piped in, "tell Nash about that time you sent that woman to the hospital."

She groaned. "It wasn't quite that dramatic."

"It *was*," Kevin insisted. "The skin on her face turned all sorts of colors after you nailed her with the tennis ball."

Nash laughed. "Remind me never to get between you and a tennis ball."

"Like I said, we're all great at some things, terrible at others." She thought more about it. "There are also plenty of things that I'm never going to get a chance to try, which I'm also okay with."

"Like what?"

"Well, there's a crazy part of me that's always wanted to go skydiving."

"That'd be so cool, Mom!" Kevin exclaimed from the kitchen table. "I would totally jump out of a plane with you."

The thought of seeing her son jump out of a plane made her stomach hurt. But before she could backtrack and say she was only kidding, Kevin held up the paper he'd been working on.

"I'm done. Want to see?"

Both Ashley and Nash walked over to the table.

Kevin had drawn a remarkably good rendition of the outside of the van, plus a bird's-eye view of the interior from the top. Maybe those video games where he built virtual houses with his friends weren't a total waste of time.

"This is brilliant!" Nash said, genuinely enthusiastic about the drawings. "I wouldn't have thought about making the upper bunk fold away into the right side of the van and become open shelving when it's not being used."

"What do you think, Mom?"

She loved that Kevin still cared about her opinion. Granted, she'd never stopped caring about her parents' opinions, regardless of how old she was. Fortunately, they were always extremely supportive.

"I think it looks amazing," she told her son. "I'm really impressed. Both with your design and your drawing."

"Thanks." Kevin turned back to Nash. "What would you do differently? And do you have any other ideas?"

Ashley was happy that he wasn't so wed to his plans that he might refuse to listen to other ideas. She hoped she could take some credit for teaching her son how to be flexible and to see more than one side of things. It was a lesson her mother had taught her and her siblings—to have goals and be determined, but also to be able to roll with whatever came, because life rarely moved in a straight line. Ashley did her best to follow that advice, although it wasn't always easy.

Especially when what came her way was a super-sexy rock star who made her pulse race...

"The only thing I might look at," Nash replied, "is making sure there's enough headroom in the bunk to sit up and read, or watch TV, or play video games."

Her son's face lit up. "What do you play?"

Nash grinned. "The better question is what *don't* I play."

"Mom, can Nash and I play Xbox before dinner?"

Knowing it would be better to allow a short time frame than to say no, which might prompt an argument, she said, "Dinner will be ready soon, so I'll give you thirty minutes, but that's it for the night."

She knew Kevin would try to push for forty-five minutes. It was the art of negotiation as a parent. Let him think he was getting away with just enough so that he wouldn't push too hard for things she *really* didn't want him to do.

"We should make sure your mom doesn't need more help with dinner or setting the table," Nash told Kevin.

"It's okay," she said with a smile, "I can take care of getting everything else ready. Go have fun, you guys."

It made her heart swell to watch Kevin and Nash

bond, first over the van and now over Kevin's beloved video games. While she wasn't going to make the mistake of thinking that tonight's family atmosphere changed anything about her and Nash's future—it was still totally out of the question that they could ever make a real relationship work when he lived on the road and she was one hundred percent devoted to her son—she did deeply appreciate Nash helping her son laugh and have fun on a night that could otherwise have been so sad.

She also appreciated Nash's big heart and selflessness. He could be on a date with a supermodel right now, or partying in a penthouse suite in a glittering city, or sitting down to eat a fancy gourmet meal with multiple courses.

Instead, he was spending the night in her tiny cottage in Bar Harbor, chopping vegetables for soup, making chocolate chip cookies, and playing video games with her son.

If she wasn't careful, it would be really easy to fall in love with him.

* * *

After dinner and then a cutthroat three-person game of crazy eights using the Empress Sisi cards from Vienna—Nash had never played before, but he picked it up quickly—Kevin went to bed, and Ashley invited Nash into the backyard for the conversation he was dreading.

He'd had a great night with her and her son. One of the best nights he could remember.

What he wouldn't give to take Ashley to bed and hold her close all night long. But from the look on her face, he knew that wasn't in the cards. Not now.

Not ever.

"Thank you for spending the evening with us," she said. "You completely made Kevin's night, both with your enthusiasm for his van design and also by playing video games with him."

"He's a great kid. I had a good time, Ash. A really good time."

Though she smiled at him, it wobbled around the edges. The same way his heart was wobbling.

"Maybe we should wait to talk," he suggested, but she shook her head.

"It will only make things harder if we do. Especially now that Kevin is going to be working with you on your van." Though her beautiful mouth was turned down, she bravely held his gaze. "I can't keep being with you the way we were yesterday. The way we were in Vienna. It's not that I haven't loved every second, because I have. So very much. But now that you're in my town, I have to think about what people around Kevin might say that could have a negative impact on—"

"You don't want to be seen with a celebrity musician who has an arrest record." He hadn't meant to sound so bitter, but he couldn't help it when he'd never been more bitter about anything than he was about having to keep his distance from Ashley.

"I know you've moved on from your past. I know you've learned from your mistakes. And I know how hard you've worked to get to where you are. You deserve to be admired and respected for your talent, which I do. It's just…"

"It's okay, I can take it. Whatever you've got to say." Lord knew, after all the names and obscenities his mother had hurled at him, other people's harsh words just bounced off him.

"People can be cruel," she said in a rush. "Especially to kids. One of Kevin's friends already asked him about your prison record."

"I'm sorry, Ash." Damn it, he'd never regretted his idiotic youth as much as he did now. He started to get out of his chair. "I'll stay away from you. And from Kevin."

"No!" He was surprised by her passionate response, especially when she grabbed his hand. "He'll be totally heartbroken if he doesn't get to work on the van with you. And even though people saw us kiss at the café, I think that if we're careful to stay in the friend zone from now on, gossip will hopefully die down. People will understand that we're just friends."

"Okay." He wanted to be so much more than *just friends* with Ashley. But if it meant he didn't have to leave her immediately, he would take it. "Thanks for being honest with me, Ash."

"The thing is, if I'm being totally honest..." She looked into his eyes, and he hated to see the pain in them. "The two of us needing to stay just friends is about more than gossip. It's about more than me worrying about whether Kevin will be affected." She swallowed hard. "The truth is that I can't allow myself to get in any deeper with you when I know you're going to leave. I can't believe I'm admitting this to you, when I've barely even admitted it to myself, but it really hurt to say good-bye in Vienna. And if we allowed ourselves to get closer while you're here working on the van..." She closed her eyes for a brief moment, looking anguished. "It would hurt even worse a second time. I know it would. And I don't think I could stand to feel that way again, Nash. Which is why we absolutely need to just be friends."

He wasn't sure he knew anyone else who could be so honest about their emotions. Which was why he had to give her back total honesty. "It hurt me to leave you, too, Ash. More than I expected it would. I wish I could tell you that I'll stay this time. But I've never been good at staying anywhere for too long." He shook his head, admitting, "The only thing I've ever been good at is leaving. Every day a new city. Every night a new bed."

He was surprised when she gently stroked his tightly clenched fist. "Do you think always leaving is still right for you?" Before he could reply, she added, "And I'm not asking you that because I'm trying to convince you to stay with me. I swear I'm not. I'm just wondering if there might be something permanent for you somewhere in the world. Something steady. Something that feels right."

"I don't know. I've never thought to look for anything permanent." He unclenched his hand and turned it over so their palms were touching. "And I do understand the reasons why you don't want us to be together again. The thing is…it's not going to be easy staying away from you. In fact," he said as he stroked the sensitive skin on her palm, and she shivered at his touch, "it might just be the hardest thing I'll ever do."

"I know. When I'm with you, I feel such a pull to be a little bit wicked." She looked down at their hands, which were practically sparking electricity, their connection was so strong. "*A lot* wicked, actually."

Nash knew it was time for him to be a good man. An honorable one. But damn it, it was difficult to force himself to lift his hand from hers and move away.

Because even that one point of contact with Ashley had been so powerful, it shook him to his core.

"That's my cue to leave. Before…"

She pushed back her chair and stood. "Yes. Before…"

Before he made love to her again, beneath the moon and the stars, with her son only a handful of yards away inside her house.

It was only through extreme strength of will that he propelled himself out of her backyard and on to the sidewalk where his beat-up van was waiting.

"Thanks again, Nash, for everything you did tonight." Her voice sounded as strained as he felt. "I'll text you the address to Rory's warehouse, and Kevin and I will meet you there tomorrow morning. Will nine work?"

In Nash's normal life, he was never up at nine in the morning, because he rarely finished after-show meet and greets with fans before two in the morning.

But while he was in Bar Harbor, he didn't want to waste any time. He had two weeks to try to squeeze as much joy as he possibly could out of his time with Ashley.

"Nine is perfect." He drank her in as she stood in the moonlight, looking beautiful in jeans and a T-shirt, her hair in a ponytail. "Good night, Ashley."

"Good night, Nash."

As he drove back to his lonely rental cabin in the woods, he couldn't help but think about the questions she'd asked him. Despite his past, could it be possible that there was something permanent for him somewhere in the world? Something steady? Something that felt right? Something that looked a heck of a lot like Ashley and Kevin and their cozy cottage in Bar Harbor?

But Nash knew better than to bother with these difficult questions. The mistakes he'd made in his past would forever haunt any future happiness that he could have had with Ashley...beyond "the friend zone."

CHAPTER TWENTY-ONE

Ashley got to Rory's furniture studio a few minutes early to speak with her brother before Nash arrived. Zara had brought Kevin's favorite homemade doughnuts as a special treat, so while her son was happily munching on his second breakfast, Ashley pulled her brother aside.

"First, thanks for offering to let Nash work in your parking lot. And second…" She paused, trying to find a way to say the next part nicely. "Please don't be all weird and overbearingly protective."

"I'd like to make you some guarantees, Ash, but the idea of you hooking up with some rock star?" He scowled. "I can't say I like it."

"Too bad, because you don't get any say in my personal life," she reminded her brother. "But even though it's none of your business, you don't have to worry. We're not together."

Her brother narrowed his eyes. "Really? Because word on the street is that the two of you were locking lips at the café a couple of days ago."

Ugh, sometimes living in a small town was just way too much to handle. "Again," she said in a stern voice, "my life is *my* life. So if I want to lock lips with someone, rock star or not, I will."

Rory looked surprised by the forceful way she was speaking to him. She tended to be less prone to outbursts than their other siblings, but that didn't mean she felt any less passionately about things.

"I just want to make sure no one hurts you or Kevin," he said in his defense.

"I know that. But do you truly think I would risk my happiness and Kevin's on a man like him, who is going to blast out of town as quickly as he blasted in?"

She stopped speaking when Rory's eyes moved to a point over her shoulder, and she knew they were no longer alone.

Nash spoke first, introducing himself to Rory while her face flamed as she thought of what he might have overheard. "You must be Ashley's brother. I'm Nash. It's nice to meet you."

Rory shook Nash's hand. "Rory Sullivan." He turned to look at the old VW van in the parking lot. "Looks like you've got quite a project ahead of you."

"It's been a long time since I've worked on building out a van. Hopefully, I haven't forgotten everything from when I was sixteen."

Although Nash was smiling as he replied, he

seemed a little tense. Probably because he'd overheard her being a complete jerk, saying how she wouldn't be stupid enough to ever risk her heart to a man like him. She'd spoken much more carefully last night when she and Nash had had their difficult discussion in the backyard. It was just that Rory had a way of pushing her buttons, acting like he knew what was best for her, just like her other brothers. Now, her chest ached. She knew her words had to have wounded Nash.

"So, what's your plan?" Rory asked.

Though her brother was gesturing to the van, Ashley couldn't help but feel that he was asking Nash a bigger question. Not simply, *What are you going to do with your van?* But, *What are your intentions toward my sister?*

Clearly, Rory hadn't been listening when she'd told him to butt out. So she elbowed him in the gut, making him groan. Hopefully, he'd heed her requests in the future.

Nash, to his credit, ignored Rory's implied question about his intentions. "I'm planning on making it livable for up to a week at a time on the road."

"Are you thinking lithium and solar?" Rory asked, quickly moving into builder mode despite his reservations over Ashley's relationship with the rock star.

"I am. I've ordered a few things online to be shipped to this location, if that will work for you."

"No problem. And Ash says Kevin's going to be helping you?"

"He's a good kid," Nash said with a nod. "Smart, too, which you of course already know as his uncle. He came up with some great ideas yesterday. I'm looking forward to working with him on the project."

Her heart melted. Though she vowed to keep their relationship purely platonic from here on out, when Nash spoke that way about her son and when she saw him be so great with Kevin, her insides got all gooey.

She didn't care that he was a superstar, or that he was rich and handsome. What mattered most was the fact that Nash was a wonderful man.

"My nephew's great," Rory agreed. "But if you do need a break at any point, feel free to send him into my workshop. I can always put him to work for a little while."

Just then, Kevin finished eating his doughnut and ran over. When Nash shook his hand and asked him how things were going this morning, she could see how pleased her son was to be treated like an adult, rather than a kid.

"I'm awesome!" Kevin declared. "I'm ready to get started on the build. I've had lots more ideas too."

Ashley was amazed by how old he sounded. Like he wasn't her little boy anymore, but was becoming a man. Although, he did have a smear of chocolate frosting from the doughnut across his upper lip.

Just then, the woman Rory was madly in love with walked up to Nash, holding a plate with two dough-nuts. "Hello, I'm Zara. These are the last doughnuts. Any interest?" she asked Nash and Ashley.

"Aunt Zara makes the best doughnuts in the whole wide world," Kevin enthused.

Ashley shook her head. Being so near Nash and not being able to touch or kiss him made her lose her appetite.

"It's nice to meet you," Nash said. "And yes, I'd love a doughnut." He took a bite, then groaned low and deep in his chest. Remembering how he'd groaned in a similar way while they were making love sent tremors through Ashley's body.

Zara shot Ashley a heavily loaded look that seemed to say, *You've got yourself a live one, don't you?*

Ashley blushed even harder now. In an effort to hide her reaction, she grabbed the remaining doughnut and shoved a bite into her mouth. Unfortunately, it ended up going down the wrong pipe, and she started coughing, spitting doughnut into the napkin Zara quickly handed her. Nash reached out to rub her back, and she instinctively moved closer to him.

By the time she'd recovered from her coughing fit, she realized Rory's eyes were narrowed again. Proba-bly because Nash's hand was still on her back.

Again, the devil leaped onto her shoulder, urging her to shock her brother by kissing Nash, just as she'd shocked Josh.

But she couldn't give in to the devil this time, not with Kevin watching—and after she'd insisted to Nash that they couldn't do that anymore.

"On that extremely embarrassing note," she said in a self-deprecating tone, "I'd better get to the café and store now." She shot serious looks at both Nash and her brother. "Keep Kevin away from anything dangerous, or it's both your heads on a platter."

They both nodded, understanding that if anything bad happened to her son, she would tear them to pieces with her bare hands.

She gave Kevin a hug before she left, one that he seemed a little embarrassed to receive in front of the guys.

"See you later, Mom," he said in a slightly gruff voice, obviously ready for her to stop hovering.

Ashley wasn't surprised when Zara walked with her to her car. "I'm thinking you're going to have some *serious* stories to tell at our next girls' cocktail night, aren't you?"

Though she supposed she could have tried to act cool, Ashley couldn't keep the smile from her face. "Being with Nash was amazing," she confirmed. "But it's over now."

"Why on earth is it over?" Zara sounded flabbergasted that anybody would willingly choose to stop rolling around in bed with Nash Hardwin.

"It's complicated."

"Because of Kevin?"

Ashley nodded. "One kiss yesterday at the café, and the whole town is already gossiping about us. If it was just about me and Nash, I could deal with gossip. After all, I've had lots of practice with that after getting pregnant in high school. But it's *not* just about me. It's about Kevin too. And his welfare is a line in the sand I refuse to cross."

"I'm assuming people are talking about Nash's arrest record from years ago? I know I've only just met him, but I have a hard time putting the person he seems to be now in the shoes of the much younger man who committed those crimes."

"I know, that's exactly how I felt when I first met him in Vienna." Ashley sighed as she realized she wasn't going to get away with giving Zara less than the whole truth. "I also can't let myself get too attached to him." She instinctively put her hand over her heart. "I really like Nash, and not just because of how incredibly sexy and unexpectedly sweet he is. But since we all know it will never work long-term, it's best to put a stop to things before they go any deeper. Otherwise, it's going to hurt too much after he's gone."

"Trust me," Zara said in a gentle voice, "I get it.

Love is really hard sometimes."

Ashley was shocked by what Zara had just said. "I'm not in love with Nash."

Zara looked doubtful. But rather than debating Ashley's feelings for Nash, she simply said, "Well, he is definitely in love with you."

"He couldn't possibly be in love with me! Especially since we've agreed to keep things squarely in the friend zone from here on out." Ashley couldn't keep the panicked tone from her voice. "The time we've spent together has been amazing, but we haven't known each other long enough to fall in love."

"I used to think that way too. But when I fell for Rory, I swear it happened in an instant. He says it was the same for him. And take Cassie and Flynn—love hit them like a lightning bolt. Lola and Duncan too." Zara smiled. "If there's one thing I can say for the Sullivan family, it's that love at first sight seems to run in your genes."

Ashley laughed despite herself. She couldn't deny it, not given the way so many of the Sullivans' relationships has played out over the years. When they knew, they knew. When it was right, it was right. And it was forever.

"Nash can have literally anyone he wants," she protested.

"I get that he has fame and fortune, but you have so much more than that. You're one of the best moms

I've ever known, you're brilliant at running the family business, and you're an amazing sister."

Ashley gave Zara a hug. "Thank you for giving me so many props this morning. I appreciate it. Keep an eye on the boys for me, will you?"

"Don't worry, I won't let them get up to any trouble. And I promise that none of us will let any harm come to Kevin."

As Ashley drove out of the parking lot, she stole a look in her rearview mirror at Nash and Kevin standing outside the van discussing their plans.

Ashley had always wanted a male role model for Kevin, to work with him and teach him valuable life skills. Her brothers and her father had done so much to pick up the slack from Kevin's useless father over the years, but she could see her son blossoming already under Nash's attention.

Could Zara be right? The question popped into her head before she could stop it. Was there any way Nash could have fallen in love with her? And could she have fallen in love with him too?

No. She couldn't let herself go there. She had to stick to the plan. The serious, smart, no-nonsense plan.

No more messing around with Nash. They were just friends. From here on out, Ashley needed to walk the straight and narrow. No matter how tempting it was to walk on the wild side with Nash.

CHAPTER TWENTY-TWO

Later that afternoon, after having checked in by text with both Nash and Kevin several times and hearing that everything was A-okay, Ashley packed a picnic for them to eat at one of her favorite ocean overlooks in Acadia National Park. The spot was secluded enough for Nash to have privacy from his fans, while also giving him a feel for the beauty of Bar Harbor.

She had just parked in Rory's lot when Kevin bounded over.

"Mom," he said as soon as she opened the door, "you've got to see what we did today. It's awesome!"

Nash looked on with a smile, and her heart fluttered at how sexy he was in his worn jeans and black T-shirt. Then she turned her attention to the van while Kevin told her all about doing demolition.

"We got to be super rough with everything inside the van. It was the best. I love demo day!"

She laughed, happy he'd had such a good time. "Looks like it was a fun job." She examined the van's innards, now in a pile in the parking lot.

"After we finished tearing things apart, we measured for flooring and ceiling planks and wall trim, and then we started cutting wood to fit."

Her ears perked up at the word *cutting*. "Who did the cutting?"

"Nash did most of it," Kevin informed her, "but he showed me how to use the saws. And he said tomorrow when we cut more wood, he's going to let me take the lead."

She rounded on Nash, scowling. "That wasn't the deal. You were going to do the dangerous stuff, not Kevin."

"Before I let you use any tools," Nash said to her son, "we always go over the safety precautions, don't we, Kevin?"

"Yeah, Mom, he's worse than my teachers. He's like, 'Repeat everything back to me. Now repeat it again so I know you were listening.'" Kevin did a funny approximation of Nash's deep voice. "But it's okay, because I get it. This stuff can be super dangerous. But I'm being extra careful, I swear I am."

"He is, Ashley," Nash confirmed. "We both are. I promised you I wouldn't let anything bad happen to him, and I won't."

Her insides were still churning, despite their assurances. "Great job on the work you both have done," she made herself say, not wanting to diminish Kevin's sense of accomplishment. She was glad that Kevin had a sense of satisfaction in a job well done today.

Her son wasn't the only one who seemed pleased. Nash did too. There was a happy glow about him after a day of working with his hands and tapping into yet another well of creativity and talent. He'd looked the same way after he'd sung "Scarborough Fair" at the garden in Vienna using the busker's guitar.

It was how she felt when one of her new strategies for the café or store paid off. This past week, she'd launched a new social media plan and had been thrilled when the images she'd worked so hard to put together got a really great reception.

"If you guys are hungry," she said, "I brought fixings for a picnic. I thought we could head up to a lookout at Acadia National Park and have it there. It's one of the most beautiful vistas in the area, Nash, one of the many reasons why Bar Harbor is so special."

"That sounds great," Nash said, while Kevin said, "I'm starved."

Just then, her phone buzzed with a text. It was Kevin's best friend's mom asking if Kevin could come over for dinner and spend the night. She was tempted to say he couldn't, if only to have him around as a chaperone for her and Nash. If Kevin were nearby, she felt confident that she wouldn't throw herself at Nash. But that wouldn't be fair to Kevin. She needed to be able to control herself whether he was with them or not.

"Sammy's mom wants to know if you want to come for a sleepover."

"Yes! I can't wait to tell him about the work me and Nash did on the van today. He's going to think it's so cool."

"Okay, then, I suppose we could grab your sleepover things at home and then drop you off at his house on the way to the lookout."

"And then you'll come get me in the morning so I can work with Nash again?"

"Of course." She turned to Nash. "Will that work for you?"

"It does," he said to her. And then to Kevin, he said, "You did a great job today."

"Thanks," Kevin said. "So did you."

They did a manly fist bump that made her grin.

Five minutes later, they pulled up to Kevin's friend's house. Normally, Kevin would have run inside without Sammy's mom coming out to the car.

"Sorry about this," Ashley said to Nash in a low voice as Louella approached, looking as giddy as a teenage girl. Clearly, she had been hoping that Nash would be with Ashley. The news about his being in town certainly had travelled fast, hadn't it?

"Don't worry about it," he said as he rolled his window down. "It comes with the territory."

"Oh. My. God. I swear I am your *biggest* fan!" Louella looked like she was about to burst with excitement. Louella didn't seem to care one whit that Nash had been to prison. Nope, all she cared about was seeing her idol live and in the flesh.

"Thanks, it's nice to meet you." Nash was as friendly as could be and didn't seem the least bit put out by her fawning adoration.

"You wouldn't mind signing this T-shirt I picked up at one of your concerts, would you?"

Nash obliged with a smile, and Ashley had a feeling Sammy's mom was going to sleep in the T-shirt from this day forward.

At last, Louella acknowledged Ashley's presence. "Thanks so much for letting Kevin come over to spend the night."

"He's excited about it. Thanks for having him. I'll be by at 8:45 tomorrow morning to grab him."

"Okay, sounds great." Louella shot one more adoring look at Nash. "Bye-bye."

Nash rolled his window up, and as they were driving away, Ashley said, "I know you said it comes with the territory, but I'm still sorry about how awkward that was."

"That wasn't awkward at all. Now, if she'd asked me to sign her underwear instead of a T-shirt, it might have been a different story."

"Her underwear?" Ashley was scandalized. "Does that actually happen?"

"More often than you would think."

She made an *ick* sound in the back of her throat, then quickly changed the subject from strangers' underwear. Because, *ew*. "Today seemed to go well, at least according to Kevin. How do you think it went?"

"Great. Just like I knew it would."

"You're remarkably good with him. Have you spent much time around kids?"

"No, but he's easy to be with. Just like you are. You've done a really great job with him."

"You're so sweet." She sighed. "And I need to apologize to you."

"I've already told you I'm fine with signing autographs for people in town."

"Not about that. It's about what you heard me say to my brother this morning. It's not that I don't think you've overcome your past. I was just trying to explain to Rory why we're not a couple and are just friends. But since he was pushing my buttons, it came out all wrong." At a stop sign, she shifted her gaze to meet his. "I'm sorry, Nash."

"You have nothing to apologize for. I understood what you were telling him. And I don't disagree with anything you've said. I screwed up too many times before I finally learned my lesson. And I am going to leave Bar Harbor once I'm done with the van. You weren't wrong on any of those counts. The thing is, Ash, I'm the one who should be apologizing to you. I didn't mean to upset or frighten you over the work I let Kevin do today. If you're still against it, I won't let him use the power tools." He paused before adding, "But I do want you to know that he is a very capable young man. Capable of doing a lot more than he even knows he can."

"I know I can be overprotective," she said softly. "It's just that he's everything to me, and I can't stand the thought of anything bad happening to him. When he was little, if he crashed his bike, or fell off the jungle gym, or another kid was mean to him, it felt like my bruise, my scare, my broken heart. I know I need to do a better job of letting him experience life, good and bad, but…" She shook her head. "It's so hard to let go of him when I've held him tight for so long."

Nash put his hand over hers on the gearshift. "You're the best mom in the world. He's going to get hurt and have his hopes dashed from time to time, just like everyone else, but I have no doubt whatsoever that he'll always be resilient. Just like you. Strong and smart and full of heart and brave as hell. So don't you dare beat yourself up for anything you have or haven't done. Because you've done a damn good job raising your son."

Good thing she was driving. Otherwise, she would have thrown her arms around him and kissed him. "Thank you, Nash."

"No, thank *you*. You've invited me into your world, your life. You've introduced me to people in your family. You've let me spend time with your son, the one person you care about most in the world. I tried to convince myself that I was just coming here to see about a van. Instead, I've had a great couple of days with you." He squeezed her hand. *"Really* great."

She didn't know how everything had gotten so serious again, so *real*. Only that whenever she and Nash were together, they didn't do small talk. Instead, they talked about things that really mattered.

Nash was right—being together was wonderfully easy. Even while the sexual tension between them thrummed higher and hotter every moment. And since Kevin would be sleeping at Sammy's tonight, if she and Nash wanted to sleep together again, there would be no chance of Kevin walking in on them.

No. She needed to keep fighting temptation. Because even if she were somehow able to stop worrying about the possible repercussions of their relationship on Kevin's life, Ashley knew better than to think there wouldn't be massive repercussions on her *own* life.

No one would ever be as capable of breaking her heart the way Nash could. Simply by leaving, which he

when he'd done tim
from trespassing to
fights while on p
known better.

But now he su
days of his past truly
And on the other e
and his success matt

Or were the onl
ship and love?

"I remember lea
"to give my parents
relived the memory
terrifying. "The wor
seeing their disappo
their hopes and goal
grades. I was aiming
breath. "But they did
only love and suppc
mirror, when I looke
disappointment. It tu
of disappointing my p
disappointing *myself.*"

Nash had told her
had for her, but that c
respect herself. Hell,
compliments sliding c

had just confirmed, yet again, was his plan.

And the last thing Ashley wanted was to be left behind with nothing but a broken heart to remember him by.

CHAPTER
_____

"I've seen a lot of beau
Ashley stood side by si
at the ocean and the
the bright blue-green
not quite, touching. "F
all."

"This is where I ca
pregnant, while I was
out at the water, at all
of blue beyond, alwa
when my problems see
part of a much bigger w

When they'd first g
seen the stunning vista
the lens of Ashley's pe
more.

She was completely
small players in a worl
any of them. Sure, he'
as a kid and a teenage

he deserved them.

"What do you see when you look in the mirror now?" he asked.

"Before Vienna, I saw a woman who was working like crazy to hold it all together and keep the pieces of her life moving in the 'right' direction." She made air quotes around _right_. "But after Vienna?" She met his gaze. "Now I see a woman who is finally starting to come into her own. A woman taking baby steps in a new and exciting direction maybe, but important steps nonetheless." She gave him a small smile. "I know it sounds like I'm talking out of both sides of my mouth, telling you in one breath that we can't be together while you're here and then saying in my next breath that I've discovered this new part of myself _because_ of the time I've spent with you."

"I get it, Ash. Life doesn't always make sense." Even if Nash felt like nothing in his life had ever made as much sense as it did whenever he was with her. "Before Vienna, I believed I was meant to spend my entire life on the road, never letting myself settle anywhere for too long or connect with anyone too deeply. But after Vienna?" He looked deep into her eyes. "Suddenly, I'm wondering if everything I thought I knew was wrong. And if maybe there's a different way to live my life."

"Both of our lives are already really great," she said

softly. "Hopefully, they'll just keep getting better from here."

He barely kept from reaching for her hand. "Mine is already better, simply because I met you."

For a moment, he thought she might kiss him. Instead, she took a step away and said, "I'm starved. Should we eat?"

Swallowing his disappointment at not getting to kiss her, he helped her lay out the blanket and the Irish-inspired comfort food from the picnic basket. Corned beef and cabbage sliders. Mini shepherd's pies. Bacon-wrapped cabbage. Guinness cheese pretzel bites.

Everything looked delicious, and when he told her so, she said, "My mom is a wonder in the kitchen. She's a wonder, period. I mean, you'd have to be to raise seven kids, wouldn't you?"

"Seven of you, wow. That must have been quite a crowd to grow up with."

"I'm the baby of the group. On the one hand, it was like having six big best friends to play with. On the other, it meant there were six people always ready to tattle on me when they thought I was doing something wrong."

"Do your siblings all live nearby?"

"Everybody except Hudson, who's in Boston with his wife, Larissa. And although Brandon has a house in town, he's usually off in some exotic locale, launching another hotel."

"Are there any other kids in your family apart from Kevin?"

"My sister Cassie is getting married this weekend, and her fiancé has a little girl named Ruby, whom Cassie has adopted. Ruby is almost two and the cutest kid on the planet. Apart from when Kevin was her age, of course," Ashley added with a grin. "Hudson and Larissa have been married a while, but don't have any kids. I don't know if Rory and Zara and Lola and Duncan are thinking about kids yet. One day, though, I hope there's lots of little Sullivans running around Bar Harbor the way we did when we were kids." She reached for an apple slice. "What about you? I know your mom passed away, but do you have any aunts or uncles or cousins or nieces or nephews?"

"Not that I know of. It was always just me and my mom."

"If you don't mind my asking, how did she pass away?"

Again, he was struck by how nice it was that Ashley didn't already know everything about his life. But even though he'd told parts of this story before in interviews, he could feel the emotions building inside of him as he prepared to tell Ashley. "The year after I left home, there was a fire in the apartment building she lived in. The official cause was a wiring issue. She was still living where I grew up in a pretty poor part of Raleigh, North Carolina, and the building was old and not very well maintained."

He was barely done speaking when she moved closer to put her arms around him and hold him tight.

"Nash, I'm so sorry."

It had happened a long time ago, and he'd sworn he was over it. But he still found himself holding on to Ashley. Breathing her in. Letting himself be comforted.

She was still hugging him when she asked, "How do you feel about your mom now?"

His arms instinctively tightened around her, and he felt something that was suspiciously like a sob moving through his chest. And then the words were spilling out of his mouth.

"I never got a chance to go back to see her again. Never got a chance to have a relationship with her as anything but a kid. I might have been able to look at her life through different, more mature eyes. I never got the chance to say I understood, or that I forgave her, if either of those things are even true. And I never got to say good-bye."

So many *nevers*. That's how life with his mom had always been. Never hearing *I love you*. Never laughing together. And never getting to forgive or say farewell.

"The last time we saw each other was the night I left town. She screamed at me, told me I was worthless, that I was just like my waste-of-space father and would never amount to anything. She told me she didn't care if I ended up dead on a street corner some-where."

He'd never cried over his mom, not even when he'd heard about the fire. He hadn't wanted to allow himself to cry over someone who had been so cruel. But cruel or not, she had been his mother. And he'd always wanted her love, even if she had been incapable of giving it.

At last, he couldn't stop the tears from falling. "I drove away that night, determined to come back filthy, stinking rich. I wanted to shove my money and success in her face. I wanted to show her how wrong she was about me." Then he admitted to Ashley what he'd never admitted to anyone before. "I wanted to come back as a star so that she'd finally be proud of me."

For a small woman, Ashley was full of strength. Her arms were still around him as she moved fully onto his lap and held him tight, absorbing his pain so that he could finally be absolved of it.

With her huge heart, she took in the sadness of his childhood, the hurt of that final fight with his mom, the pain of losing her in such a horrific away, the trauma of having worked his entire life to try to find the love and support and respect he'd never had as a child.

When she finally drew back, her cheeks were wet.

"Your mom might never have said it, but I'm going to say it right now, because it's the truest thing of all." She stared into his eyes and let him see everything she was feeling, holding nothing back. "You are worthy of love, Nash. You are a beautiful person, inside and out. And I love you."

All day long, he'd steeled himself to keep from kissing her, touching her. But now he had to crush his mouth to hers.

He needed her to know that by expressing her love for him in the most genuine and sweet and compassionate of ways, she'd given him a gift beyond measure.

The greatest gift he'd ever had.

But then she tore her mouth from his, clearly intent on saying more. "I didn't say that to try to make you stay in Bar Harbor, or to influence you in any way to be with me. I just needed to say it because you have to know how lovable you are. And also because it's what I'm feeling. I've always been honest with you, and I always will be."

He put one hand on her cheek while holding her tightly around her waist with the other. "Ashley, I—"

She shook her head. "Please, don't say anything back to me right now. It's okay for me to give you my love, and for you to accept it, without you owing me anything in return. That's how love works when it's unconditional."

He stroked her cheek, gazing at her in wonder. "What did I ever do to deserve this time with you?"

She smiled at him, then simply said, "You're you. That's all you've ever needed to do. That's all you've ever needed to be. Just *you*."

This time, she was the one kissing him, and when they finally came up for air, she whispered, "Make love to me, Nash. One more time. Here, in my favorite place. So that after you're gone, I can come back here to remember the magic between us."

He hated hearing her talk about him in past tense, like he was already gone. But if he didn't have the words to say he loved her, how could he possibly find the words to tell her he would stay?

Because he wouldn't stay. He couldn't. They both knew that.

But right here, right now, he could give her his body. His pleasure. And so much more of his heart than he had ever given to anyone else. More than he would ever give to anyone but her. Nash couldn't imagine ever trusting anyone the way he trusted Ashley.

Their picnic spot was surprisingly private, as they'd had to walk a narrow path through the forest to get to it. Still, it was too risky to strip off all their clothes. They'd have to be a little stealthy in case anyone came upon them.

Fortunately, she was wearing a skirt, one that flowed around her calves when she walked. If he were a better man, he would have forced himself to keep his hands off her. But no matter what she'd said about his having a good heart, there was a core of wickedness in him that was undeniable. And he needed her so badly, too damn badly, to resist her request to make love to her one more time.

Holding her face, he kissed her deeply. Her hands roamed over his chest and abs before reaching his belt buckle. He loved when she took his clothes off, loved watching her elegant hands work so diligently to get what she wanted. What they *both* wanted.

Moments later, his erection sprang free into her hands, and she made a sound of deep pleasure, one that seemed to say she'd never seen nor touched anything so wonderful.

He felt exactly the same about her as he ran his hands up her bare legs, from her calves to the backs of her knees, making her shiver as his fingertips traced a wicked path up her thighs and over her hips.

She rocked into him, and he used his hands and the movement of his body to help her grind even harder into him. If he pulled her panties to one side, he could thrust into her. No protection, just skin-to-skin. But she'd already had one unexpected pregnancy, and he would never put her in the position of having to deal with that again.

Still, he hated to take his hands off her to reach into his back pocket and pull a condom out of his wallet. He'd had to replace his supply of condoms, because he'd run out.

Thinking of the two of them using up all his condoms made him smile, and as she helped him open the wrapper, she asked, "What are you grinning about?"

"How sexy you are, how much I want you, and how I had to restock my condoms in the hopes that maybe, just maybe, you'd let me make love to you again."

"Hoping I'd be a sure thing, were you?" There was a teasing lilt to her voice.

"More like *praying*."

With protection on, unable to wait another second, he gripped her hips and brought her down over him. Hard enough that they both gasped, then groaned at the intense pleasure of coming together.

She took over from there, using her leg muscles to move over him, against him. And as they made love on the hill overlooking the ocean and the great wide expanse of blue beyond it, Nash never wanted the moment to end, never wanted to let her go. But there was no stopping pleasure. Not when it was this good. Not when it was this wild. And perfect. So damned perfect it blew his mind.

At the exact moment that he felt her inner muscles begin to tighten over him, he gave her all of himself. She'd told him that she loved him. He'd never been this close to anyone before. And knew he never would be again.

Because no one would ever matter to him as much as she did.

They held each other for a long while after the final waves of ecstasy had crested. Her head was on his shoulder, and he rested his on top of hers, breathing her in, relishing her heart beating hard and fast against his chest.

Somewhere in their lovemaking, they'd knocked over the bottle of sparkling water and the containers of food. They both noticed at the same time and laughed.

"I know I said this was supposed to be our last time," Ashley said, "but since I have the house to myself tonight, how about we make it one final night instead?"

CHAPTER TWENTY-FOUR

Every part of their evening together was magical to Ashley—making love with Nash, lying warm and sated in his arms, resting her head on his chest and listening to his heartbeat.

She had never felt so relaxed. She hadn't realized just how tightly she'd been wound all these years, until kiss by kiss, touch by touch, orgasm by orgasm, Nash unwound her like a spool of thread.

A thread that felt like it had changed from muted pastels to all the vibrant colors of the rainbow.

After leaving the vista point, they had stopped by his rental cottage to pick up clothes for the following morning so that no one at Rory and Zara's warehouse would see him wearing the same outfit for a second day and guess that he hadn't gone home. It also meant Nash was able to stay longer with her in the morning, because he didn't need to rush home to change before going to work on the van.

She loved showering with him in the morning, reveling in the sensuality of wet skin against wet skin...and the sounds of their ecstasy reverberating against her bathroom walls as they made love again.

Having breakfast together was absolutely wonderful too. She scrambled eggs while he squeezed oranges for orange juice, then Nash pulled her bare feet onto his lap as they ate at her little kitchen table.

Ashley's family, and a therapist she'd seen for several years after becoming pregnant with Kevin, had tried to help her stop beating herself up for the mistake she'd made. But it wasn't until she was with Nash that she finally felt like a better version of herself. She felt full of so much love that there was enough go all the way around the world and back.

Love.

Zara had been right—Ashley was head over heels in love with Nash. Still, she hadn't expected him to say the words to her. Not given his past and knowing how difficult his relationship with his mother had been, how little love he had been given as a child.

But even without hearing him say that he loved her, she swore she could *feel* it every moment they were together. She hugged this feeling to herself, savoring it.

Whether or not the words ever fell from his lips, she would never doubt that he cared deeply for her. And after he left Bar Harbor—what she truly believed would be their final farewell—she felt certain that the deep affection they had for each other would never go away.

She'd told her sisters and Zara that she needed to keep her distance from Nash while he was in town, because she wouldn't be able to withstand the pain of letting him go again if they grew any closer. But while the ache inside her chest remained beneath the joy and the laughter and the lovemaking, she couldn't help but be immensely grateful for this unexpected extra night with him. Of course she knew she needed to live in the real world, but being with Nash had made her life infinitely sweeter for a few more precious moments.

After they'd finished breakfast and were about to head out to pick up Kevin, Nash drew her against him and gave her a sweet, lingering kiss.

"I already know what you're going to tell me," he said once he let her lips go. "We can't do this again. There won't be any more sleepovers while I'm here. And last night was our final night together."

She looked into his eyes and saw so much beauty in them. "I wish it could be otherwise."

"I do too." He looked as sad as she felt.

When he kissed her one more time, she gave herself over fully to their final kiss. Let herself memorize his taste. His touch. All the delicious sensations he made her feel.

Then the alarm on her phone went off, and it was

time to go.

Time to leave the fantasy and return to reality.

From that point forward, the day moved quickly for Ashley. Picking Kevin up from Sammy's house and hearing about the fun he'd had at his sleepover. Dropping Kevin and Nash off so they could continue their van build. Immersing herself in work as she kept the Sullivan Cafés and stores flourishing throughout Maine.

Throughout the day, she daydreamed about Nash, reliving their laughter and their lovemaking. But whenever she caught herself getting lost in sensual memories of him, she did her best to refocus on her work.

Unfortunately, she was also distracted by Josh. Only, those thoughts were furious instead of joyful.

As soon as he returned from his gambling trip with his friends, she was going to read him the Riot Act. But she didn't want to lose herself in fury over what a terrible father he was while she was still floating on a cloud of love and lust. Knowing she'd see Nash again tonight and that they might have dinner together was something to look forward to. It didn't matter that they wouldn't be able to kiss or make love. It would be lovely just to listen to him tell her about his day and to share her day with him.

When she got back to the warehouse later that afternoon, Nash and Kevin were huddled over Nash's phone. They looked like they were conspiring, two boys making a plan.

"Hi, how's it going?" she asked.

They looked up at her as if she'd caught them out, and she laughed as she took a mental picture of the two of them.

Kevin looked so happy with Nash, happier than he likely would have been if he had gone camping with his father.

"You don't have any plans tonight that you can't break, do you?" Nash asked.

She had been planning to check in with Callie and Flynn to see if there was anything more she could do to help with their wedding. But her mother had called on the drive over to let her know the wedding plans were well in hand for now, though there would be plenty to do in the final days.

"Nope, no plans," she replied. "Why do you ask?"

Kevin looked like he was bursting to tell her. "It's a surprise, Mom."

She looked from her son to Nash. "A surprise?" She'd always loved surprises. Good ones, of course.

"If you're up for letting me drive your car for a half hour," Nash said, "we have somewhere we'd like to take you."

It was a bit of a shock to hear Nash say the word *we*

in reference to himself and her son. For eleven years, *we* had been Ashley and Kevin. But she was surprised to realize how much she liked including Nash in their tight group.

"Okay, I'm game." She handed her keys to Nash.

They got in the car, and after Nash had pulled out of the parking lot, she handed them the snacks she'd brought from the café. Ravenous at the end of a busy day, they munched on mini Reuben sandwiches and potato bites and filled her in on what they'd accomplished. She was impressed by how quickly the work was going and couldn't wait to get a better look at the van. A part of her couldn't help but wish they would work more slowly—if only to keep Nash in town for a little while longer.

Before she knew it, Nash had stopped the car. "We're here."

She looked around her, not recognizing where they were.

"Look up, Mom," Kevin said.

Oh my. They were in the parking lot of a zip-line course. Her breath caught in her throat. "Are we going to ride zip lines?"

Nash smiled. "It's as close as we can get to jumping out of a plane today."

Though the thought of zip-lining was more than a little terrifying, she was amazed that he'd listened so carefully when she'd talked about dreaming of jumping out of a plane. Even better, Nash and Kevin had decided to do something about it and try to give her one of her dreams that she had given up on.

She wanted to throw her arms around both of them. As soon as they got out of the car, that's exactly what she did.

First, she hugged her son. "This is super exciting. Thank you, honey."

And then she hugged Nash, even though touching him was extremely risky given that she never, ever wanted to let go.

"I'm super nervous," she admitted as she forced herself to step out of his arms rather than burrow in closer. "What if I can't do it? What if I'm not brave enough?"

But Nash didn't look at all worried. "You're the bravest person I've ever known, Ash. There's nothing you can't do."

CHAPTER TWENTY-FIVE

Matt, the manager of the zip-line course, measured and fitted them for the harnesses, then walked them through the safety protocols. Thankfully, both Matt and his assistant were low-key about meeting Nash. Though it was obvious they knew who he was, they didn't ask for autographs or gush all over him. Thus far, nearly everyone in town had given Nash space to be a normal guy, rather than treating him like a celebrity. After their experience with the huge crowd of Nash's fans on the streets of Vienna, Ashley had a feeling there weren't many other places in the world where this would have been the case.

Ashley's heart was pounding like crazy as they walked over to the ladder that would take them up to the first zip line. Kevin was bouncing up and down with excitement, but she couldn't quite read Nash's expression. It wasn't until they were standing on the landing, about to take their first ride on what Matt had called an "easy line for beginners," that she realized Nash looked green around the gills.

Had he brought her here despite his own fears?

As Kevin got ready to jump off, she said quietly to Nash, "Are you okay? Do you want to do this?"

He nodded, though it looked like he was clenching his teeth.

"You're brave too," she reminded him. "And I'll be waiting for you on the other side."

He leaned forward as though he was going to kiss her, but pulled back when he obviously remembered that they weren't alone. She deeply regretted missing out on his kiss. But, as she reminded herself for the thousandth time, it was for the best.

No more blurred lines between her and Nash meant no blurred lines for Kevin. There was no way Ashley and her son were going to uproot their lives to follow a musician around the world in the hopes that it would all magically work out. She knew far too well how harsh reality could be. Staying safe in Bar Harbor would be smarter than risking everything on a man who had made it perfectly clear, more than once, that he wasn't the staying kind. Nash was simply a friend of the family.

"Mom, make sure to get a video of me, okay?"

Her hands shook a little as she held up her phone to take the video. She couldn't quite shake her instinctive fear for his well-being.

"All right, whenever you're ready," the instructor

said.

With a whoop, Kevin launched himself off the platform. Though Ashley's heart was in her throat as she watched her son fly through the air, her worries were mitigated by the joy and exhilaration on her son's face.

She wished she had done this sooner. Although honestly, she couldn't imagine being here without Nash.

Watching Kevin spin around in the air to give her a thumbs-up and a massive smile, she wanted her son to always be this happy. She never wanted him to have regrets or experience sadness. But she realized with a jolt, as he made it to the landing on the other side and high-fived the second instructor, who was waiting for him, that wasn't always going to be up to her, was it?

The truth was—and this was something she was only just starting to accept—as Kevin grew older, he'd come more and more into his own. Regardless of how hard she might work to keep him safe, there would come a time when his life decisions would be entirely up to him, and he would fly the nest just as he'd flown from the tall platform today.

There would be times in his life when he'd be exhilarated and thrilled. And there would also be times when he'd be sad or frustrated or angry. All she could do as his mother was celebrate his wins and be there to comfort him after his losses.

Actually, there was more she needed to do. Instead of clinging so tightly to him, as she had for the past eleven years, she needed to start letting him make decisions on his own, even if some of those decisions might be ones she didn't fully agree with.

The realization reminded her of what she'd said to Brandon in Vienna when she'd told him it was time for her to stand on her own two feet and have some adventures, and that even if some of her adventures ended in tears, she wouldn't regret any of them. Only, now Kevin was the one who had to use his own two feet to jump into adventure. She was so proud of him for taking the literal leap away from safety into the unknown today.

Letting Kevin seek more adventure on his own would also free Ashley up for more of her own dreams, her own desires, her own passions. If she didn't spend more time focusing on herself and her own life, if she didn't work on being more than Kevin's mom, she was going to feel hugely lost and alone when he went to college. She didn't want to make the mistake of holding on too tight, for either of their sakes.

The instructor's voice brought her back to the present. "Kevin did great! Are you ready now, Ashley? I triple-checked your harnesses, and everything looks good."

She tucked her phone into her zippered pocket,

gave Kevin a double thumbs-up, then turned to smile at Nash before saying, "Yes, I'm ready."

Moments later, she jumped off the platform with a wild scream. And as she opened her arms wide to fly even faster, she realized she wasn't just ready for this...she'd been *born* ready for this.

Ashley had always been an adventurous child and teenager. She hadn't been afraid of swinging on a rope tied to a tree branch and dropping into a lake. She'd loved the rush of riding her bike down a hill with the wind in her face. She'd craved the thrill of being nearly horizontal over the ocean in a sailboat as the sea sprayed up from beneath her.

She hadn't done any of those things since becoming a mother. Partly because she'd told herself she had to behave in a certain way once she was a mom. But also because her one big mistake had convinced her that she should never put herself in a position to make another one.

On the far platform, Kevin was clapping and yelling her name. "Mom, you look awesome out there!"

She felt awesome. She felt completely alive. So wonderfully in the moment.

Exactly the same way she felt in Nash's arms.

Using the hand brake, she made a perfect landing.

"How did you like it?" the second instructor asked.

"I *loved* it! I can't wait to do the next zip line on the course."

The instructor grinned. "As soon as I met you, I had a feeling you and Kevin were going to love it." Then the instructor looked across at Nash, who was waiting his turn on the other side. "I didn't want to make a big deal about seeing Nash here. But it's really exciting to have such a big star zip-lining with us today. I hope he enjoys himself."

"Me too," Ashley said before giving Nash a thumbs-up. And then, before she could think better of it, she added one more gesture, using the fingers of both hands to make a heart.

Suddenly, he smiled. A beat later, he jumped off the platform and into the air. As he rocketed toward them, Ashley and Kevin called out his name and told him how great he was doing. At the last second, she remembered to pull out her phone, catching the final ten seconds of his ride on video before he landed.

Thankfully, he no longer looked green around the gills. "Heights aren't really my thing," he admitted, "but I have to say it was pretty exhilarating."

"It was the best!" Kevin exclaimed.

Before they headed to the next zip line, she reached out to hug both her men.

Because somewhere along the way, that's what Nash had become—another one of *her* men. No matter what, he would always be extremely important to her, and she would always want him to be happy.

Even if his future happiness couldn't include her.

CHAPTER TWENTY-SIX

Nash had loved seeing the thrill of excitement on Ashley's and Kevin's faces. Though he usually avoided heights, for them he'd been willing to face a few minutes of airborne terror. Fortunately, it hadn't been nearly as bad as he'd imagined. In fact, he'd actually enjoyed himself up there, hearing Ashley and Kevin cheering him on.

"I'm starved," Kevin proclaimed as they got back in the car, his cheeks slightly chapped from the wind. He was tired but satisfied from their adventure.

"How does pizza sound?" Ashley asked.

"Awesome!"

"Great, because we'll be passing by that waterfront pizza place on the way home."

During the drive, they compared their impressions of the various zip-line routes, each picking a favorite and laughing at their memories of one another's expressions and reactions. Ashley had been a screamer, Kevin had been a giggler, and Nash had tried to act like he wasn't holding on for dear life.

Soon, they were at the pizza joint, and though it was little more than a shack, the views of the sunset were extraordinary, and the pizza coming out of the ovens smelled even better.

The two guys running the zip-lining organization had been easygoing and relaxed around Nash, waiting until the end to ask for an autograph and a picture. The owners of this restaurant immediately asked for him to sign something, but after that, they treated Nash no differently than their other customers. The other diners didn't pay much attention to them either, as Kevin, Ashley, and Nash found a table by the water. Probably because they were all too focused on devouring their delicious slices of pizza.

Nash had always assumed big cities were the only places he might be able to blend in—wearing a baseball cap and sunglasses, of course. Now he wondered if he'd had it completely backward. Maybe it was only in a small town like Bar Harbor that he could have some privacy. Almost as though Ashley and Kevin and the other Sullivans he'd met, like Rory and Zara, had created a protective barrier around him that everyone else in town knew not to breach.

Nash had never had a family to look out for him before. His chest ached as he thought of leaving them.

Their personal pizzas came quickly, and the three of them didn't say much as they ate. It was one of the best pizzas Nash had ever eaten—the crust was crunchy, the toppings were fresh, and the cheese was from a nearby farm. On top of that, the views from the restaurant were astonishing.

But though the sunset over the water was stunning, Nash couldn't stop staring at Ashley. She was so beautiful. The most beautiful woman he'd ever known.

"Are you guys dating?" Kevin asked suddenly.

Ashley's head spun from the view to her son so fast that Nash was half afraid she would have whiplash. "What?"

"I was just wondering since you guys kissed at the café, if you are boyfriend and girlfriend?" Before either of them could reply, Kevin added, "Dad is actually the one who wants to know, but I'm kind of wondering too."

Nash watched Ashley deliberately try to control her reaction to learning that her ex was pestering their son for information about her personal life. What a douchebag that guy was.

"Nash and I are good friends," she said primly. "But although people did see us kissing in the café, we are not dating."

Kevin thought about her response for a minute. "Okay. I mean, that would be cool if you were. But if you're not, that's okay too."

Ashley seemed more than a little surprised to hear

her son say it would be okay with him if the two of them dated.

Nash tried not to let his hopes rise. Of course he wanted to be with Ashley again, rather than staying in the friend zone for his remaining time in town. But he also understood her reasons for not wanting to get romantically tangled up with him.

His rock-star life was unreliable.

He was unreliable.

Nash had never been a man who stayed in one place. And constantly moving from one location to another on the road was no life for Ashley or Kevin.

Then why not stay? Where do you have to go?

The voice inside his head jarred him to attention.

He'd first hit the road to get away from his mom and had stayed there to chase his dreams of music stardom. But the truth was that his roving life had gotten old a while ago, with one five-star hotel blending into another, every city looking the same.

The voice popped up again. *What if staying in one place with one person is the* real *adventure? What if staying is the way you can prove yourself to be the man you've always wished you could be?*

Right then, Kevin yawned so loudly that Nash snapped out of his crazy thoughts.

"We should get this guy to bed," Ashley said to Nash. "I want to make sure you two are rested for your workday on the van tomorrow."

Nash tried to pay the bill, but Ashley insisted that since he'd paid for zip-lining, she would take care of dinner. On the drive back to town, Kevin nodded off in the backseat, and though Nash wanted to hold Ashley's hand, he couldn't risk Kevin waking up and seeing it. Especially after they had said they were only friends.

"How are you feeling about our surprise now that we've all lived through it?" he asked in a low voice.

She smiled, looking radiant in the moonlight that poured through the windshield. "I had the best time zip-lining. Thank you so much for setting it up, Nash. It was such a great surprise and such a treat. Something tells me it won't be the last time Kevin and I do that course."

Working to ignore the ache in his chest from the way she'd just said *Kevin and I* instead of *the three of us*, Nash told her, "I had a great day with you and Kevin, Ash. A *really* great day."

She reached out to touch his hand, although she didn't let her fingers linger over his, unfortunately. "You've been amazing these past few days. Actually, the whole time I've known you, you've been amazing." But then she scowled. "If only I could say the same for my ex. I can't believe he asked Kevin to gather dirt on me. Josh has no business whatsoever poking around my personal life." She checked to make sure Kevin was still asleep, keeping her voice low as she added, "As soon as he comes back to town, I'm going to lay down some major new ground rules with him."

Nash had plenty to say about her ex. None of it good. But he knew better than to weigh in. Or to fight her battles for her.

She could handle Kevin's father just fine on her own. Of that he was certain.

Ashley dropped him off in Rory and Zara's parking lot so that he could pick up his van and head to his rental cottage.

He wanted to kiss her. Wanted to hold her close. But since he couldn't do any of those things when Kevin might wake up any second and see them together, he simply said, "Good night, Ash. I'll see you guys tomorrow morning."

She reached out and put her hand briefly over his again, squeezing it, filling him with warmth. "Thanks again for the zip-lining adventure. Sleep well, and we'll see you in the morning."

Nash had walked into countless empty hotel rooms. But he had never felt as lonely as he did walking into his rental cottage ten minutes later.

Soon, he would head off on a cross-country adventure. But what had once seemed like the perfect escape no longer sounded particularly good anymore. And if he was being totally honest with himself, had it ever really sounded that great?

All his life, remaining alone—even in a crowd—had been the safest way for him to live.

Alone meant he'd never be attached to anyone as full of bitterness and anger as his mom.

Alone meant keeping the risk to his heart as low as possible.

But until he'd met Ashley, he hadn't realized that *alone* also meant his chances of finding love—real love—were nonexistent.

For the first time since he'd gotten off tour, Nash found himself reaching for his guitar. He hadn't been planning to write any songs during this break. On the contrary, he'd been feeling burned out enough to let music go for a while.

But as he started strumming some basic chords, he was surprised when words started coming with the melody.

Words he'd never thought could come from him.

Words of *love*.

CHAPTER TWENTY-SEVEN

The next morning, Ashley dropped Kevin off with only a wave for Nash. Her supplier meetings at the café were to begin in ten minutes, and she told herself it was for the best that she couldn't get close enough to Nash to breathe in his delicious scent, or to look into his beautiful eyes.

All night long, she'd dreamed of him. Breathtakingly sexy dreams that only made her want him more. If she'd had the time to get out of her car and say a proper hello, she wasn't convinced she would have had the self-control to keep from kissing him.

For the next three hours, she did her level best to focus on the next quarter's orders for the store. As soon as her meetings were concluded, she fired off a text to Josh, inviting him to have lunch at the café on the house. Having a meal with her ex was the last thing she wanted to do, but since she'd heard he was back in town, she didn't want another day to go by without confronting him about his inexcusable behavior toward their son.

Josh arrived at noon on the button. Considering how unreliable he was with Kevin, it was funny how he managed to be perfectly punctual when it came to a free meal.

He started in on her before she could say a word. "If you're going to give me hell about not being able to make it on the camping trip with Kevin—"

She held up her hand, cutting him off. "Why don't we pick up our lunches from the kitchen and take them to the park? Annie has already put our usual orders in to-go boxes."

As they walked across the street to the park, she noticed that a few women's heads turned. Josh was still a good-looking guy, just as he'd been in high school. She heard enough via the local grapevine to know that he went out on plenty of dates with young women who didn't know they should avoid him. Even so, she'd never interfered in his personal life, beyond trying to make sure he'd be there when Kevin needed him.

As soon as they sat down, she told him, "Don't you dare ever again take money—*my* money—that's meant for our son and spend it on anything but Kevin. He was heartbroken when you didn't show up."

Josh's expression was like thunder, although his anger didn't stop him from chowing down on his free chicken fillet roll. "I told you something came up."

She hadn't yet taken a bite of her sausage roll, and she was glad she hadn't, because her stomach was getting tighter with every second she spent with her ex. "I don't want to hear your excuses," she replied. "And don't you *dare* ever again put Kevin in the middle when it comes to my personal life. You should never have told him to ask if Nash and I are dating. It's none of your business."

But Josh didn't look the least bit remorseful. "After the way you were sucking face with Nash at the café a few days ago, I needed to know for sure if it was true that you're not quite the Goody Two-shoes you've always made yourself out to be."

"I can't believe your nerve!" Steam was practically coming out of her ears. "You actually think you can weigh in on my life when you've gone from woman to woman the whole time you've been back in town?"

"At least I'm not pretending to be holier than thou," he spat. "At least I'm not hooking up with someone with a prison record. At least I'm not dating someone who has been in the press countless times over the years for partying and womanizing and drugs."

"Watch yourself," she warned, her voice coming out as a low growl. "Nash's life, past or present or future, has nothing to do with you."

"It sure as hell does," Josh countered. "If you're

hooking up with a guy with an arrest record, that puts Kevin at risk. What if Kevin sees the two of you partying rock-star style and decides to start drinking or doing drugs? What kind of a role model is a guy like Nash Hardwin for our son?"

"A hell of a better role model than you!" Ashley snapped, losing her patience once and for all. "And Nash doesn't drink or do drugs. So that ridiculous scenario you just came up with will never happen."

"So that's how it is? You're talking shit about me to our kid, while building up the new guy, even though he's got a rap sheet?" Josh stood up, making sure he took his food with him, of course. "You've left me no choice, Ashley. If you continue to see Nash in any capacity at all, if your eyes so much as meet across a room, I'm going to take my case to the courts."

"What case would that be?"

"The case that you're an unfit mother. The case that you should lose custody of Kevin. The case that I should be his sole parent and provider from now on."

She jumped to her feet, her meal flying off her lap and onto the lawn. "You wouldn't dare."

"Want to bet? You've given me nothing but attitude since the day I came back. And now look who's on the back foot." His eyes were bright with something that looked a heck of a lot like revenge. "Now look who's creating a bad environment for our son. It's not me. It's you. One wrong move, and it's over for you, Ashley. *Over.*"

With that final shot, he walked away, leaving Ashley standing there with grilled onions from her sandwich sliding down her leg. Her heart was pounding, her stomach was twisted in knots, and she felt like she was going to vomit.

All of her worst fears felt like they were coming true.

* * *

When lunchtime rolled around, Nash and Kevin ate the sandwiches Ashley had made for them, then Kevin went to model for Zara in a photo shoot for her new line of glasses frames for teens.

Nash was working on connecting the plumbing under the kitchen sink in the van when a car pulled up nearby. A man who looked vaguely familiar stepped out of it.

"Hi, I'm Flynn Stewart. I'm engaged to Ashley's sister Cassie."

As Nash shook his hand, his face and name suddenly rang a bell. "We've met, haven't we? You're a screenwriter, right?"

Flynn nodded. "I left Hollywood last year and moved to Bar Harbor. Best decision I ever made."

"I've only been here for a few days, but the town

seems pretty great," Nash agreed.

"It's not just the town," Flynn said. "It's the people. Living in Hollywood for so long, I didn't realize how cynical I'd become. But moving to Bar Harbor helped me see that there are still plenty of good people in the world."

Nash nodded, having already learned that very thing.

Flynn gestured to the van. "This is quite a project you've got going."

"It's gone faster than I thought it would," Nash told him. "Kevin's been helping, and he's good with his hands, especially considering he's only eleven."

"He's a great kid. My daughter, Ruby, adores him." Flynn suddenly looked a little uncomfortable. "About why I'm here today… Considering I was just complaining about people in Hollywood, I can't believe the favor I'm about to ask you."

"No worries," Nash said. "I'm happy to hear what's on your mind." Though he didn't know Flynn well, anyone who had fled Hollywood for Bar Harbor felt like a kindred spirit.

"'Missing Piece' is Cassie's all-time favorite song." Flynn looked even more uncomfortable now. "And Cassie mentioned that you're in town and have been spending time with Ashley and Kevin—"

Since Nash could easily guess what Flynn was hoping for, he decided to spare him further discomfort. "Would you like me to sing it at your wedding?"

"If that's too much to ask, especially from a stranger, I totally get it."

"Anybody related to Ashley and Kevin isn't a stranger," Nash replied. "I'd be happy to sing for Cassie."

Normally, he was offered seven figures to sing at a wedding or birthday, though he normally turned down those offers. But for Ashley's family, he was more than happy to do it. Not only would it mean Nash would get another day with Ashley, but now he would also get to meet her entire family. It would be a privilege to get to know the people who had helped shape her into the incredible woman she was today and who had done so much to help her as a pregnant teen.

Flynn looked hugely grateful. "I'm sure your fee is well beyond my means, but I hope we can work something out."

"There's nothing to work out. Consider it a wedding gift."

"I owe you big time for this," Flynn said. "If there's ever anything I can do for you, please let me know."

"No payback necessary," Nash told him. "Just let me know where to be and when, and I'll show up with my guitar."

"We'll be getting married in our own backyard on

Saturday at noon. And if you don't have anything else planned for that day, I'd be honored if you would stay for the reception. If I tell Cassie you're coming to the wedding as Ashley's guest, hopefully she won't guess you're going to serenade her."

"I'd be happy to accept your invitation. Although," he found himself saying before he could think better of it, "if it's all right with you, there might be a new song I could debut too."

"Two songs would be even better than one," Flynn said. After giving Nash another handshake, he drove off, grinning.

Last night, when Nash had picked up his guitar, a fully formed song had poured out of him. A song that he hadn't been able to stop singing in his head all day long. A song he'd named "Hold On To My Heart."

Nash hadn't thought that he was capable of loving anyone, or of fully giving his heart to another. But he could no longer deny the truth.

He'd fallen in love with Ashley Sullivan.

Kevin came bounding back, and though Nash felt like his entire life had changed, he knew if he didn't pay attention to the work they were doing on the van, he was likely to screw something up.

That afternoon, they worked on plumbing the interior and underside of the van. Kevin had an impressively long attention span, although they did take a short break to play a video game on Kevin's phone.

All the while, however, Nash kept repeating the same five words to himself: *I'm in love with Ashley.* Five words that changed everything.

The sun was starting to fall in the sky when Ashley texted to say that Sammy and his mother would be there in five minutes to pick Kevin up for soccer practice—and that she was hoping Nash would be free too, so they could talk.

His heart leaped as he realized he would be seeing her tonight. She was right—they did need to talk. He needed to tell her how he felt. That he loved her as much as she loved him.

Was there a way to actually make things work between them? Could the small-town single mom and the rock star get their happy ending against all odds?

She arrived thirty minutes later, wearing dark sunglasses and a hat. Almost as though she was trying to disguise herself.

Swallowing his declarations of love, he asked, "What's wrong, Ash?"

She shook her head. "Not here. People might see us."

He frowned. Why did it matter if people saw them together when they were just talking?

She gestured for him to follow her into Rory's

workspace. Her brother had already left for the day, so they had it to themselves. She made sure the doors were closed before she spoke again.

"I saw Josh today. I asked him to lunch so that I could lay down some new ground rules about his behavior with Kevin. But then..." She took a shaky breath. "He threatened to take Kevin away from me. To declare me an unfit mother."

"What the hell?" Fury lit up inside of Nash. "On what grounds?"

She took off her sunglasses and lifted red-rimmed eyes to his. "*You.* He says he'll tell the courts that I'm dating someone who's been in prison. He says he'll prove that you're notorious for drinking and partying and doing drugs."

"I was barely more than a teenager when I did all those things," Nash protested. But he couldn't be sure that a judge would care how old he'd been when he'd behaved so recklessly. Only that he had. Still, he had to tell Ash, "It's just a bluff. There's no way Josh would be able to prove this case."

"Maybe," she said, but doubt and fear were crystal clear in her voice.

"Ash, I never would have come here if I'd thought you or Kevin would end up being hurt."

"It's not your fault," she said. "It's mine. I knew better than to kiss you the way I did at the café. I knew better than to make love with you that afternoon, or again at the vista point. I knew better than to try to break out of my shell, even if just for a handful of days. I couldn't help myself. But now I wish I had. Because if Josh were to succeed at taking Kevin away from me, I'd never forgive myself."

Nash could easily hear what she hadn't said. *And I'll never forgive you either.*

He'd planned to tell her that he loved her. He'd hoped they could maybe even find a path to forever with each other, if they just looked hard enough for it.

Instead, he found himself saying, "Are you going to let Josh keep calling the shots forever? Are you going to keep letting him live his own life however he damn well pleases, while he makes the boundaries around your life tighter and smaller?"

She erupted. "You're not a parent! You have no idea what it means to take care of someone! You have no idea what it takes to love someone! The sacrifices you have to make for people you love. All you know is running, leaving. Looking out for number one."

She wasn't saying anything that wasn't true. Nash had never taken care of anyone but himself. He'd almost given in to the fantasy of taking care of her and Kevin. But now he saw that was all it had been—a fantasy. He was, and always would be, a tiger incapable of changing his stripes.

It didn't matter that he loved her. He'd destroy both her life and Kevin's if he refused to let them go.

"You're right," he said in a low voice. "Coming here was selfish of me. And if I stay, I'll only make things harder for you and Kevin. I'll leave immediately so Josh won't have any more ammunition against you." But then he remembered... "Flynn came by earlier and asked me to sing for your sister at the wedding. If you'll give me his number before you go, I'll let him know I won't be able to do it after all."

"He asked you to sing 'Missing Piece,' didn't he?"

"He did."

Ashley closed her eyes as though looking inward for strength. As soon as she reopened them, she said, "You have to sing at the wedding. Hearing you perform her favorite song just for her will be the gift of a lifetime for Cassie."

"Are you sure?"

"I am. But afterward—"

"I'll leave. And I won't come back." Then something occurred to him. "Kevin can't work with me on the van anymore, can he?"

She shook her head. "No, he can't." Worried it would break her son's heart, she thought fast. "I'll find something to distract him so he's not too upset. Maybe a day at a local amusement park tomorrow with his best friend."

"He'll like that," Nash said.

She nodded, though they both could guess that Kevin was going to miss continuing their work on the van. Over the past several days, Nash had loved watching the boy's growing confidence around the tools and the overall project.

Two fat tears rolled down her cheeks. "I wish things could have been different, Nash."

"I do too."

And then, though he knew it would only make things harder, he couldn't stop himself from reaching out to hold her. He needed to feel the wonder of her in his arms one last time before he had to let her go.

CHAPTER TWENTY-EIGHT

Ashley felt completely numb as she zipped around town, checking off a dozen final details for Cassie and Flynn's wedding. The wedding was small enough that the café staff was going to cater the event, and normally Ashley would have helped out in the kitchen. But she couldn't risk facing anyone in her family right now, especially her mom. One look at Ashley's face, and Beth Sullivan would know something was wrong. Something big.

Perhaps Ashley should have been stronger, tougher, more ready to face her emotions. But she was afraid if anything pierced the numb shell encasing her heart, her sorrow over having to say good-bye to Nash might overflow.

And she might never recover.

No, it was far better to stay deadened to everything.

A bigger wedding celebration would happen later in the year that would involve the entire extended Sullivan family from around the world. But this

Saturday, Cassie and Flynn would say their vows in front of their nearest and dearest family members—and Nash, as well.

Josh had threatened that if Nash came anywhere near Ashley and Kevin in the future, he would set the legal wheels in motion to have her declared an unfit mother. Which meant the wedding could be a potential problem if word got out that Nash was there. But how could Ashley take away Cassie's surprise from Flynn when she knew how much it would mean to her sister? Being at the wedding with Nash was the final risk she had to take for the sake of her sister's happiness.

Ashley had mulled endlessly over Josh's threats. And while she'd pretty much convinced herself that no judge worth his or her robe would award sole custody of Kevin to Josh, she also believed that severing ties with Nash—after the wedding—was the right thing to do. It was one thing for her to weather Josh's snap judgments about being a bad mother. But it was another thing entirely to subject Kevin to other people's judgments. He was just a kid, and she needed to make sure she protected him from that.

All along, she'd known that a real relationship with Nash was an impossibility. And yet, when he'd appeared in Bar Harbor from out of the blue, she hadn't been able to stop herself from impulsively kissing him.

Nor had she been able to resist jumping back into bed with him when the opportunities had arisen.

Still, there was one thing she absolutely refused to regret.

Telling Nash she loved him.

It was the one thing she knew for sure and that she would keep with her long after he left Bar Harbor. She loved him with her whole heart and soul. And the time she'd spent with him had been some of the most important, rewarding, amazing moments of her life.

Maybe that was why the idea of moving forward without him felt so empty.

Every time Ashley thought about seeing Nash at the wedding, she lost track of where she was on her to-do list. Fortunately, she was armed with a detailed spreadsheet. She'd been crossing off tasks as she completed them, so she was fairly certain she hadn't screwed anything up thus far.

Over and over, Ashley reminded herself that once she got through the wedding, and Nash had played his song for Cassie, she'd be on the other side. The side where no one's harsh judgments could possibly harm her son. The side where she wouldn't have to control her urges to kiss Nash all the time. The side where her emotions wouldn't constantly be a roller coaster of ups and downs. The side where she would settle back into her regular, boring existence in town and force herself to be happy about it, even if it killed her!

* * *

Nash had always been a master at hiding what he was feeling, not only from other people, but also from himself. It was something he'd learned as a child. His mother's moods had been so unpredictable that if he made one wrong move, she would explode. While he was growing up, it had been easier to act like nothing mattered, like he didn't care about anything.

But for the first time in his life, Nash couldn't push away his emotions. Since Ashley had told him about Josh's threats, his insides had felt black and blue. Because she was right.

It didn't matter that he'd anonymously given millions of dollars to charity over the years, or that he'd put dozens of kids through college, or that he'd secretly sponsored at-risk families in his hometown for more than a decade.

It was easy giving money to strangers. It was a million times harder to actually take care of someone else. To put someone he loved first. To give up his time to someone, rather than live his life exactly the way he wanted to. He'd never completely changed the course of his life to make another person happy.

Even if he was no longer a stupid kid getting into trouble with the law, he still wasn't good enough for her or for her son.

If only he'd learned how to give, rather than always take, maybe Ashley wouldn't have been compelled to kick him out of her life. Maybe his future could have been full of love. Instead, he was staring down the barrel of such devastating loss that it felt like he'd been shot straight through the heart.

If he hadn't promised Flynn that he would play his song for Cassie as a wedding gift, Nash would have been gone in a flash. He would've driven away in the van and finished building it out somewhere else. Moving on was the only thing he'd ever been good at.

But he couldn't move on until the wedding was over. Somehow, some way, he needed to keep his distance from Ashley when they were together again in Flynn and Cassie's garden. He couldn't steal a kiss. Nor could he get down on bended knee and beg her to reconsider, no matter how desperate he was for her to change her mind about them.

Nash would never forgive himself if his presence in Ashley and Kevin's life led to a custody battle. Even if Josh didn't win—and Nash couldn't imagine any judge on the planet giving Kevin to Josh—Nash still didn't want Kevin to have to go through a court battle.

Kevin was a great kid. As they'd worked on the van all week, Kevin had not only been a big help, he'd been a good companion too. And all of it was down to

Ashley and what a great mother she was. If Nash were in her shoes, he'd make the same choice to kick him to the curb.

That didn't make losing both of them hurt any less, though.

On the way home, with the Sisi key chain hanging from the van's ignition making his gut twist as it reminded him of their perfect day in Vienna, Nash picked up some Chinese takeout. But when he got back to his rental, instead of eating, he reached for his guitar.

The last time he'd played it, he'd written his first love song. For Ashley. Now, he could barely resist the urge to go stand outside her window to serenade her with the love he'd only ever felt for her.

No. He couldn't do that. Back in Vienna, he'd promised to pay her back for her help at some point in the future. He'd never thought that leaving her would be the only way he could fulfill his promise.

Nash put the guitar down and reached for a pair of sneakers. He had to get out of here. Had to outrun all these goddamned emotions. An hour later, though his heart was racing and his body ached from sprinting through the forest, the song of love still played inside his heart.

But even if he told her how he felt, even if she knew she was the only one for him, even if she knew she'd changed him in a way he'd never thought he could be changed, it wouldn't mean they could be together. Even if he confessed that her love had shattered all the walls he'd put up around himself, she still wouldn't change her mind. Even if he told her that he hadn't fallen in love with just her, but that Kevin also held a huge piece of his heart, Nash's dark past would still be an ugly thing for people to gossip about.

From the first moment he and Ashley had put on disguises and snuck out of the Vienna hotel together, the ice surrounding Nash's heart had begun to thaw. Being with Ashley had given him a taste of how good life could be. She'd shown him joy. And adventure. She'd taught him to risk. And to care.

And most of all, she'd given him love.

Love he'd never thought he'd be able to give back.

But he did. He loved her. He would always love her.

Even if she could never be his.

CHAPTER TWENTY-NINE

Cassie and Flynn's wedding day dawned bright and beautiful. The sky was so blue that there wasn't a cloud in it, a rarity for Bar Harbor. The weather had a tendency to change from sunshine to rain in the blink of an eye, but Ashley had a feeling today would remain absolutely perfect.

Years ago, Cassie had purchased a wooded property on a hundred acres fifteen minutes from downtown. The Sullivans had helped her fix up the cottage over the years, and now Cassie and Flynn were expanding it for their growing family. It was the perfect place for a wedding. The garden was in full bloom, as though the universe were intent on making it look as heavenly as possible for their special day.

Cassie had intended to design her own wedding cake, but her family had insisted that she shouldn't turn her big day into another project. Though she loved transforming sugar into edible creations, her family wanted her to be able to focus completely on one of the most wondrous days of her life.

Ashley had pitched in to help Cassie and Flynn wherever she could in the final runup to the wedding. She'd cleaned their cottage and cars. She'd weeded their garden. She'd cooked meals for them and Ruby. She'd babysat her sweet little niece-to-be. And when she'd run out of tasks to take care of for the bride and groom, Ashley had whipped out paint cans and brushes and painted her guest bedroom. She'd been planning the project for months, but hadn't gotten around to it until now.

She supposed it helped that she'd barely been able to sleep, snatching just enough rest here and there to keep from keeling over. Though she had zero appetite, she'd made herself eat at mealtimes. And she most definitely had avoided seeing anyone in her family, apart from Cassie, Flynn, and Ruby, who were too wrapped up in their impending nuptials to notice that anything was wrong with her too-bright smiles and forced laughter.

For any other family members who had tried to reach her, she'd replied via text, rather than calling or seeing them in person. God forbid the tone of her voice or the bags under her eyes should alert them to her emotional state. The last thing she wanted was for her problems to overshadow Cassie's wedding. What's more, if her brothers or father had thought Nash had broken her heart, they'd hunt him down. Even if she

explained to them that none of this was Nash's fault—
and that if she'd had the choice to do it all over again,
even knowing the pain that would come, she would
still give Nash her body, heart, and soul—they would
think they needed to avenge her.

"There you are." Lola found Ashley standing beneath the rose arbor and looped elbows with her.
"How have you been? I've been dying for an update on
your sexy rock star, but things have been too crazy
with work and doing Cassie's final fitting." Lola pinned
her with a look. "I really hope you decided to have
some fun with Nash after all."

Fun. It had been so much more than *fun.*

Ashley was trying with all her might to hold herself
together, but she knew all it would take was one word
out of her mouth for Lola to see what a complete and
total mess she was. Even without Ashley saying
anything, unfortunately, Lola was starting to look
seriously concerned.

"Hey, Ash—"

But Ashley wasn't listening. Because Nash had just
walked into Cassie's backyard.

Oh God. She'd been trying to prepare herself for this
moment. But nothing could have prepared her for the
impact of seeing him again. She felt like all the breath
had left her lungs, her skin was on fire, and her brain
had ceased to function.

How on earth was she going to pretend throughout the wedding ceremony and reception that she didn't love him with everything she was? How could she possibly act like her heart wasn't shredded to pieces?

Kevin ran up to Nash, talking animatedly. Nash grinned and put an arm across his shoulders. They were good friends after working together on the van.

But when Nash looked up and saw her watching them, he dropped his arm from Kevin. She'd told him that her son was her first priority and that she couldn't allow her relationship with Nash to jeopardize Kevin in any way. It sickened her that it had come to this—that Nash was afraid to make even the slightest friendly gesture toward her son in case Josh found out and tried to take Kevin from her.

Anger simmered inside her, hotter than ever. But though she was furious with Josh for trying to control her life with his threats, this wasn't just about her ex.

Ashley told herself that a good mother wouldn't fall in love with a rock star with a checkered past, even if he was so handsome it took her breath away. On the contrary, a good mother would do whatever it took to ensure her child's happiness.

But even as Ashley reminded herself about the rules she'd lived by for the past eleven years, she couldn't hide from the fact that her mother had managed to raise seven children without subjugating who she was in the process. Beth Sullivan hadn't been perfect, she hadn't been faultless, but she'd always been an amazing mother. Although, since Beth hadn't gotten pregnant in high school, she hadn't needed to spend the rest of her life trying to atone for such a big mistake the way Ashley had.

"Ash, what's wrong?" Lola finally got her attention.

But Ashley couldn't talk about it, or she'd break down in tears. And then she'd ruin her sister's big day. "I promise to tell you everything later. Today is about Cassie, not me." When it looked like Lola might argue, she insisted, "I can't. I just can't. Let's focus on Cassie and Flynn and Ruby and make sure they have the best wedding ever."

Lola studied her face for several long moments before finally nodding. "Okay. But whatever is going on, I'm here for you. We all are. Promise me you won't forget that, Ash. You don't need to hold it all inside."

Her family had always been there for her. Just as she'd been there for them. But if Lola said one more sweet thing, Ashley was going to start bawling.

"I think you should know something about Nash, though, in case you don't already."

"Lola, please—"

But Lola kept speaking over her protests. "He's given a *ton* of money to charity over the years. We're talking millions and millions of dollars. Evidently, he does it anonymously, but Duncan says it's easy to trace the money back to Nash. It's an open secret in Hollywood that if you need help, or know someone who does, Nash is the man who will give it, no questions asked."

Ashley's head spun. Not because she doubted anything Lola said, but because she knew instinctively it must be true. Despite Nash's transgressions as a teenager and young man in his twenties, at his core he was a good man. And he always had been.

Just then, Ruby ran up and tugged on her hand. Knowing it was her cue to pick up the little girl, Ashley snuggled her close.

"See my pretty dress?" Ruby asked.

Ashley nodded. "Your dress is beautiful, honey. And I love the wreath of flowers on your hair."

Lola also snuggled Ruby, putting her arms around Ashley at the same time.

"Isn't this exciting, Ruby?" Ashley asked. "Your mommy and daddy are getting married today. They're going to say beautiful words of love to each other." Ashley's throat was so full of emotion she could barely get the words out. "We all love you so much, sweet girl."

"Love you too," Ruby said.

Flynn and Cassie's daughter was a bundle of light,

and she reminded Ashley of what was important. Loving and protecting Kevin, no matter what.

And yet, it was getting harder and harder to ignore the voice in her heart that wouldn't stop insisting that pushing Nash out of their lives would only cause both her and Kevin *more* pain, not less.

CHAPTER THIRTY

It was killing Nash to be this close to Ashley, and yet, they were further apart than they had ever been. He was barely holding himself back from striding across the lawn and pulling her into his arms. Only the knowledge that he'd never forgive himself for hurting either Ashley or Kevin was keeping him from giving in to the urge to touch her, kiss her.

"What the hell are you doing here?"

Nash turned at the growled question and came face-to-face with Brandon Sullivan. Everyone else in the family was in on the wedding song surprise, but Brandon must not have heard.

"Flynn asked me to play a song as a surprise wedding gift for Cassie."

Brandon looked absolutely furious, no different from his expression when he'd realized Nash had spent the night with his sister in Vienna.

"Don't worry," Nash told him. "I'll be out of your family's hair by tonight. As soon as the wedding is over, I'm hitting the road. And I won't be coming back."

Brandon looked at Ashley, then back at Nash. "My sister looks miserable. It's your fault, isn't it? Why the hell couldn't you leave her alone?"

Before Nash could reply, a woman whom he assumed must be one of Ashley's sisters, given the resemblance around the eyes and mouth, walked up and held out her hand to him.

"I'm Lola, Ashley's sister. I've heard so much about you, Nash. I'm glad to finally get this chance to meet you in person."

Her smile seemed genuine as they shook hands, and strangely, he almost felt like she was on his side.

A tall man in a suit put an arm around Lola's waist, then held his free hand out to Nash.

"I'm Duncan, Lola's other half."

As Nash shook his hand, another man entered the circle of Sullivans, introducing himself as Turner, another of Ashley's brothers.

When Nash shook his hand, he noted that while Turner wasn't angry like Brandon, nor nearly as welcoming as Lola, it seemed he was trying to gauge if Nash was a good man or a bad one. It was easy enough to decide, Nash figured. He'd made a hell of a lot of mistakes in his past. And now he was paying the ultimate price for them.

Another man came into the group. "I'm Hudson,

and a big fan of your music. It was a huge surprise to hear you were going to be here today."

Nash said his thanks as he shook Hudson's hand, then met Hudson's wife, Larissa, who said she was also a fan. But despite liking his music, that didn't seem to make them any more favorably inclined toward him as a possible partner for Ashley. Not if there was any chance that he might hurt her. Nash was so glad she'd had her family to lean on through the years.

At last, the man and woman he assumed were Ashley's parents approached. Her father's expression was perfectly transparent—he didn't like the look of Nash and would clearly prefer he got the hell away from Ashley and Kevin sooner rather than later.

"You must be Nash. I'm Ethan Sullivan." Ethan's grip was bone-crushingly strong. "I understand you've been working with my grandson these past few days building out a van."

"Yes, sir. Kevin's been great to work with."

Kevin beamed. "It's been tons of fun, Grandpa. Nash is awesome, and he even lets me use the power tools."

Though Ethan patted his grandson's shoulder approvingly, his eyes narrowed as he turned back to Nash. "Power tools, eh?"

Thankfully, that was when Rory and Zara ambled over. "Nash repeatedly drilled Kevin on safety procedures," Rory said. "Turns out, Kevin's got such great hands, he's been a big help in my studio this week too."

Though Rory and Zara had been busy this week running their design businesses, from the little time he'd spent with them, Nash liked them both a lot. On the surface, they didn't look like they'd be a good fit. Zara was the quintessential artist, while Rory looked like an all-American jock. But they were a perfectly matched couple.

It struck Nash that some people might think he and Ashley would be an odd pairing, as well, simply because they'd mistakenly assume a rock star like him wouldn't have any interest in a sweet single mother from a small town.

How wrong those people would be. With Ashley, Nash felt like he'd finally found the one person he trusted.

"I'm so pleased to meet you, Nash." Ashley's mother had a lovely, lilting Irish accent and a welcoming smile. "I'm Beth, and it seems you've already met everyone else. Flynn is over the moon that you agreed to sing Cassie's favorite song. Ethan and I need to head back into the house now to see if Cassie's ready for her walk down the aisle, but I wanted to make sure you knew how glad we all are that you're here."

Nash sensed this was Beth's way of warning her sons and husband that they'd better play nicer with

Nash than they had so far. For some reason, Ashley's mother seemed to agree with Lola that he wasn't a bad seed. But why? Had Ashley spoken to her mom about her feelings for him?

No, he didn't think she had. Not when throughout her family's introductions, Ashley had remained on the other side of the garden, rearranging baskets of flowers and straightening ribbons on chairs. He hated the distance between them, but he knew if she came any closer, he wouldn't be able to keep from holding her, kissing her, begging her to let him stay and try to prove himself to her and Kevin.

The officiant took his place beneath the rose arbor, then directed them to take their seats. Nash sat in the back, and when Ashley took a seat in the opposite front corner, he couldn't stop staring at her and drinking her in.

He wouldn't forget a single thing about her after he left. The brightness of her smile. The flush that came over her skin whenever he kissed her. The sweet little sounds she made when he made love to her.

Just then, Ashley bent down to whisper something in Kevin's ear, and his heart turned over as he watched mother and child. He'd never seen a more beautiful sight and knew he never would. Nash snapped a mental picture of Ashley and of Kevin sitting beside her. The two people he'd come to care about most in the world.

A string quartet began to play the "Wedding March" and they all stood as Cassie emerged on the arm of her father.

Everyone gasped at the sight of Cassie in her wedding gown. She looked almost otherworldly, in large part because of the enormous smile on her face.

Flynn, waiting for Cassie under the rose arbor, looked equally as happy.

Ruby stood beside her, holding a basket of flower petals. She looked up at Cassie as she asked, "Can I throw roses now, Mommy?"

Cassie laughed, bending down to hug her little girl. "Yes, honey, you can throw the rose petals now."

With adorable abandon, Ruby skipped down the aisle, flinging flower petals this way and that. Nash's gut twisted as a clear vision hit him of the child he and Ashley might have had if things were different. If *he* were a different man.

His life, *his* career, *his* past—those were the reasons they couldn't be together.

When Flynn broke away from his spot beneath the rose arbor to meet Cassie halfway up the aisle, Nash was brought back to the present moment and away from his impossible longings to erase his past.

There were tears in Ethan's eyes as he kissed his daughter on the cheek and hugged her tight. Nash felt his chest grow tighter at the display of parental devotion. Something he'd never personally known. Then Ethan put Cassie's hand in Flynn's, shook the other man's hand, and took a seat.

Flynn kissed Cassie, long before *I do*, and as they walked hand in hand the rest of the way to where the officiant stood, there didn't seem to be a dry eye in the house.

Ruby had gone to sit on Beth's lap after she'd emptied her basket of rose petals, but when she saw her parents standing together beneath the rose arbor, she scrambled off Beth's lap and moved between Cassie and Flynn so that the three of them could all hold hands.

It looked exactly right to Nash. Flynn and Cassie weren't complete without Ruby.

It was how Nash felt about Ashley and Kevin—he couldn't imagine the woman he loved without her son.

Just as Nash could no longer imagine his future without either of them in it.

CHAPTER THIRTY-ONE

Cassie looked so beautiful. So did little Ruby. And Flynn looked like the proudest man in the entire world. They were the perfect family, meant to be together.

Ashley was barely holding back a flood of tears, the numbness of the past two days having disappeared as soon as she'd set eyes on Nash. But today wasn't about her impossible feelings for Nash, or his for her. Today was about Cassie, Flynn, and Ruby and the rest of Ashley's family, all of whom were thrilled by their union.

Flynn cleared his throat as he prepared to speak his vows. "I never dreamed of meeting a woman like you, Cassie. I never believed I'd be lucky enough to fall in love with someone who radiates goodness the way you do. But then there you were, at one of the darkest points of my life, with your smiles and laughter, your help and support, and most of all, your love. Not only love for me, but also for my little girl."

"I love you, Mommy and Daddy!"

Everyone laughed at Ruby's declaration, even as

they wiped away tears.

"I vow to love you with all that I am," Flynn continued, "and try to bring just as much light into your life as you've brought into mine. You and Ruby mean everything to me, along with the new little one we'll have soon." He paused to place a gentle hand over Cassie's slightly rounded belly. "I love you, Cassie. Now and forever."

Ruby tugged on Cassie's hand. "Don't cry, Mommy."

Cassie bent down to kiss Ruby's cheek. "They're tears of joy, honey. So much joy."

Then she looked into Flynn's eyes. "From the first moment I set eyes on you holding Ruby in the doorway, I knew you both were meant for me. And though the road wasn't always smooth, I never doubted for one single second that we were meant to be together and that I was meant to love both of you, just as you were meant to love me. You and Ruby are the brightest lights in my life and my heart. Every morning when I wake up, I can't wait for our next adventure. And every night when I go to sleep, my heart is full, because I have been blessed with so much more than I could ever have imagined. I love you, Flynn." She smiled down at Ruby. "I love you, sweetie." Cassie's smile for Flynn was radiant as she told him, "I can't wait to be your wife."

And then they were kissing again as the officiant proceeded to declare that, under the laws of the state of Maine, they were now Mr. and Mrs. Stewart. As everyone cheered, Flynn and Cassie lifted Ruby to hold her between them. When the little girl puckered up to give them both smooches, it was the sweetest wedding scene imaginable.

Tears ran down Ashley's face as she applauded the newly married couple. Happy tears, just as Cassie had said to Ruby.

But if Ashley was being totally honest with herself, they were sad tears too. Because although Ashley had also found love at first sight with Nash—and knew that the love she felt for him ran to the furthest depths of her soul—the two of them weren't going to get a happy ending.

After everyone hugged Cassie, Flynn, and Ruby, and champagne and sparkling apple juice were poured and passed around for her parents' toast, their father asked for everyone's attention.

"To Cassie, Flynn, and Ruby. May you forever be as happy as you are today. My heart is full to the brim knowing that the three of you will always love and support each other, through good times and bad, through bright days and dark. Flynn, I have not only given you my trust to be there for my daughter and grandchildren, I also want you to know that I now and forever think of you as a son."

Everyone clinked and drank, then Beth lifted her glass. "I'll keep it short and sweet with a traditional Irish blessing. Otherwise, I'll be blubbering long after the cake has been cleared away." She already seemed to be on the verge of tears as she lifted her glass to the wedding couple. "May your hands be forever clasped in friendship and your hearts joined forever in love. I love the three of you so much."

Ashley was so overcome by her parents' beautiful toasts that she didn't notice Nash had picked up a guitar and was standing before them until he spoke.

"Cassie, Flynn asked me to play your favorite song for you as a special wedding gift."

Though Cassie had been told that Nash would be there as Ashley's guest, her eyes grew huge as she turned to Flynn. "I can't believe this. Did you really ask Nash to play 'Missing Piece'?"

When Flynn grinned and nodded, Cassie kissed him again before turning to Nash to give him her rapt attention as he began to play.

"Missing Piece" was a beautiful song about holding on to hope that your dreams would one day come true, even if the road was bumpy and rough, and it looked like all was lost. It was a song about never letting your dreams go, against all odds. It was a song about how a little love and attention could turn any dream into reality, as long as you kept on believing.

Ashley sank to the nearest chair, her legs no longer able to hold her up. A part of her wanted to flee the garden and all of the emotions that were battering her, but a bigger part couldn't bear to leave. Not when she felt as though she was suddenly seeing straight through to Nash's heart.

She'd heard this song a thousand times, but it had never meant so much to her before. Not until now, when she finally understood that Nash had put his deepest longings into these lyrics. His whole life, he'd wished for love that he didn't believe he was worthy of. But he *was* worthy. And she would never stop loving him.

When Nash finished the song, Cassie was all smiles. "Thank you, Nash. I absolutely loved it."

Though he told her how glad he was to hear that, he didn't put down the guitar. Instead, he turned his gaze to Ashley. "There's one more song I'd like to play, if that's okay. A song I just wrote."

Ashley's mother replied before anyone else could. "Please," Beth said, "we'd love to hear your new song."

Ashley couldn't move, couldn't think straight, could barely breathe as Nash gazed at her with his heart in his eyes.

"This one is called 'Hold On To My Heart.'"

Even before he began to sing, the notes from his

guitar tore at Ashley's heart. They were from the beginning of "Scarborough Fair," but the song quickly turned into something new.

I swore I'd never trust my heart

And I'd never fall in love

Until you walked through my door

I never knew my heart could be so full

I never knew love could be so true

Until the first time I saw you smile

I always swore I'd keep moving on

And the road was the only home I'd ever need

Until your love became my home

I wish I could undo my mistakes

I wish I could be the man you need

I wish you could hold on to my heart

The way I'll be holding on to yours

Until the end of time...

By the time Nash came to the end of his song, the hush among Ashley's family was almost deafening. Her heart was pounding so hard, she was sure that everyone could hear it. And with Nash's eyes still holding hers, and his heart laid out before her and everyone she loved, on a sob, she ran blindly through the garden.

As she ran through Cassie and Flynn's forested

property, his lyrics played in her head. Words so full of love she'd never be able to forget them, no matter how far away he went.

Gasping for breath, she sank to the ground beneath a copse of birch trees that obscured the sky above her. She didn't know how much time passed before she felt warm arms come around her. Her mother's arms.

For a long while, her mother simply held her while Ashley finally cried the tears she'd been desperate to keep inside.

"I love him, Mom."

"I know you do. I could see it in your eyes when you looked at him. And I can see that he loves you too. We all can."

Ashley's heart shattered even more as she said, "But I have to let him go."

Her mother drew back, wiping away Ashley's tears with her gentle fingers. "Why do you think you have to do that?"

It was all so obvious to Ashley. Why wasn't it obvious to her mother? "He's an amazing man, but he made mistakes. Mistakes that were big enough to land him in prison more than once. Josh threatened me, saying that he'll fight to take Kevin away from me if I spend any more time with Nash. He said he'll have me declared an unfit mother." Before her mom could respond, Ashley added, "I know it would be an almost impossible battle for him to win, but it's not just Josh. It's everyone in Bar Harbor and beyond who would talk behind our backs and say things that could affect Kevin. He could get caught in the middle of it all, and the last thing a child going into middle school should have to deal with is stress like that. Life is stressful enough at that age. And a good mother would never willingly put her child in that position."

"Ashley, you're the best mom I've ever known." Beth's voice rang with conviction. "For the past eleven years, you've given Kevin everything he could possibly need. He's a wonderful boy, and he already has everything inside of him that it will take to be a fine man one day. Nothing you do from this point forward is going to change that. And if he ever has any questions about anything that anyone says about you or anyone else he cares about, he knows where to go for answers. He won't hesitate to ask either, because that's how you've brought him up."

"But after coming this far with Kevin, how can I deviate from my plans now? How can I even *think* about doing anything as wild and crazy as being with Nash?"

"You never did like deviating from your plans," her mother said with a small smile. "Even as a child, you would fight big changes. You have such a strong will, Ashley, and that strong will has held you in good stead all these years as a mother to Kevin, as our wonderful daughter, and as a loving and giving sister. But sometimes in life, you come to an unexpected fork in the road, and you're forced to make a difficult decision. Do you follow your heart, even if some people may think it's leading you astray? Or do you stay on the straight and narrow path that you've told yourself is the only way, even if that path no longer makes you happy?"

Ashley knew her mother was speaking straight from her heart. Nearly four decades ago, Beth had made the decision to leave Ireland with Ashley's father. Ethan Sullivan had been divorced, which had automatically made him persona non grata in her family. And yet, she'd still followed her heart, even though she'd had a difficult relationship with her parents for many years after she'd come to the United States.

How brave her mother had been, Ashley thought, before remembering that Nash had said that about her too. *You're the bravest person I've ever known, Ash. There's nothing you can't do.*

She'd discounted his words at the time, but now she had to ask herself, Was he right? Was she as brave as her mother? Could she be brave enough to choose this unexpected and terrifying path into the unknown? Could she follow her heart, even if other people might think that was the wrong thing for her to do? Could she fight whatever battles came from choosing to be with Nash, because fighting for love was always worth it, no matter how long and difficult the struggle might be?

She'd told Kevin that everyone should be given a chance to grow and learn from their mistakes and that their mistakes shouldn't define the rest of their lives. But she hadn't really meant it, had she? Not only with regard to Nash and the mistakes he'd made, but also *her own* mistakes.

She'd never truly forgiven herself for getting pregnant in high school. Nor had she given herself credit for how much she'd learned about life *because* of that.

"I thought it was the only way," Ashley said softly. "I thought living a completely straight and narrow life was the only way I could make up for the mistake I made in high school. I hoped if I did everything right from the moment I found out I was pregnant with Kevin, that nothing would ever go wrong again." She looked into her mother's eyes. "But that's not true, is it? I can't protect myself forever, and I can't protect Kevin forever either—not even if that's what I most wish for. And the truth is that I'm a better person *because* I made a mistake. Instead of holding me back, my past enabled me to be who I am, and learn, and have so much more. And the same is true for Nash and his past. Everything he's been through, the ups *and* the downs, have helped make him the amazing man he is today."

"That's right, honey." Beth gently pressed her forehead against Ashley's the way she used to when, as a little girl, Ashley was feeling confused or sad. "As much as your father and I have tried to protect all of you over the years, we know our only real choice is to celebrate watching you spread your wings and fly...even if we're afraid you might fall. We have learned again and again that the most important thing we can do as parents is celebrate and support you, no matter what." She smiled into Ashley's eyes and squeezed her hands. "Whatever you decide about Nash, I want you to know we will love and support you as we always have and as we always will. All I'm asking you to do today is to promise me that you'll make the right choice for *you* and not for anyone else."

After so many weeks of tormenting herself over her feelings for Nash, everything finally felt clear.

"I promise," Ashley said, coming quickly to her feet. At last, she knew *exactly* what she needed to do. Right away. Before it was too late. "I need to tell Nash that I'm sorry, that I love him, and that I'm willing to face any and all battles if it means we get to be together."

Her mother rose and said, "Go find him, honey. And know that your father and I are with you every step of the way."

CHAPTER THIRTY-TWO

Ashley ran back through the forest, taking off her heels so that she could run faster, ignoring the leaves and sticks poking her bare feet. Her family was still gathered in the garden, but Nash was nowhere to be seen.

"Where's Nash?"

Lola reached for her hand. "He's gone, Ash. I'm so sorry."

No! He had told her he loved her in front of her entire family—and then *because* he loved her, *because* he cared so deeply about Kevin's well-being and future happiness, he'd done what she'd asked him to do, and he'd left.

Pulling her hand from Lola's, Ashley whirled and ran out of the garden, down the driveway, and out to the road. She would find him, damn it, no matter what it took. No matter how far she had to run.

And then, *thank God*, she saw his busted-up old van on the side of the road a quarter of a mile away. It looked like it had a flat tire.

Divine intervention.

"Nash!" She yelled his name as she ran, calling out to him again and again until she was close enough for him to finally hear her.

At first, he looked like he couldn't believe his eyes. And then he got up from where he'd been changing the tire and started running straight for her.

Seconds later, they fell into each other's arms in the middle of the road. And just as she'd known all along, no matter how hard she'd tried to fight it, there in Nash's arms was *exactly* where she was meant to be.

"I'm sorry, Nash. I was wrong. I never should have asked you to go. I never should have cared what other people think about our relationship. All that matters is what we think. And that we love each other." She cupped his jaw and drank in the face that had become so very dear to her. Not because he was her fantasy lover, but because he was real, and wonderful, and had made mistakes. Just like she had. "Thank you for writing the most beautiful song in the world for me. Thank you for putting your entire heart on the line for me. You are so full of love. You're such a wonderful person, not despite your past, but *because* of your past. The things you've been through and the choices you've made, both good and bad, have made you the man you are today. I'm so proud of the man you are, and I'll happily shout it to the rooftops from this moment forward. Because I love *everything* about you,

Nash. I'll always love you. Past, present, and future."

"I love you, too, Ash." There was wonder in his eyes as he held her. "I love you so damned much. More than I knew it was possible to love anyone or anything. And Kevin too. I love your son. I want to stay and be with you. Both of you. In Vienna, you said that you weren't the woman for me, but you are. I think I knew that from the very first moment I set eyes on you."

"I knew it too," she told him, "just from talking with you. I felt so comfortable. Like I could be myself with you in a way I had never been able to be with anyone else, not even my family. And then when you kissed me, for the first time in my life, I knew what it was to be completely alive."

"You brought me to life, too, Ash. I thought I was coming here to buy an old van with the potential to be more so that I could keep being free forever. But now I know that freedom is nothing but an illusion without love. And as soon as I showed up in town, and you kissed me at the café, I couldn't stop secretly hoping that you might see *my* potential, even if I'd never been able to see it in myself. The fact that you can accept me for both the man I am now *and* the idiot I used to be means everything to me. But I still could never forgive myself if my being in your life ever hurts you and Kevin in any way."

"First of all, you might have been an idiot at times,

but that didn't happen for no reason. You were hurt. And you were scared. So you lashed out at the world. But you made it through the darkness with an even bigger heart than you would have otherwise had. You downplay everything you've done to help others, the charities you've anonymously funded, the families you've supported, the way you give endless joy to people all over the world with your music, and how you've brought such joy not only to my life, but my son's life too. And I want you to know that possibly getting hurt in the future is a risk I'm willing to take, both for myself and my son. With you, I finally understand that love—true love—is worth the risk. And I want Kevin to see it too. That when you find the one person you've been looking for your whole life, you shouldn't hesitate to risk *everything* for them."

She knew words weren't enough, though. She needed to erase the rest of his worries, his fears—and all of the worries and fears that she'd so foolishly let take over her heart and mind—with a kiss.

A kiss of trust.

A kiss of hope.

A kiss of love.

A kiss that said she no longer cared what anyone else thought. Because Ashley knew deep in her heart that she, Nash, and Kevin were as meant to be as Cassie, Flynn, and Ruby.

"I know we can make it work, Nash. We already *were* making it work, but I was too scared to spread my wings and fly. Scared that I'd end up hurt again, the way I was when Josh left me to fend for myself. Scared that I'd feel like I made another mistake. But I always knew, deep inside the part of my heart that couldn't help but love you from the very start, that you weren't a mistake. Even if it isn't always easy, I'm not going to back down. Because you were right when you said I'm brave. And I want my son to be brave too. So whether you're here at my side in Bar Harbor, or if you're on the other side of the planet, playing shows to thousands of fans who adore you, what you and I have will always be strong. Strong enough that nothing can ever come between us again. Especially not my ex and his threats. I was just using those as an excuse to stay in my safe little box."

"We'll make Josh see sense, Ash, whatever it takes. And you should know that I'm not planning to go halfway around the world anymore, not unless you and Kevin are with me." He looked deeply into her eyes. "I'll never stop loving you, Ash. *Never*. My heart will always be yours."

"And my heart will always be yours," she whispered.

Their kiss solidified the vows they'd just made, vows to stand together no matter what, come hell or high water.

As they held on to each other, Ashley had never felt so happy in all her life, apart from the first time she held Kevin in her arms. She wasn't blind to the fact that there were going to be struggles. Being in love with someone famous wasn't easy—she knew that from talking with her own celebrity family members. But she didn't care about any of that anymore.

Because she loved Nash. He loved her and Kevin.

And those were the only things that truly mattered.

"What do you say we go back to the wedding?" she said between kisses, "and show everyone again that true love really does conquer all? The same way it did for Cassie, Flynn, and Ruby."

Nash looked at her with such love. And utter devotion. "Love is stronger than anything. You showed me that, snuggle wuggle."

Laughing at the silly pet name he'd given her in Vienna, she said, "I can't wait for all the adventures and all the fun the three of us are going to have, honey bunny."

He drew her into his arms, and as he swung her around, her laughter was full of joy.

After one more lingering kiss, they headed back to the wedding, with Nash insisting Ashley jump onto his back so that she didn't bruise her feet any more than she already had from running through the forest and down the road.

Once they were back in the garden, she hopped off onto the grass, and they walked toward her family, hand in hand. Ashley's mother, Lola, Rory, and Zara were beaming, clearly pleased to see that Ashley and Nash had decided to make things work. And if Brandon, Hudson, Larissa, Turner, and Ashley's father looked like they needed more convincing, well, there'd be plenty of time for that.

Because from this moment on, though no formal vows had yet been spoken, Nash, Ashley, and Kevin were *forever*.

* * *

After the wedding, Beth suggested that Kevin spend the night at his grandparents' house so that he could teach Ethan how to play the new video game Kevin had been raving about. Though Ashley's father didn't look particularly pleased to know that Ashley and Nash would be completely alone for the evening, he knew better than to object.

Ashley's mom had put her foot down with the family—she believed Ashley and Nash were meant to be together, and she wouldn't hear a word against him.

Kevin had accepted the news that Ashley and Nash were a couple as if it was no big deal. "I figured you guys would probably start dating at some point. I could see how happy you make my mom," Kevin said to Nash.

"She makes me just as happy," Nash told Kevin. He grinned and put an arm around the boy. "And so do you."

After they'd all seen the bride and groom and Ruby off—the little girl was thrilled to be joining her parents on the honeymoon to Hawaii—they called a tow truck for Nash's van. Then Ashley and Nash decided to head to Josh's house in her car.

Not only did she refuse to let her ex's threats hang over them any longer, it was time to finally shut down his nonsense, once and for all.

★ ★ ★

As a younger man, Nash would have solved the conflict with Josh with his fists. But Nash was no longer that guy who threw drunk punches and ended up in jail. He was better than that now.

So when Ashley said that she wanted to be the one to inform Josh that his threats to seek sole custody wouldn't be tolerated, Nash promised to stand beside her and not step in unless absolutely necessary.

Josh's apartment wasn't a terrible place, but his slightly run-down home didn't have a hint of the character or warmth of Ashley's cottage.

Her ex opened the door wearing only boxer shorts,

and there were women's clothes strewn across the floor behind him. He looked surprised, and none too pleased, to see them. "I'm busy. I can't talk right now."

The woman he was *busy* with didn't look much older than a college student, and when she saw Nash, her mouth fell open.

"Oh my God, you're Nash Hardwin!"

"This conversation is none of your business," Josh snarled at her. "Put your clothes on and wait in the bedroom until I'm done here."

Though she gathered up her things, she pulled out her phone before she headed out of the room and took a picture of Nash standing in the doorway.

"Kevin isn't here right now, so I can do what I want with whoever I want," Josh said, already on the defensive before Ashley had said a word.

"Honestly, I don't care what you do or who you do it with when Kevin isn't here, as long as it's legal. However, I do care about your irrational and unforgivable threats." Ashley reached for Nash's hand. "Nash and I are a couple. So if you want to sue for sole custody, I dare you."

Josh's face lost its color. "You're together for real?"

Nash nodded, baring his teeth at the other man in a not-quite-smile. "We are."

"I'm not afraid of you, Josh," Ashley informed him. "What's more, I think you know, in your heart of hearts, the damage a custody battle would do to Kevin. Especially given that the odds of you winning are very, very slim. And also given that the legal battle would be very, very expensive." Her voice softened slightly as she said, "Even though you are constantly making our son promises you don't fulfill, I know you love Kevin and truly wouldn't want to hurt him. It's your decision, of course. But if you decide to pursue legal action, or if you ever threaten me again, I promise I will fight you every step of the way, no matter what it takes. And I will *win*." She paused before saying, "I just hope that you can put Kevin above your own desire to beat me at something. You and I don't have to be friends. But we do have to be partners in parenting." She had just started to walk away when she turned back to say one more thing. "Oh yeah, and I want my money back for the RV rental. All of it, by Friday, in cash."

With that, they turned and left Josh standing in his boxers at the open door with an open mouth. Though it took every ounce of Nash's self-control, he held in check his urge to protect and avenge Ashley. If it did come down to a legal battle, however, Nash would throw the full weight of his money and connections behind her and Kevin. If Josh had even half a brain in his head, he would grovel the next time he saw Ashley and promise never to threaten her again.

★ ★ ★

A short while later, they arrived back at Ashley's cottage. It was the first time they would be crossing the threshold as a bona fide couple, rather than as "just friends" or secret lovers.

Nash lifted Ashley into his arms, and she held on, laughing, as they walked inside. But instead of putting her down inside the door, he carried her into the bedroom.

"Do you have any idea how much I love you?" He punctuated each word with kisses that went deeper, and hotter, every time their lips touched.

"I do," she whispered. "Because I love you just as much."

He laid her on the bed, and as he stripped her pretty dress away, he worshiped her with first his eyes, then his hands, and finally his mouth as he loved every inch of her body. "You're so beautiful. And you're all *mine.*" With his hands and his mouth, he brought her to another incredible peak again and again, relishing every time she cried out beneath him, against him.

"I love you," he said again, knowing he'd never get tired of saying the words and of feeling so much love deep within his heart.

Soon, she was stripping away his clothes, having already stripped the walls away from his heart in a way no one else had ever been able to. And in the same way that he'd worshiped her with his body, she now worshiped him with hers.

She gave him untold pleasures with the touch of her lips on his skin, with the press of her breasts against his chest, with the slide of her tongue over his erection. She teased, tempted, and amazed him.

And when they finally came together, with her hands in his, drinking the breath from each other's lips as they kissed, they became one in every possible way.

At last, Nash knew true love.

Love so sweet and true and wickedly hot that he gave himself completely over to Ashley—the bad and good, the dark and light, his past, present, and future. They were all hers now. And she gave him the same. Her mistakes and her triumphs. Her sadness and her joy. Her worries and her hopes.

From now until the end of time, they would always hold on to each other's hearts.

EPILOGUE

Two months later...

Brandon, Turner, and Hudson sat around the fire ring in their parents' backyard, nursing glasses of Irish whiskey. Beth had just served a delicious farewell dinner for Nash, Ashley, and Kevin, who would be hitting the road in the morning in their fully built-out camper van during summer vacation from school. Everyone else was inside the house, watching a movie in the TV room.

"I don't know who's more excited about their road trip," Turner said. "Ashley or Kevin."

"You'd think it would be the eleven-year-old boy," Brandon said, "but I'm pretty sure Ashley is taking the cake on this one."

Hudson nodded. "I sometimes forget the only time she's ever really traveled was when she went to Vienna."

"If I had known she'd hook up with Nash, I would have thought twice about insisting she come to the hotel launch," Brandon grumbled.

Though they were all still getting used to the fact that their sister was in a serious relationship with one of the most famous bad-boy rock stars on the planet, Hudson pointed out, "She's happy, and that's what matters most."

"You're right," Brandon agreed. "It's good to see her so carefree and excited about going on an adventure in the van. And I suppose Nash has turned out to be a pretty good guy after all. A hell of a lot better than her ex, that's for sure. I still can't believe Josh threatened to take Kevin away from her."

"Good thing the dirt bag apologized," Turner said, scowling.

"I don't buy that guy's apology for a minute," Brandon said, a cynical glint in his eyes. "I'm guessing he belatedly realized it's a far better play to make nice with the zillionaire rock star than to be on Nash's bad side. Plus, I'll bet Josh is bragging to the women he wants to sleep with that he knows Nash."

Sipping their drinks, they all silently wished their youngest sister could have had it easier over the past decade. It was only fair that she'd finally gotten the happy-ever-after she deserved.

"Did you guys know Nash was going to ask Dad to help him build a recording studio on the acreage he just bought?" Hudson asked his brothers.

"Nope," Turner replied. "It's a brilliant way to get his potential father-in-law on his side, though, since there's nothing Dad likes more than building something. What do you bet he's already on the Internet doing research for the new project?"

"Now we just need to find Mom a project," Turner said with a raised eyebrow in Brandon's direction. "Otherwise, I have a feeling she's going to turn her attention to us two sad-sack sons of hers who haven't been lucky in love yet."

Brandon gave his brother a cheerfully evil grin. "I'm leaving the country at the end of the week, so that means you're the only one with the target on his back."

Before Turner could reply, their father opened the door of his backyard office and walked toward his sons, holding a piece of paper. His expression didn't look quite right.

"Dad," Hudson said as he got out of his seat to move to his father's side, "is everything okay?"

Ethan Sullivan's face was pale as he took the whiskey glass from his son's hand and polished it off in one gulp.

Finally, he spoke. "I just got an email from a man who says he's my older half brother." He turned the paper around so his three sons could see the picture on it.

The man could have been Ethan's twin, the resemblance was so distinct.

All four men looked at each other in the firelight, surprise written on all their faces. Of all the ways they'd thought the evening might end, none of them could have predicted that their father would hear from a sibling he'd known nothing about.

* * *

ABOUT THE AUTHOR

Having sold more than 9 million books, Bella Andre's novels have been #1 bestsellers around the world and have appeared on the *New York Times* and *USA Today* bestseller lists 93 times. She has been the #1 Ranked Author on a top 10 list that included Nora Roberts, JK Rowling, James Patterson and Steven King.

Known for "sensual, empowered stories enveloped in heady romance" (Publishers Weekly), her books have been Cosmopolitan Magazine "Red Hot Reads" twice and have been translated into ten languages. She is a graduate of Stanford University and has won the Award of Excellence in romantic fiction. The Washington Post called her "One of the top writers in America" and she has been featured by Entertainment Weekly, NPR, USA Today, Forbes, The Wall Street Journal, and TIME Magazine.

Bella also writes the *New York Times* bestselling "Four Weddings and a Fiasco" series as Lucy Kevin. Her sweet contemporary romances also include the USA Today bestselling "Walker Island" and "Married in Malibu" series.

If not behind her computer, you can find her reading her favorite authors, hiking, swimming or laughing. Married with two children, Bella splits her time between the Northern California wine country, a log cabin in the Adirondack mountains of upstate New York, and a flat in London overlooking the Thames.

Sign up for Bella's New Release newsletter:
bellaandre.com/Newsletter
Join Bella Andre on Facebook:
facebook.com/bellaandrefans
Join Bella Andre's reader group:
bellaandre.com/readergroup
Follow Bella Andre on Instagram:
instagram.com/bellaandrebooks
Follow Bella Andre on Twitter:
twitter.com/bellaandre
Visit Bella's website for her complete booklist:
www.BellaAndre.com

Made in the USA
Coppell, TX
26 September 2021

63026173R00198